GEE WHIZ!

m

DERBY DUGAN'S
DEPRESSION
FUNNIES

Also by Tom De Haven

Funny Papers
Freaks' Amour
Sunburn Lake
The Last Human
End-of-Everything Man
Walker of Worlds
Jersey Luck

Walter Geebus's "Derby Dugan," Sunday, October 11, 1936

DERBY DUGAN'S DEPRESSION FUNNIES

A NOVEL BY

TOM DE HAVEN

METROPOLITAN BOOKS

HENRY HOLT AND COMPANY   NEW YORK

Metropolitan Books
Henry Holt and Company, Inc.
Publishers since 1866
115 West 18th Street
New York, New York 10011

Metropolitan Books® is an imprint of
Henry Holt and Company, Inc.

Library of Congress Cataloging-in-Publication Data
De Haven, Tom.
Derby Dugan's depression funnies / Tom De Haven. — 1st
Metropolitan ed.
p.   cm.
I. Title.
PS3554.E1116D4   1996   95-47237
813'.54—dc20   CIP

ISBN 0-8050-4445-0

Henry Holt books are available for special promotions and
premiums. For details contact: Director, Special Markets.

First edition—1996

Designed by Art Spiegelman with Kelly Soong

Printed in the United States of America
All first editions are printed on acid-free paper. ∞

1   3   5   7   9   10   8   6   4   2

FOR ART SPIEGELMAN

ACKNOWLEDGMENTS

Derby Dugan's Depression Funnies has been a long time in the making, but it would still be a novel-in-progress if it hadn't been for the inspiring friendship, good comics talk, and decade-long encouragement of Art Spiegelman. For that, and for his superb cover painting, frontispiece, endpapers, and book design, my deep gratitude.

I also want to thank Santa, Jessie, and Kate De Haven for their love, patience, and moral support. Thanks as well to Michael Naumann and Sara Bershtel for giving my orphan boys a real swell home.

Finally, thanks—and praise be—to all those great newspaper cartoonists of the Golden Age, especially Harold Gray and Chester Gould, whose work, I'm proud to say, invented me.

—TDH

Any man can count his real friends on the fingers of one hand, even if he has a couple of fingers cut off.

— "DADDY" WARBUCKS, 1931

DERBY DUGAN'S
DEPRESSION
FUNNIES

That year, Walter Geebus, the famous moneybags cartoonist, lost all his teeth all at once to gum disease and it just about killed him to wear clackers. Then he got shingles. Then a peptic ulcer, a lazy colon, then rheumatoid arthritis. Some days the poor guy's fingers were so tender and sore he couldn't pick a pencil up, much less draw with it, and that, along with every other god-damn thing, made him as cross-tempered as Attila. Oh, was he ever miserable to his studio help—he was a real bastard!—and they all kept quitting. Hardly anybody stayed longer than a month. Pros like Charlie Flanders, Ed Kellogg, Nat Edson, Jim Raymond: in and out through the revolving door. Poor Walter. Walter the Hun. He'd snap and snarl at me, too, but no matter what, he couldn't get my spunk up. Sticks and stones. Nobody could sore me. Nobody ever could. My name is Al Bready.

I guess Walter was around sixty that year, although he may've been younger, I don't know. He never let on how old he really

was. In fact, he could be as touchy on the subject as your great-aunt Mary. Once, when his fingers were too achy to write, he asked me to fill out a questionnaire for him from the *Who's Who.* So he dictates all the career statistics but ignores his date of birth. So I ask him, "Walter, what year were you born?" and he says, "Leave that blank." There you go. He was colossally vain. He used to be handsome, you know, and I think it broke his heart the way his face had gotten so lined and puffy and bloodless. If some doll he tried to make gave him the cold shoulder, he sulked for days. Actually sat around the studio and sulked, then ended up going out to a cathouse and paying for stuff.

Besides everything else, Walter had trouble sleeping. And if he got sick of his own company, which he often did in the fall of 1936, he'd just ring me up in the middle of the night. "Al? Say, Al, there some bug floating around? I feel so lousy."

He always felt lousy, and he always felt low. And he never smiled, and he never laughed. And here was a guy who'd danced goofy rumbas on the St. Regis Roof!

"Al? Do I sound congested? Listen."

"You sound fine."

"How could I, you're crazy—I'm congested!"

"Glad you called, Walter," I'd say. "Good night, buddy."

Jesus God, he was driving me nuts, demanding far too much of my time. His wasn't the only strip that I wrote, I wrote five others. What, you thought all these birds dreamed up their own stuff? Think again. I wrote six comic strips all together, as well as four 75,000-word novels a month for *Thrilling Marriage* magazine. That's right, *Thrilling Marriage.* I specialized in that junk. Every Sunday I turned out a complete novel of married love, starting at six in the morning and finishing up by eight at night, when I always listened to the "Ritz Cracker Mystery

Theatre," featuring Derby Dugan and Fuzzy, His Dog That Talks. I wrote that, too, the radio script.

If it was the advertising director at Ritz Crackers calling me up in the night, I might've been sympathetic. He paid a good rate. But Walter paid me just thirty bucks a week, and thirty bucks, which half the time I had to badger him to get, didn't give him the right to interrupt my sleep. You understand what I'm saying? I wasn't his friend.

I'd been hooked up with the great Geebus for more than five years by then, since the morning he'd telephoned to say that he'd read a story of mine in *Argosy* and liked it. An aviation novelette. "Oklahoma Air Ace." This was back in July of '31. Calls me up and says, "Mr. Bready? I'm Walter Geebus," pronouncing his name with a hard *g*. Ghee-bus. Walter Ghee-bus. Now, I'd been seeing that name in the funny papers since I was a kid, and always I'd assumed you pronounced it with a soft *g*, like gee whiz. "I'm Walter Geebus," he says, and wants to buy me a drink. So naturally I'm flattered—strip guys back then were big celebs, you'd see their names in the chatter columns—and the following afternoon at a speakie down on Barrow Street I'm more flattered still when he asks me to write his comic strip.

Up until that time, "Derby Dugan" had been a slapstick funny, Sunday only, and hadn't changed one single jot since the days of goldbugs and Bill McKinley. Christ, it was already in the paper when papers were drumming the Spanish-American War. But Walter's new syndicate—King Features, which had bought his contract, along with legal title to the strip, from the just-defunct New York *World*—had decided to launch a daily "Derby" and they'd told him to make it a story strip. Give it some drama, some danger. That was the new trend. Look at "Tarzan," they said. Look at "Buck Rogers" and "Little Orphan

Annie." With a depression on, even the funnies were turning grim. Even Mickey Mouse was tied up and tortured every couple of weeks.

Walter was keen on changing his strip's format, eager to double his workload, and not just because it meant an extra seventy, eighty grand a year. "Derby Dugan" had become stale and predictable, and he'd grown weary—that's the exact word he used, good and goddamn *weary*—of dreaming up and drawing practical jokes. Derby and his smart alecky yellow mutt had run out of pep. "Mr. Bready," he said, "if I have to draw one more pie on one more windowsill, I swear to Christ Almighty you'll have to roll me to the nuthouse in a wheelbarrow."

Turning "Derby" into a continuity strip, into a slam-bang daily cliff-hanger, struck him as the perfect, and the safest, cure for his blahs; he wished he'd thought of it himself. "But here's the problem," he says to me. "I'm strictly vaudeville. I'm not a good story man, I need somebody to write scripts. I can't do that sort of thing myself."

Afterward, of course, he always insisted for the record that he could and did. He grabbed all the credit for my stories, but to be fair, he'd made it plain from the start that he would. So it didn't bother me too much. And besides, to be fair again, Walter did contribute a lot of ideas. I wrote the episodes, but he came up with at least half the plots, and the conservative politics were all his. I may've written the anti-union speeches and the soliloquies about the homely virtues of hard work and self-reliance, but the sentiments were strictly Walter's. Strictly.

The daily strip premiered on October 26, 1931, and in just the first three weeks, the little bald kid in the high yellow derby was tossed into an orphan asylum and promptly mistreated, then ran away and nearly drowned in a flash flood. Walter was delighted. "More, Al, more! This kid is gonna *suffer.*"

And did he ever! He was kidnapped by racketeers and shanghaied by foreign agents with Vandyke beards, he lost his memory and he lost his dog—he lost his dog several times. He was paralyzed, and blinded, and shot in the forehead; he was framed for murder, stabbed with a bayonet, sold into slavery, mauled by an ape, and sunburned to leather, crawling on his stomach through the Gobi Desert.

Who knows why the daily succeeded as much, and as quickly, as it did; there were dozens of other adventure strips launched that same year that to me seemed just as good, even better, but for some reason none of them grabbed readers and tickled them like ours. Week after week we kept picking up new client papers.

So that's how Walter Geebus and I became partners who clicked. But why the two of us did I couldn't tell you, and for a long, long time now I've thought about it. It's always seemed to me just one of those mysteries that can't be solved, and you shouldn't even try. When people all by themselves are a baffling mystery, which in my opinion they surely are, then two people yoked together, hell, that's practically the mystery of mysteries.

With the other cartoonists that I scripted for—it was funny, but the ones I found it easiest to be around, who never bothered me and took whatever I gave them and drew it right up, you'd think those would have been the best partnerships, but they weren't.

You take me and Walter Geebus, though. He was, bar none, the biggest pain in the ass, and the worst meddler, but "Derby Dugan" was the only strip I felt proud of writing. I mean, Joe Palooka I liked as a comic-strip character far better than I liked Derby Dugan and his insufferable talking dog, but that dog and that kid—"That's me, that's mine," I could always say with absolute truthfulness.

And Palooka, the stuff that I wrote for "Joe Palooka," every panel was drawn exactly as I'd described it, every line of dialogue was lettered as I'd typed it, yet for my money that Sunday-page Palooka was dead on arrival. I was happy to cash the paychecks, but I couldn't have cared less about the strip. "Derby Dugan" I would've written free of charge. Not at first, but once it got going. You can be sure I never told Walter that, although I bet you he knew it, the bastard.

Another thing. Not for "Radio Patrol" or "Ted Towers" or "Tex Thorne" or "Fu Manchu" did I ever create a gimmick half as good as Derby's yellow magic wallet with its self-replenishing sawbuck. I never came up with anything *really* snazzy for any strip except the Dugan strip. Or created a character remotely as popular as our crippled acrobat Tim Topp— "the suffering guy who refused to cry."

But Tim Topp and Derby Dugan weren't the only chronic sufferers that first year, year and a half of the Geebus-Bready partnership. Walter was forced to put in seventy hours a week at the drawing table. Each daily had four panels; four times six is twenty-four. Walter was penciling and inking twenty-four extra panels a week, and doing it in a brand-new style: he'd switched from cartoony to semirealistic, and he wouldn't skimp on details. It was far too much work to handle by himself, but he flatly refused to hire any help. While most of his peers used assistants, and many of them—some of the biggest names in the field, with the most popular strips—had ghost artists slaving in the attic while they played golf or lunched at the Union League Club, Walter insisted on going it alone, as he'd always done.

The strip was his calling, his monumental enterprise, his only child, and had been for more than forty years. He may've gone through five wives and been a notorious skirt chaser—as rooty as a rabbit!—but his work ethic was still engine age

Protestant. So Walter held out and held out, practically living at the board, till finally, worn to a frazzle, he cried uncle. And hired Frank Sweeney.

During my first years with him, Walter Geebus was quite a different guy, not nearly so grouchy. He could be very funny, as a matter of fact—quite a kidder. And he wasn't a bad mimic. He could do Bela Lugosi, Fannie Brice, Ed Wynn, and Mrs. Roosevelt, and he did a great Bert Gordon as the Mad Russian—"How *do* you do?" But even so, I never much warmed to him. Never did. Never could. Why? Well, I don't know why, really. Maybe it was all of his money, it may've been as petty as that, petty jealousy. Or because he was a Republican. Or a skirt chaser. Or maybe it was purely a chemical reaction. I don't know. I can't say. I could work for him, no problem. I just could never feel too friendly toward him.

I respected him, though. He was good at what he did. I mean, Walter had the hard job. All *I* had to do was type "Derby surrounded by dozens of angry cannibals," but he had to draw the damn tribe. His assistants (beginning with Frank, then one after the other) ruled panels, lettered balloons, and blacked in the big spots—a coat, a car, a doorway, a tree—that Walter had marked with a small blue X. He drew everything himself, both figures and backgrounds, and never missed a deadline. I respected him for that.

Still, I wasn't his friend. Even though the son of a bitch always remembered my birthday and bought me something extravagant, like an acoustical radio, the biggest one made, or a white linen suit with a train ticket to Miami Beach stuck in the breast pocket, I wasn't his friend.

EPISODE ONE

I MEET HOWARD BLUM

Walter was living by himself in a townhouse on West Seventy-seventh Street, near Riverside Drive, and along about ten in the morning on the first Monday in December 1936, I dropped up to see him about an exchange of paper. He owed me sixty bucks and I owed him panel descriptions and dialogue for a week of daily strips and one Sunday page.

The front door was opened to my ring by a tall young man with brown crinkly hair and clotted acne along his jawline. His eyes were bright and black and desperately earnest. He wore his pegged woolen trousers beltless, and his dress shirt was speckled with tea or coffee and India ink. I'd never seen him before. I could guess what he was, though.

"Mr. Bready?" he said, glancing at the string envelope in my left hand. "Mr. Geebus said you should just leave the script."

"Give you a check for me?"

"No."

"Then I want to see him."

The young man wet his lips and looked grave. Then his ears turned pink on the curvatures when I stepped through the doorway. In the vestibule hung a large oil painting of several black-and-white grazing cows bathed in celestial light. I can't stand pictures that don't have people in them. People doing something. Call me a Philistine, but who cares a fig about cattle? About clouds in a dramatic heap? Vistas. God, spare me *vistas*. "He in the studio?"

"His office. But there's a lady with him."

"Yeah? Who?"

"How should I know?"

I started up the stairs, the new assistant following close behind. Framed under glass on the papered wall were several enlarged banquet snapshots, one every two or three steps. Walter with Bing Crosby. Walter with Jimmie Walker and Rube Goldberg. Walter with George Gershwin, with Harry Houdini, with Jascha Heifetz. Walter with Gene Tunney. Walter with Kitty Carlisle.

"What's your name?"

"Howard Blum."

"When'd you start, Howard?"

"Last Wednesday."

"Has he paid you any wages yet?"

"This Friday."

"Well, okay. Just don't let him fall behind. All these millionaire guys are in another world."

"I'll get paid," said Howard Blum. We were standing outside Walter's office. "He said you should just give me the script. Really."

"Don't worry about it."

"I'm not worried," he said, then went on up to the studio with an irritable scowl on his face. Not a bad-looking boy, I thought. Too bad about that acne. Then I stood in the hall for half a minute, patting myself for cigarettes. I must've left them home, though, or in my other topcoat. The hell with it, I knocked.

"Howard? What's the goddamn problem?"

"It's me, Walt." Nobody called him Walt. I turned the knob and walked in.

The room had chestnut paneling, a high ceiling, and lots of decorative books bound in leather. There was a world globe nearly as big as a buoyant mine, a mahogany table with a green-shaded lamp, and the mounted head of a black bear. Walter was curled up in a leather club chair with his shoes off. His full head of grayed black hair had just been trimmed—big clumps of it had tumbled onto the carpet. His face looked pale as putty. His swimming eyeballs said hangover. He had a package of Lucky Strikes in his shirt pocket. I could see the red bull's-eye.

"Al, I can't talk to you now. You have to wait."

"Sure thing. Hiya, Sadie."

"Hello, Shakespeare." Across the room, the fifth ex–Mrs. Geebus was fitting her barber shears back into a leather cosmetics case. She zipped it up, then held out her arms. But I didn't walk over there and take the hug. I just blew her a kiss.

"Walter, if you got my check, I'll take it and go."

"I'll mail it to you. Hey, Al, come on. Mercedes and I are having a discussion."

"I want money, too," she said.

"Yeah? Maybe we should join forces. I hold him, you give him the hotfoot. Walter, could I bum a smoke? Old buddy?"

He flipped me the package and a paper of matches, then braced his arms and got out of his chair. He dusted hair clippings from his trousers, then squeezed his eyes closed tight. Opened them, rolled them, and began to rub his shoulders. While I lipped out a cigarette and lighted it, he poured himself a cup of coffee. There was a complete silver service on a lacquered table. He added cream and several lumps of sugar, and stirred and stirred and stirred.

Sadie was standing by the window. Even in a bar of anemic daylight, she looked as robust as ever, and as glamorous—in a tailored black suit and a red blouse that matched her lipstick. Single-pearl earrings and a seed-pearl necklace. She used to edit some fashion magazine. I forget which one. "I'm going to Havana tonight, Al."

"That's nice."

"Have to find another husband."

"Bud Fisher's still between wives."

"Thanks, but he likes them young. Besides, no more cartoonists."

"They're not all like Walter here."

"Let's hope not." She parted the curtains and glanced down to the street. "Between friends, how's he doing, Al?" She looked back around.

"Same as ever. Mr. Warmth."

"He seeing anybody?"

"Not that he's told me. You seeing anybody, Walter?"

"Are you two clowns just about finished?" He was sunk back in his club chair. "You finished now? Then get the fuck out of here, Bready."

"He thinks he's going to die, Al."

"I know." I glanced at Walter again and shrugged. "Yeah, I know."

"Al?" Walter was shaking his head incredulously. "Al. What say you go smoke that someplace else, all right? I'll be with you when I can."

He was, I could tell, about five seconds this side of blowing his topper, so I obliged him. "Have a good trip, Sadie. Invite me to the wedding."

"Absolutely."

I went out then, and on up to the studio, a big chilly attic with too many inclined drawing tables and a set of patio furniture—Adirondack chairs and a picnic bench. Howard Blum sat inking with a loaded brush and listening to a breakfast-show tenor sing a nativity song. He peeked at me, then turned back to his work.

"You should bring a sweater, kid. He'll never turn up the heat.

"I'm not cold."

As he finished spotting a Sunday page, I moved around behind him and ran my eyes from left to right, one panel to the next, three panels to a tier, four tiers all together. Derby Dugan and his dog riding a boxcar into a city, talking to hobos, scrambling off at a siding, running from yard bulls. In the next-to-last panel, Walter's florid signature and the date—2/14/37—appeared on a patch of white tape. My name, of course, didn't appear anywhere.

In the last panel, poor Fuzzy got clubbed on the head.

Happy Valentine's Day.

"How did Walter find you?" I asked Blum, to start a conversation.

"I wrote him a letter."

"You a Derby fan?"

He seemed highly insulted and turned a ray on me. "It wasn't a *fan* letter. I was looking for a job. I'm a professional."

"How'd you know he needed somebody?"

"I didn't. Well, I did and I didn't. I was working at the *Daily News,* in the art department, and this new fellow started. I heard he used to work for Mr. Geebus, but he got fed up and quit."

"Ray Catlow?"

Blum nodded. "So I took a shot and wrote a letter. I thought Mr. Geebus maybe hadn't found another assistant yet."

"How come you call him *Mr.* Geebus? That what he told you?"

"No, he didn't say anything. I just—until I know him better I'll call him Mr. Geebus."

"You can call me Al."

"Yeah?" He smiled impudently. "Why, thanks. But I already figured I would."

"You live in the city, Howard?"

"Thirty-eighth Street."

"East?"

"West."

"What number?"

"Why?"

"Don't worry, kid, I'll always phone you first if I'm dropping by for supper."

He laughed. "No phone." Then he said, "Four-forty-one," and removed a strip of tape from each corner of the Sunday board, rolling them all together between his thumb and first finger to make a sticky little ball which he flicked into the wastepaper basket. He lit a candle in a candlestick and carefully passed the board, art side up, over the flame several times, to dry the ink.

"How old are you?"

He looked at me for a moment, then blew out the candle. "Twenty-two. And you sure ask a lot of questions."

"I'm just interested. We're *colleagues*," I said, "practically family." Then I said, "Your father still alive? What's he do? Are those Florsheims you're wearing? Where'd you buy 'em?" and he grinned in spite of himself.

"I'm serious. Those Florsheims?"

"Jesus."

"You drive? What do you drink? Do you like everything you see? What *don't* you like? Ever been persecuted?"

"Je-*sus!*

"You interested in women, Howard? Married already? Got a little bride back home on Thirty-eighth Street?"

"No."

"No what? No bride? Or no interest in women? Well? Which is it?"

Howard Blum clicked his teeth together and looked at the ceiling. "You come here a lot, do you?"

"Every Monday and every other Friday."

"Gee, that'll be great." He set his mouth and shook his head, he cleaned his brush and dried it.

Well, I guess he'd thought he was a pretty hot sketch, hadn't he? Making that crack about his figuring already to call me Al; I guess he had. Well, I guess I'd shown *him.*

"You a good ghost, Howard?"

Blum looked at me again, very carefully that time. "Pretty good. I can do most anybody's style, I figure." He switched off the radio and sat back down at his drawing table. "Why?"

"Just wondering."

"You mean his hands."

"Noticed that, have you?"

"Who wouldn't? Man soaks them for twenty minutes every morning." Blum stood up. "I could ghost him, sure. But for

right now," he said, baring his teeth a little bit, "I'm just the letterer and the background man."

I'd run out of things to say and there wasn't much sense in needling him any further, so I started to prowl, looking for Walter's cigarette box. Blum had a package of Old Golds stuck in his pencil jar, but I didn't feel I should mooch till I knew him better. Or else liked him more. I couldn't find Walter's smokes, so I picked up and pocketed a tin of Bayer aspirin that was on top of the filing cabinet.

There was an electric percolator in the bottom drawer, and I was taking it out, along with a canister of coffee and the scoop, when Blum said, "He likes to make it himself."

"What?"

"He likes to make the coffee himself, when he gets here."

"That's not exactly right," I said, lifting out the brewing basket. "He doesn't want *you* to make the coffee." The kid's eyes narrowed slowly and studied me. "But *I* can." And did.

Then Sadie called to me up the stairs, saying good-bye. I went to the door and called down after her, "Don't come back with any Cuban, all right?" and I heard her laugh. "The most recent former Mrs. Geebus," I told Howard Blum, who briefly quirked his mouth, like saying "Who gives a damn?"

I walked to the window and stood looking down at a maroon taxi idling in the street. The driver jumped out and opened the back door on the curb side. Why, sure. Handsome woman like Sadie Geebus. From twenty feet she looked twenty-five. Face to face, not a day older than forty. But she was fifty-one, and said so. I watched her go briskly down the stoop and across the pavement and climb into the cab. Probably I sighed. "Do you know Ray Catlow?"

"You talking to me?"

"No," I said, "I'm talking to myself. Ray Catlow—the guy at the *News*. You know him, right?"

"You mean are we friends? No. Why?"

"Just—if you see him, tell him he still owes me three bucks."

"I won't see him. Why should I see him?"

"Well, I'm just saying *if* you do."

"Yeah. Sure thing, Al, I will." He gave me a wise-guy sneer. With it still frozen on his face, he got up and carried the Sunday board to Walter's table. He was still standing there looking at it—he was *admiring* it, was what he was doing—when Walter came in a few minutes later.

"From what I'm paying that woman in alimony, she ought to give me french every time she sets foot inside this house. So what do I get? My hair cut." He plucked a check, deliberately crumpled, from his trouser pocket. Waggled it. "Here you go, Albert." He knew it wasn't Albert. "Your wages."

"Gee, thanks, boss. Can I sweep up, do anything else before I go?" I put down my cup of coffee and took the check. Then I gave him my scripts. "You want to look 'em over while I'm here?"

"Later. Fucking headache is killing me."

"Well, I didn't change anything from what we talked about. The kid meets an honest lawyer who's being threatened by some big-shot politician."

Last Monday Walter had told me, "Have the kid meet an honest lawyer who's being threatened by some big-shot politician."

With a casual flip, he tossed my envelope on the picnic table, sat down on the bench, and untied his shoelaces. He always did that, first thing coming into the studio. Untied his shoes, then undid his belt buckle. "So Al," he said, tipping his

head toward Howard Blum, "you've met the new brat. What do you think?"

"Seems all right. I notice you taught him the candle trick."

Walter grunted. "He won't last long."

I looked at Blum. He was back sitting at his own table, staring at the wall. No expression, none, on his long face. But his ears, once more, glowed red. I don't get embarrassed easy, but I did right then. And I felt sorry for the kid. Kind of admired him, too. That stone face. I liked that stone face. Even though I couldn't stand to look at it for another second. "What's the matter with him?"

"The kid has designs." He got up and walked to the sink, ran the cold water faucet, and filled a jelly glass stenciled with characters from the Dugan strip. "He *watches* me, like Frank used to."

"Cut it out, Walter, for Christ's sake."

People who knew nothing else about Walter Geebus knew he was the cartoonist who'd once had an assistant who tried poisoning him with arsenic. Frank Sweeney was the guy. He was the guy all right, he was the goddamn Bluebeard of the ink pots!

Before he joined Walter in January 1933, eighteen months after I started writing the strip, Frank had been a bullpen artist with the NEA Service, a features syndicate in Cleveland. He was twenty-five, and a sweeter, more genial man you never met. Honest to God. He was a charmer. Bright red hair, disheveled pompadour, and a lopsided grin on a clear-cut, brought-up-right kind of face. An Eagle Scout. Coming in by subway every day from Queens—thanks to coolie wages, he lived with an older sister and her husband over the drugstore they owned near Crotona Park—carrying a cheese or a ham salad sandwich for lunch, and always dressed in red- or blue-check shirts and

riveted dungarees. His shoes were scuffed so fantastically raw at the toe caps that it seemed like somebody'd had a mad go at them with a cheese grater. Walter used to tease him about those shoes, but good naturedly. He liked Frank. He truly did. Liked him, trusted him, depended on him.

They worked together more than a year without a single argument, as far as I know, and then—then Frank starts in to spiking Walter's morning coffee, day after day, granule by granule. I may be wrong, but I don't believe Frank ever intended actually to *kill* Walter, just make him so miserably sick that he had to give up the strip—to Frank Sweeney, of course.

I discovered the arsenic myself, in Frank's portfolio, and the reason I became suspicious was that I'd just read a pulp novel with a plot involving arsenic poisoning, and the symptoms in the story fitted Walter's exactly. The chronic nausea, the burns in the mouth, and so forth.

It was funny, but when I told Walter, when I showed him proof, he accepted the truth at once. He never couldn't believe it—not for one second did he think that Frank Sweeney was possibly innocent. He went from thinking the guy was his best friend in the world to knowing—to fully accepting the fact— that he was his worst enemy. And his feelings weren't hurt, either. He just got mad.

Naturally, I'd called the cops, and there was a juicy front page of a trial in the early autumn of 1934. Day after day Walter sat in court glaring. Upon conviction, Frank turned around, sniffling and shaking like a third grader, and begged Walter's forgiveness. Walter sneered and flipped him the bird. And when Frank was sentenced—to fifteen years, no parole for ten—Walter applauded. It was ugly as hell, the whole business, and very goddamn pathetic. But as a result of all the publicity, twenty newspapers picked up "Derby Dugan," so it wasn't a to-

tal disaster, though Walter always blamed the arsenic for his subsequent ailments, and I was inclined to agree with him.

Relatively late in life, Walter Geebus had discovered evil, and it shook him. He wasn't ever going to get over Frank Sweeney, not ever. And to be honest with you? I probably wasn't going to, either . . .

"Give Blum a chance," I said.

"Oh, I will. I'm not saying I won't. I'm sick of hiring new brats. He watches me? All right. So I'm going to watch *him*, Al. Like crazy."

Carrying the water glass, he went over and stood in front of the filing cabinet. When he frowned, Howard Blum said, "If you're looking for the aspirin, Mr. Geebus, Al took them."

When I'd got going in the writing business, I was even younger than Howard Blum—twenty years old with an idiot job selling classified ads over the phone for the New York *Graphic,* Macfaddan's dirty rag. Evenings, I'd go up to Harlem with some friends, maybe with a girl, stay out all night. That ended me up in the hospital with alcohol poisoning. I almost died. I almost did. It wasn't funny, let me tell you. And when the hospital finally booted me out, my old job wasn't there anymore, they'd given it to a colored man with a white man's voice. I was flat broke and still shaky, so I went to live with my older brother Donald on Staten Island.

Next to Pius the Pope, Donald—you could never call him Don—was probably the holiest guy on earth. He and his fat, pale wife were always reading the New Testament together on the davenport, always going to early mass and making novenas, praying for the conversion of Russia. I stayed with them for six

weeks and never touched a stick of reefer or a seidel of beer. I was good and all, good as gold, I even went to church on Sunday, but Donald finally decided that I'd turned into a shiftless mooch and told me to pack. No hard feelings. Not on my part, at least. I was glad to get out of there and back to the city. There's recuperation and then there's suffocation.

So I left, and got a studio in the old DeSoto, an apartment hotel on West Twenty-fifth Street, corner of Sixth. Not swell, believe me. Not even okay. Its canvas awning was faded to pink and badly tattered, and both T's in the electric sign were burned out. The other letters fizzed and flickered. Oh, you know the kind of place. Four bucks a week that I covered, though only just, by running diluted and rebottled prescription whiskey from drugstores in Chelsea to several clubs in Harlem owned by a cheerful gangster named Marty Planet. And it was at one of those places, late one evening, where I picked up a few pulp fiction magazines. Somebody'd left them lying on a table in the cloakroom.

I read a Doc Savage novel—or maybe it wasn't Doc Savage, no I guess it wasn't, the Man of Bronze wasn't around then; so maybe it was a Khlit the Cossack story, or some Foreign Legion adventure by Theodore Roscoe. Whatever, I was hooked. On the idea of writing similar crap, I mean.

I'd finished high school, I knew about subjects and predicates, I'd read most of Jack London, and I figured to make up the kind of stuff you found in those dimers, you didn't need to know too much about the real world. Which I didn't, and maybe still don't. Plus, two cents a word sounded good to me. And if you don't think so, think about this: the paragraph that you're reading right now? In 1924 could pay for breakfast, lunch, *and* dinner.

I found an Underwood machine with carriage return at a hock shop and bought a ream of sleazy yellow paper at Wool-

worth's, then, in one marathon session, sixteen hours, I wrote a
lost-city novelette. "Adventure in the Ruins of Gold!" By Alfred O. Brady. Except when it got published in *Smashing Danger* two months later, the byline—thanks to a typographer's
error—read: Bready. Alfred O. *Bready.*

I kept the name, though, adopted it, mainly because I didn't
think there was anybody else in the world named Bready; still
don't—so I'm unique. Overnight I was a new person, alone in
the world. Something I'd desperately wanted to be since I was
a boy of fifteen.

So that was a dozen years earlier, and a dozen years later I
was still living in the same old dump, still writing the same old
bunkum. All I ever had to do was sit down at the table, I sat
down and something always came, and I never got stuck or
needed a stiff drink, or ten. If I woke up lazy, I'd just start
chopping away at the machine before I even brushed my teeth.
Or say it was a glorious sunny day and I felt tempted to run
outside and wander the city—what would I do? Pull the tin
bathtub from under the sink and partly fill it, then take my
shoes and drop them in, so's I couldn't. My shoes kept shrink-
ing, they looked like puckered hell, but at least I ate regular, always made the rent the first of the month, and could afford to
buy new shoes. Temptation, time and again, may've decked
young Al Brady, but it never laid a glove on Alfred O. Bready.

EPISODE TWO

NOT THAT
JIMMIE RODGERS

After I left Walter's house, I went straight to the public library on Forty-second Street and spent an hour taking reference notes on the island of Borneo for a sixty thousand–word adventure novel that I'd promised *Blue Book* the first week of January. Then I borrowed some lithos and photographs, mostly of cannibals, from the circulating picture collection, and walked home.

I got back to the Hotel DeSoto around twelve-thirty, quarter of one, and Jimmie Rodgers—not the yodeling brakeman, the other one, the one who owned a lunchroom in the Midtown Bus Terminal and was married to my dear friend Jewel; the tall, handsome, square-jawed bowl of nervous pudding with china blue eyes and a deep, nasty crease in the back of his skull; the one who always smelled of chlorine bleach from swimming twice a day in the pool at the Twenty-third Street branch of the YMCA, *that* Jimmie Rodgers—was waiting for me in the

lobby. He sprang from his chair. "I was just going to leave, Al, but I said no, five more minutes. I was just going to leave."

"Been waiting long?"

"Not so long." He shook his head from side to side. "Not so long. A little while."

"What's the matter?"

"Nothing." But he avoided my eyes, and in fact looked all around, then all around again, like he was actually searching for something. Then he blushed and said oh, he'd forgot, and handed me a small, bulked-out brown paper sack. "I brought you a couple sandwiches. They're pork. Just a couple sandwiches. All right?"

"Yeah, Jim, that's fine."

"On Vienna rolls." He shuffled his hands into his overcoat pockets, then pulled them back out. When he caught me looking at one of them—at the skin between his thumb and first finger where he'd copied down a telephone number in blueblack ink—he stuck them both away again, pronto.

"So what's doing?" I said. "You want to come upstairs?"

"And we could talk? That'd be good. We should talk."

"Then let's go up." Which we did, taking the stairs, since the elevator was stuck between the lobby and the basement, and had been since 1931. Or two.

"Is Jewel all right?" I asked him.

"Oh sure. Jewel's all right. Jewel's—all right." But he didn't seem convinced, and neither, suddenly, did he sound so friendly anymore. Charged up and dithering, he was *always* that, but not as friendly by half.

I threw my coat on the bed. Jimmie didn't take his off, though, and I knew how come. Because he was wearing his white counterman smock underneath and didn't want me to see it. He left his hat on, too. "Sit down, Jim."

He said thanks but remained standing, shifting his feet and looking slowly from the upholstered chair to my swivel chair, then at my typewriter on the bridge table. Then at the bed. Then he looked at the pictures on the wall, one a crayon portrait of Sacco and Vanzetti, the other a silly ad I'd cut out of *Collier's* showing George Cukor and the cast of *Dinner at Eight* standing around on the set drinking Coca-Colas. (Yeah, I just *bet* that's what they drank, all the time.) And then, since there was nothing else in the room to look at, besides me, Jimmie looked out the window.

"So nothing's wrong," I said. "You just figured I needed a pork sandwich."

"I don't *blame* you—"

"Sit. Because I'm going to sit and I'd rather you weren't standing." Then I sat on the bed. "You don't blame me for what?"

"Could I ask a favor? If you don't mind—would you mind not coming up the apartment tonight for supper? I know it's Monday, it's Monday, I know it, but—"

"That's all right, Jim, sure. But you could've called me, no reason to come down here to say that. Was there?"

"Well, there was," he said, biting a fingernail. "Maybe there was." He dropped his hand and pursed his lips and stared gloomily at a spot above my head on the wall. If you knew Jimmie Rodgers, you learned patience. I patiently waited till he quit jigging on the balls of his feet and finally sat in the upholstered chair.

"Jimmie, what's going on? What happened?"

"Nothing. It's not that something happened. It's not that something *happened*. It's just—well, maybe *you* can say."

"Me?" I was surprised, of course, but not nearly as much as I hoped that I sounded.

"I'm not saying I think—you know, the worst. All I'm saying is that she's stuck on you, and that's that. And you know it. And I know it. And Jewel knows it. Jewel knows it best."

"Cut it out."

"That's what I'm trying to do!" he said in a kind of fury. "That's just what I'm trying to do, Al. If you'll let me."

"So I'm not welcome anymore. Not Mondays, not anytime."

"I guess not." He looked miserable, picking at his little ginger mustache. "I guess not."

"This is stupid."

"You think so? I don't. You think so?"

"Good and stupid. You seen yourself in the mirror lately? Or don't you look at yourself when you brush your hair?"

"I look. Sure I do. I look at myself all the time. Only she doesn't. She looks at you. So what's it matter? The hell with my face! The hell with it. It's not everything. It's not anything."

"I'll tell you what's not anything. You want me to, I'll even put it in writing. I'll type it up for you. I never touched your wife. Period."

"I believe you. I believe you, Al—'cause if I didn't, you'd be on the floor right now. So I believe you—but so what? You think about her. You stare at her. You think about her."

"Oh, grow up."

"You want to tell me you never did that? You want to tell me that? You want to say it?"

"I won't say it."

"All right. That's enough. That's enough for me."

"Sure I look."

"Sure you do."

"And I think about a lot of things. And right now I think you're nuts."

"You said that already." Jimmie stood up and walked to the door. "And you think I'm stupid. But I'm not. Stupid *or* nuts." He lifted his arm and pointed a finger. "Just stay away from us. You got that? Just stay away!"

"Something happened, Jimmie. What? Sit down."

He gave a small jerk of his head, and there was a note of sadness in his voice when he told me, "I'm sorry, Al."

"Yeah?"

He screwed up his eyes and wrinkled his forehead, then he turned suddenly and walked back toward me. "And I guess I'm saying it's not a good idea if she keeps typing up your stories. I don't want her typing up your stories anymore. That's out."

"That's business."

"Sure, everything's business. Everything's business." Then he added resentfully, "I don't know how you make up those stories anyhow. What do you know about marriage?"

I thought about standing up and knocking him down, but I let him go. The hell with him. Maybe he wasn't stupid, but he wasn't very bright, either, and he was so full of self-pity that he made me sick. And he said everything twice. He said everything twice.

I ate one of his sandwiches, then put on a fresh shirt and went out to see what Jewel had to say about all this.

When I first laid eyes on Jewel Rodgers—it was November of '34; November *sixth,* 1934, a Tuesday—she was sitting up straight, with her shoulders squared and her back arched, behind an ugly Remington typewriter in a tiny office on West Forty-third Street. Top-Drawer Periodical Publications, Inc. Her hands were poised correctly over the keyboard, just like they teach you at those secretarial institutes. But in all candor, it wasn't them I noticed first. It took me awhile to get down to her hands.

Not that Jewel was by any stretch beautiful. She wasn't. Her face was too long, and her eyes were too small, and the pencil in her brows just emphasized that. Also, she had a bit of a problem complexion; what I mean to say is that she had *had* something of a problem complexion, as a girl, and that her cheeks, under the rouge, were pitted. Not terribly, just—to a certain

degree. Her jet black hair was brushed across her head at a sharp angle and salon-curled in the Harlow style.

She was a conventionally attractive woman in her middle twenties—till she smiled, that is. With her lips pressed together. Then she was special. *I* thought. She had the warmest smile I'd ever seen, and it was genuine. You couldn't fake a smile like that. I stood there staring at her red mouth like some guys in the subway'll stare at a woman's breasts if she has big ones.

I took a long breath, let it out. "Mr. Kamen in?"

"Your name?"

"Al Bready."

When she stood up, I was surprised by how tall she was, and how slender. Practically no hips, and a small, rock-hard bottom. She had on a gray sweater blouse and a plaid woolen skirt, and she crossed the room on military heels (patent leather four-eyelet shoes—I looked). She tapped on a door with pebbled glass and went directly in.

While she was gone, I examined the top of her desk—ratty manuscripts, three-ring binders, bills on letterhead—and found a package of candy-coated Beechies. I shook one out, to keep. (And all these years later, I still have it—linty, and crazed as ceramic—in my cuff link dish.)

She returned a minute later, smiling. "Go right in."

So I thanked her, and did, and found Clark Kamen perched on a window seat, just staring out at the gloomy day. He was about fifty, a stoop-shouldered man with a horsey face and bushy black eyebrows. His hair was silver—it gleamed—and hung shaggily around his collar. He wore suits and shirts and ties that were expensive, and likely tailor-made, when he'd bought them years ago, but that were now starting to look shiny or frayed—not wrinkled, though, never wrinkled. His

shoes were always polished, and regularly soled and heeled. "Al Bready! Didn't I read someplace you were indicted for perjury?" He hopped up to shake my hand. "Or was it murder?"

That was Kamen's social and commercial trademark: the crude, insulting, insensitive, absurd hello. *I heard you had cancer. Somebody told me you'd turned wacky. I thought you were in prison.* It was always a joke, though he'd deliver it deadpan, absolutely straight.

During Prohibition, Clarky made his living as a bootlegger, though he'd always been a small-time smallie. After repeal, he'd taken his savings and gone into the publishing racket—started things up with a fat dimer called *Top-Drawer Criminal,* then followed that with *Top-Drawer Detective,* then *Top-Drawer Western, Top-Drawer Pilot,* and finally *Top-Drawer Marriage.* "Blistering Tales of the Indissoluble Union." I'm not kidding you, that was the title tag.

He unwound the envelope string and slid out the manuscript he'd commissioned a few days earlier by phone. "How's the spelling this week? That giant snowman story? You spelled glacier wrong about ten times."

"Your rates? You're lucky it was typed."

"Glacier with an *a!* It's *e-r,* Al, *e-r.* Jewel caught it."

"Jewel?"

"The new girl, my secretary, you seen her coming in. Jewel," says Clarky, "and is she ever that!" Now there's a speller, he says, a *great* speller, best he'd ever met, never needed a dictionary. Some speller! And could she ever type! Like the wind! And she never minded working late, either. He was high on Jewel, Jewel Rodgers, but when I made some casual remark about her smile, he seemed puzzled. Smile? Well, sure, of course she smiled—she worked for him, didn't she? "She's *happy,* Al. She's making twenty bucks a week."

And that's all he said about Jewel; after that we talked a little about Frank Sweeney's trial and the sentence he'd just pulled, and then we talked business. Could I do a novel a month? Sure. Did I care what kind it was? No. Then did I want to make it a love-and-marriage job? Fine. Clark Kamen thought I had a real knack for love-and-marriage jobs, not that he was knocking my other stuff, mind you. The cowboy and detective stuff were good, too, but . . .

"You married yourself, Al?"

"No."

"Ever been?"

"No."

"You just make it all up, huh? Probably why it's so hot, huh? Without being dirty."

"Probably," I said.

On the way out I stopped by Jewel's desk while she wrote me a check. And that's when I finally had a good look at her hands. They were long and smooth, and white as cream, and the nails weren't lacquered. Jesus, though, the left one had a stark gold wedding band, and that ruined me, just about, for the rest of the day.

I walked uptown to the Paramount and saw a picture; it was set in the past, when people still wore powdered wigs. Charles Laughton, I think, was in it. But what it was about, I couldn't tell you. I kept thinking, That's that. Well, that's that. That's all there is to *that.* Jewel Rodgers was married, and so that was that. The way I saw it, a married woman was like an electrified fence. Only a real dope walked over and touched it.

All that week, though, she stuck in my head, so bad that I even mentioned her to Walter Geebus. And what did he say about the situation? "Take five dollars from your piggy bank and go get laid." The great romantic. What did I expect,

though? Sadie's lawyer had just served him with divorce papers, thanks in large part to an item that had livened up Nosy Natwin's column the previous month: "Wasn't that Derby Dugan's Papa having sea-food with Leona Utley—Mrs. Herbert S. Utley—at Le Poissonnier?" There. You see what I mean about electrified fences.

"Get laid, Al, then send your crap to this Kamen person by messenger. Al? Do it."

I took his advice—well, the first part of it, anyway. And I very nearly took the second part, too, except that by the time I'd finished my second blistering tale of the indissoluble union for *Top-Drawer Marriage,* I had come around to thinking that I'd acted pretty goddamn silly. Al Bready thunderstruck? By a typist's smile? Go on, get out of here. So early the next Tuesday morning I went back to Forty-third Street.

There was a colored man in deli whites and a bib apron standing at Jewel's desk. She was picking out nickels from a petty-cash envelope and snapping them into his outstretched hand: ". . . thirty-five, forty, and"—eyes lifting, crinkling, smile flashing—"that's for you."

Now, I'd intended just to plonk down the novel and go. Walk in, walk out. But what did I do? Laid a hand on the colored man's sleeve, and like I was George Raft or somebody, I said, "Lady's got some great smile. Don't she?"

So he glances back around at Jewel, pushes out his bottom lip, and nods. But then he gives me what I almost take—I *do* take—as a freezingly cold side glance. "Yes, sir. Very nice."

Off he goes then, and Jewel says—says after she's taken out two coffee cartons and a corn muffin from the deli sack: "Now, why did you do that, Mr. Bready?"

"What'd I do?"

"Embarrassed him."

"Him! But not you?"

She laughed. *"I'm* flattered. Did you *want* to embarrass me?"

"No," I said, "of course not. I was just . . . passing a compliment."

"Thank you."

"You're very welcome."

I was staring at her again. My mouth had gone dry, and I was out of breath and starting to perspire, and then I was sure that my clothes were all disarranged, horribly disarranged—that my shirt had pulled out of my trousers, that my belt was twisted, that my shoelaces were untied, that my zipper was down. It was nuts! "Mr. Bready? Mr. *Bready?*"

Jewel cocked her head to one side. She was still smiling, but with her lips parted for a change. She looked at me, *really* looked, and there was a moment, one second when—

I don't know. I'll never know. Because I opened the door and went out, then I closed the door and stood in the corridor and smoked a cigarette. Two cigarettes. Then I walked back in.

"Hi, Jewel!"

"Oh, hi Al," she said, prying the lid from one of the coffee cartons. "You want half a muffin?"

"Yeah, that'd be nice. Yeah, I would. Thanks. So how've you been?"

"Good. Yourself?"

"Not too bad."

"Here. Let me clear a place for you. Sit down, Al. Sit."

And that's how we became, for lack of a better word, friends. That's exactly how it happened. I've left nothing out. I've put nothing in. And I never made a pass, not then and not later. There were times, though, many goddamn times, that day and

every day afterward, when I thought—well, you know what I thought. But you can't keep a grown man from thinking his private thoughts, that's no crime. The imagination never heard of the Ninth Commandment. Or the other ones, either. She got into my dreams. I lost sleep.

And Jimmie Rodgers could just take a flying fuck at a rubber duck!

JEWEL OF
ST. JOSEPH'S

It was scarcely two o'clock when I left the DeSoto that December afternoon, so I took my time walking across town. Browsed a few newsstands, stopped by a stationer's for an Underwood ribbon, watched a fire, had coffee at a Greek's. I've always loved killing time, it never has bothered me.

At quarter to three I found myself dawdling in front of an appliance sales and repair, just looking over the window merchandise. Thom toasters, with the patented E-Z-UP Toggle, were draped in silver garland and sale priced at $2.29. Now, that was an outstanding bargain, if you knew about these things, which I did. No special reason, I just liked to read advertisements.

I went in and bought a Thom toaster, is what it comes down to, and had it gift wrapped. Then I footed it the rest of the way over to St. Joe's, where Jewel had been teaching ever since Clarky's publishing company went belly-up. I loitered by the

schoolyard fence, hearing the steady hum-throb-and-hiss of the Kip's Bay steam station directly across the street.

At three o'clock sharp, schoolbells rang. Half a minute later, side doors burst open in the old red-brick building, and several hundred teenage boys came surging out like incited workers from the lower depths. I stood clear, boundlessly glad not to be them.

By the time Jewel came out—she was by herself, and wearing a reefer coat and a dressy peaked hat with a swooping brim—the hordes had almost entirely dispersed. I let her walk down the front steps before calling to her. She looked quizzical for a beat, then smiled.

But she frowned when I handed her the square box in the red shiny wrapper.

"What's this?"

"What's it look like? It's your Christmas present."

"Little early, don't you think?"

"'Afternoon, Mrs. Rodgers," said a passing boy. "Mr. Rodgers."

"Good afternoon, Thomas," Jewel said. Then said, "Isn't it? A little bit early for Christmas presents? Al?"

"Little bit."

"So? How come?"

"Because I thought I might not be seeing you again for some time."

"Why not?"

"Have a nice evening, Mrs. Rodgers. You too, Mr. Rodgers."

Jewel said, "Thank you, Lawrence." Then said, "Al, I don't understand what you're saying. You're going someplace?"

"No."

"Jimmie called you. Didn't he?"

"Better yet. Came and saw me."

Smiling morosely at the gift package, Jewel said, "I hope this is a gun, baby. 'Cause I'll shoot him."

"It's a toaster."

"You're kidding."

"Yours is kaput—remember?"

"You're not kidding."

"He came and warned me away. So to speak."

"A *toaster?*"

"He thinks we're in love."

"Well sure, but—a *toaster?*"

"See you, Mrs. Rodgers. Hi, Mr. Rodgers."

I said, "Hiya, son," then took Jewel by the arm and started to walk her home from school. I carried her books, of course.

For the last nine months I'd been having my supper at Jewel's place every Monday—a weekly ritual that began as an indirect result of Walter's pigheaded malice toward President Roosevelt and the mild calamity that it caused us both. So I had laughing boy Geebus to thank. Or to blame. I'm still not sure which.

But one thing I am sure of, there was no way in hell Walter Geebus ever could have gotten away with that crazy tax-the-wallet story. I'd been dead set against doing it, I'd *warned* the guy, but he wouldn't listen. So typical. You couldn't tell him anything, and trust me, there'd been dozens of times since FDR took office that I'd tried to keep him from glutting up our strip with his grouchy politics.

No matter what the adventure, though, Walter could always figure out some way, somewhere, to needle trade unions and canonize big businessmen, and to sneak in some nasty crack about the New Dealers. Remember "Little minds with big

mouths?" I wrote it, Fuzzy said it, and to Walter's giggling delight, the Republicans used it—against the Democrats. Derby Dugan became the nation's most conservative fourteen-year-old (H. L. Mencken dubbed him "Kid Mussolini") and his dog commenced to rant like Father Coughlin, the radio priest.

I hated writing that stuff, it was embarrassing and mean-spirited, and I beefed to Walter about it almost every Monday. I even threatened to quit, but I never did. I never would. And Walter realized that. I think he enjoyed watching me squirm whenever he'd compliment some vicious monologue I'd put into his hero's balloon, and I know for certain he took great pride in being attacked by the liberal press; he'd clip out for his scrapbook every denunciation he could find, in union papers, socialist weeklies, the *American Mercury,* the *New Republic,* whatever. He figured he must be doing something right if he'd made enemies of those guys.

From time to time, one of our stories, or some blustering dialogue, would rankle the publisher of a client paper, who'd complain to the syndicate and yank an offensive daily, even make noises about canceling the strip altogether. But Walter never took much notice. He was working for William Randolph Hearst, he'd say, and William Randolph Hearst supported him—had in the past, would in the future—since "Derby Dugan" melodramatized (Walter's verb, not mine) what the Old Man and his flunky Arthur Brisbane carped about every day in acres of print. And it was true: Hearst did support him, annually with contract sweeteners, often by chatty telegram: THAT KID HAS BALLS. KEEP UP GOOD WORK.

Still, it was bound to happen that someday Walter Geebus would go too far, and when he finally did, even William Randolph Hearst couldn't—he wouldn't have dared—spring to his defense.

Since the Seventy-fourth Congress had passed the administration's new tax bill in August 1935, the Hearst papers nationwide had been referring to it as Roosevelt's "Soak the Successful Act," and Walter had been itching to get in dibs of his own. After all, his income put him in the most vulnerable tax bracket, and he'd be goddamned if he'd just sit back and let those Bolsheviks in Washington rake off his hard-earned dough to put another thousand loafers on the public dole. He'd been seething for months, and it came to a boil late in February 1936, just after the first-ever Social Security checks were mailed out—all to the undeserving, naturally.

In the daily strip, one story was coming to a close, it was time for a new adventure, and I'd worked up some jazz about a daffy scientist who'd invented a miracle vitamin—vitamin G, the genius pill—but Walter wasn't in any mood for that. He was feeling plundered and wanted everybody in America to know it. "Forget vitamins, Al, listen to me. The kid hits some new town, it's a nice place, a friendly place—good solid stock. But they're all headed for hard sledding. Are you getting this?"

"Yeah, I'm getting it."

"Write it down. They've elected a new mayor. Hah-vid man. And he's in a wheelchair—but that's phony. That's all phonus balonus. He can walk, he just sits there *playing* crippled, to get sympathy."

"Walter . . ."

"Meanwhile, the kid starts helping out at a grocery store. Sweeping up. Or maybe it's a farm. I like a farm. Make it a little farm. Decent people. But times are tough—and once the mayor jacks up property taxes, they're in big goddamn trouble. So out comes Derby's magic wallet, he starts peeling off ten-spots like they're loaves and fishes. To help the folks out. Tide 'em over. It's a loan, it's not a free ride, it's a loan. I don't see you writing."

"I'm writing. See? I'm writing."

"All right, the brat's making some low-interest loans—"

"Low interest? He's *living* with these people, for crying out loud."

"Okay, *no* interest. Happy? So everything's fine till the mayor's wife, ugly as sin but hoity-toity—the broad gets wind of it. Maybe sees the wallet, or could be she hears about it from some busybody—a neighbor. Whatever you like. She goes running to her husband, and they decide to grab the wallet for themselves. Only they figure on using the law to get their hands on it. They sic the sheriff on our boy—saying he's never paid any taxes on all those sawbucks."

"Well, he never *has*."

"He shouldn't *have* to—it's miracle money! All right? Got all that? This should be good for at least three months."

"Or ten years in Leavenworth. You're not seriously thinking of putting this mayor in a wheelchair, are you?"

But he sure was, and he did, and he even gave him a long cigarette holder, even drew him to *look* like the president, then named him—over my violent objections—"Boss Rascalvelt."

Which brings me to the crisis that first brought me to Jewel's for supper.

On Monday, the second of March, I get a call at nine-thirty in the morning, it's Walter in a panic. He's in a lather, is what he's in. The six dailies he'd sent over to Pete Laudermilch at King Features last Friday—the entire first week of the Rascalvelt story—had just come back to him by commercial messenger. Torn in half. Well, surprise, surprise. "Walter, I told you so."

"Screw you, it's a good story."

"Sure—if you like a little treason with your entertainment."

"What treason? You see what that privileged son of a bitch has done to this country? You can't even poke a little fun!"

"Stow it, Walter, would you? So what do you plan on doing now? Call up Joe Connolly?" President of King.

"I already did—and he's siding with Laudermilch! Maybe I should call the Old Man."

"Save your dime. He'll agree with Connolly. You're doing a comic strip, remember? And most of the papers that run it don't belong to Hearst. So let me ask you this again: what're you going to do?"

"New story. What else *can* I do? I need a new story—today."

"Tomorrow."

"And what am I supposed to do in the meantime? I got nothing to draw and already I'm a week behind."

"Use the vitamin story."

"I don't like the goddamn vitamin story! Vitamin story. Give me something else."

"Tomorrow."

"Today!"

"Today I got other commitments."

"What do you got that's more important?"

"Kamen phoned me up Saturday—I promised him a long Western by this afternoon, and I haven't even started yet."

"You're going to let me down? You're really going to let me down like this? On Monday I pencil dailies. That's what I do, Al. That's my schedule."

"What about mine?"

"What about it? I already heard about it. Go ahead, write your fucking Western. I'll write my own comic strip."

"Give me half an hour," I said. "I'll be there."

And there I went, and there went the morning. I showed up at Walter's house with a bialy and a cup of tea, and pitched him ideas till he heard something he liked. Derby gets temp work at a roadside zoo. And the tiger breaks loose. "Make it a lion, Al."

"It's a lion."

"So let's do it."

I extemporized two days' worth of dailies, panel by panel, and while I yakked, he doodled on vellum. Then, soon as Walter started roughing in figures on bristol board, I used a typewriter to script and title another ten dailies, stopping every few minutes to dictate dialogue and captions to a guy named Tommy Malloy, who was lettering. (Malloy, who'd been at the studio for less than a month, wouldn't last the week; I forget why, exactly—was he the guy who quit after Walter threw a T square at him? Or who got fired for blowing his nose once too often? Whatever the reason, by Thursday or Friday, Malloy was gone. Another man down.)

It was a hell of an anxious morning, the catch-up pressure made worse by Walter's sizzling anger—which he took out on Malloy and me in a series of crazy little tantrums. "Who said you could turn on the goddamn radio? Turn it off—and next time, ask." "Somebody cut a fart! Jesus Christ, it's like working with barnyard animals! Open the window, Al. And while you're there, do the world a favor and jump." Good old Walter. You would've thought (and maybe he did think, for all I know—maybe he'd actually convinced himself) that *we*'d been the ones, Malloy and me, who'd cooked up that crackpot tax-the-wallet story. He was incredibly nasty. A real son of a bitch. Malloy was ready to strangle him, but I shrugged it all off, as usual. The man was humiliated, and I felt sorry for him. I could sympathize. What the hell.

"Bready, if I wasn't up against it, I'd never've done this shit. I hate drawing lions!"

"So make it an alligator."

"You're a man of real integrity, Al."

"See you later, Walter."

By the time I left, it was almost noon, but instead of going back to my hotel, it was too late for that, I taxicabbed it straight up to West Forty-third Street.

"It's Bready! I heard you beat the rap, Al—good man! Al, here, murdered his brother with an oar. But they couldn't prove it, Jewel. So a boating accident they're calling it now."

Jewel rolled her eyes and laughed. And my knees got weak. It felt like whatever is there—is it bone? or cartilage?—turned suddenly into a couple of big gelatin molds. She had that effect.

"So, Mr. Speed. What d'you got for me today?"

"Clarky," I said, "can I borrow a typewriter?"

He loaned me a Remington, then Jewel set me up at a bridge table out in the hall opposite the elevators. *Top-Drawer Western* was short its featured "novelette," and since Clarky had said I could do whatever I wanted, I made it spicy: gunfighter, blizzard, isolated cabin, and a pretty young widow from way back East. The first several thousand words came easy, like dreaming. Then I looked up and there stood Jewel.

"Anything I can get you? Roll or something? Donuts?"

"Coffee'd be good," I said.

"Nothing to eat? You look hungry, Al."

"I'm fine," I told her and went back to work.

Ten minutes later Jewel delivered the carton of coffee. She said, "Whenever you get hungry—"

"I'll give a whistle," I said.

Then she was gone again, and my attention, but not my imagination, flagged badly: I'd stop, stare at the keys, start, stop, start again, stop again, feeling all fidgety knowing that Jewel Rodgers was sitting at her desk not ten feet away, on the other side of the door. Jesus, that smile. I walked down the corridor, found the gents', took a stall, and surrendered to the bachelor's bad habit. After that, the story zoomed.

All day, people kept passing me by, on their way to and from the cut-rate lawyer, the painless dentist, the private shamus, but even when some of them stopped to stare, like I was dressing a window at Gimbel's, it didn't slow me up. I was out in Montana.

By three-thirty, four o'clock, Jewel had come back a half-dozen times more, offering to run downstairs and get me something to eat. Bowl of soup, Al? Piece of pie? I felt like a heel, always saying no, but the practical fact was, I fantasized better on an empty stomach, and best when it started squeezing out cramps. So I stuck to black coffee and my Herbert Tareytons. I smoked a whole package. When Clarky left to go home at five minutes till five, I bummed three of his Luckies, to tide me over.

"Be much longer, Al? Not that I'm pushing you."

"Figure another half an hour."

"Just give it to Jewel, she'll cut you the check."

"Speaking of which . . ."

"I know, I know. But that was a fluke. This time there's funds, Boy Scout's honor. Got to run, Al. Talk to you soon."

After he'd gone, I hunkered back down and finished the damn story. Big shootout in the snow.

"You look pooped, Al."

"A little. I guess."

Jewel was dressed for the street, and she was sitting behind her desk touching up her lipstick. I folded down the bridge table, stood it in a corner. "This is for you," she said. I looked to see it was made out proper, and signed.

"I'd cash that quick, I was you."

"What do you know?"

Jewel shook her head, shrugged. "Just . . . get thee to a bank, first thing tomorrow."

"I'll do that."

"Make sure you do."

"If he goes under—"

"I didn't say that, Al. And I don't want it spread around."

"'Course not, but *if* he goes under, just say if, what're you going to do?"

"I'll be fine. I'll do what I used to do."

"And what was that?"

Jewel laughed. "Taught grammar and typing and business math. High school." She switched off her lamp. "Hungry, Al?"

"Starving."

"Finally!"

"Finally?"

"We're having macaroni and cheese. That all right with you?"

"You inviting me to supper?"

"You're starved, aren't you?"

"Well . . . yeah."

"Then I'll feed you. I've been trying to all afternoon. What do you say, you ready to go?"

"If it's—if you don't think your husband'll mind."

She gave a slight but unmistakably dismissive wave with her fingertips. "Oh, don't worry about him," she said. Then she said it again, "Oh, don't worry about him," and laughed.

It wasn't till after I'd met Jimmie Rodgers that I got the gag.

EPISODE FOUR

THE QUARREL

It was a distance of just seven blocks from St. Joseph's to where Jewel lived in one of the twelve Tudor City high-rise buildings decorated outside like English cottages and grouped around a private park. On the walk there, I asked her for some explanation of Jimmie's behavior at my hotel, and she said, "Oh—you spelled 'exaggerate' wrong. As usual."

"What?"

"In your manuscript. Double *g*, not double *r*."

"What's that got to do with Jimmie?"

"Nothing."

"So why—"

"I'm just *saying*. That you spelled 'exaggerate' wrong. And 'delicatessen.' *E*-n, not *a*-n. Big dope."

"All right, okay. But what'd you think of the story?"

"I didn't read it, Al, I just typed it."

We went inside Jewel's building. The lobby had a stained-glass window, like in a church or a funeral parlor, and criss-crossing heavy timbers overhead. The automatic elevator had red velveteen walls, a chair rail, and dark wood paneling; Anne Boleyn wouldn't have felt out of place taking a ride.

"Hold that, would you?" A guy was trotting across the lobby with his right arm stretched. He was short and curly haired, a middle-aged guy in a gray nubby topcoat that practically touched his shoes. "Thank you, folks. Al! For crying out loud. Good to see you."

"You too, Ed. What floor?"

"Three. Thanks." The car rose smoothly with a tweeting of cables. "So what're you doing here?"

"Just visiting. This where you live?"

"I wish. Caniff's got his studio here. You know Milton?"

"No."

"I do his lettering now. Just started. And I tell you, everybody in that damn strip talks too much. 'Specially the Dragon Lady." He laughed. "Well, here's where I get off. Nice seeing you again, Al. And tell Walter I said—no, never mind." He laughed again, touched me on the elbow, nodded to Jewel, and stepped off the elevator.

Once the doors sealed, Jewel asked me who that was.

"Ed something."

"Oh," she said, "thanks a lot."

"I forget his last name. He used to work for King Kong. They didn't get along."

"He doesn't look well, does he?"

"He drinks."

"I'm sure he must."

"Kellogg," I said. "Ed Kellogg."

"Poor man."

We were at her door, and she was hunting up her key, and I said, "Maybe you should just hand me out the manuscript. I don't think I should come in."

"You'll come in. And you'll stay, because today is Monday and on Monday you eat supper with us. Excuse the mess."

She always said that, excuse the mess. And the funny thing was, her apartment was always neat as a pin. You could never find so much as a cigarette butt in an ashtray, and even the slick magazines fanned on the black-mirror table were exactingly fanned. Oh, it was neat all right, and decorated according to the latest advice from Dorothy Draper, as excerpted in *Good Housekeeping:* ming green walls and white blinds. White rugs, white plaster lamps, white leather picture frames around Maxfield Parrish prints. And every damn interior door was painted a different color. Orchid. Ivory. Chocolate brown. Scarlet. The bedroom door was scarlet.

Jewel took off her coat and asked for mine. As she hung them both in a hall closet, I watched the hem of her dress rise about an inch in back, revealing her slip. I stared at her calves and thought my thoughts. And then we went through to the kitchen.

"Oh, this is lovely," said Jewel, lifting the toaster from its box and setting it down on the table. "It's a Thom. Thank you." She kissed me on the cheek and sat down.

"Merry Christmas."

"God, silly, you're not *really* thinking of staying away, are you? Al, he's a little boy—he's a baby. Don't pay any attention to him."

I filled the kettle and lighted a gas ring. "What happened?"

"Nothing."

"That's what *he* said."

"Is it?" She rested her elbows on the tabletop, made a chin stirrup with two thumbs, then leaned forward. I waited. "It's the same old thing, Al. It really and truly is. He started in again this morning, so I told him, *sell* the lunchroom, go ahead if you hate it so much, if it's not good enough for a man of your talents."

"So *he* said?"

"Nothing. At least nothing intelligent. Because, Al, he doesn't have the slightest idea *what* he'd do if he didn't have that silly lunchroom. I shouldn't call it silly. That's not fair. It's a nice place. It does a good business. It's clean."

Jewel got up and poured the boiling water into a ceramic teapot. She brought over cups and saucers and a can of evaporated milk, remembered spoons, and finally sat down again. "Just let that steep."

"I still don't get it. How what you're saying happened ends up with Jimmie at my door."

"So maybe I said something about you. Maybe I compared the two of you."

"*Maybe* you did?"

"So I did! I can't say what I think?" She poured the tea.

"Compared us how? There's no comparison."

"I'll say."

"He looks like a blond Robert Taylor, *I* look like Joe E. Brown."

"You do not!"

"Compared us how?"

"You have a cigarette?"

"No."

"I think Jimmie has some."

"Compared us *how?*"

"I only said the truth. That there's not a damn thing in the world that he wants to do anymore except jump in the damn swimming pool. Or jump into bed for you-know-what."

I took a sip of tea rather than look into her eyes at that moment. "What else did you say?"

"Nothing."

"Come on. What else?"

"I don't know! His stupid feelings got all hurt. And you know how he is. You know how Jimmie looks when he gets that way. You want to smash him."

"What else?"

"He *started* it!"

"What *else?*"

"Oh, don't shout. He says to me, 'What are you, his girl-friend?' And since I'm your friend and I happen to be a girl, I said yeah—so what?"

"Christ, I'm lucky he didn't throw me out the window. Hearing that."

"Jimmie wouldn't touch you. He wouldn't lay a hand on you. Once upon a time, but not anymore. He's learned one lesson, at least."

"I don't know about that. He sounded sincere."

"Words. Words, words, words."

"Maybe. But Jewel? I wish you hadn't said them."

"I just say what's on my mind."

"No, you don't."

"What?"

"Not all the time you don't. Say what's on your mind. Neither one of us does."

She put down her cup, and stood, and went into the bedroom. She came back tearing the blue tax stamp from a package of Chesterfields.

After I'd watched her light up, I said, "I'd better be leaving."

"It's Monday."

"Got to go home and give Joe Palooka something to say. He's lost in the Sahara."

"Let him burn."

"Can I get that manuscript now?"

Jewel nodded, not looking at me, looking instead at her cigarette coal. "You didn't bring me the new one."

"I didn't finish it yet." That wasn't the truth. I'd finished it all right, my latest love-and-marriage job, I just—hadn't brought it. "So what do I owe you? Jewel? Could I get the manuscript? How much do I owe you?"

"Shut up, Al. Please?"

So I did, and Jewel suddenly reached with both hands, lifting the Thom toaster and then setting it down in front of her. "This was very thoughtful of you," she said, depressing the toggle. She inclined her head. "Would you like a slice of toast?"

I began to laugh, then realized that Jewel's whole face, but especially around her eyes, had turned a blotchy bright red. She was trying valiantly to smile.

"Jewel . . ."

She released the toggle, and up it shot with a twang.

The way Jewel's eyes welled up slowly that Monday afternoon, it reminded me a lot of how my little sister Jeannie used to cry. Whenever our mom and dad got into another screaming-and-punching match, Jean would appear at the door of the bedroom that I shared with Donald, and no matter what day of the week it was, she'd be dragging a Sunday comics section like it was a nursery blanket. Jean saved the comics from weekend to weekend, and by the time she was six or seven there was a huge pile of supplements stacked in her bedroom closet.

Jean would stand in the doorway and plead with both Donald and me—she wanted somebody to read her the funnies. She kept asking us long after she herself had learned to read. Donald never said yes, he never indulged Jeannie; all his life he was a son of a bitch. I never could understand how he could be so dismissive of our sister, she was such a cute little kid. But Donald acted like she wasn't there, wasn't alive.

So I'd read to her. "The Katzenjammer Kids." "Foxy Grandpa and Little Brother." "Mr. Twee Deedle." "The Newlyweds."

Meanwhile in the kitchen, something would smash or there'd be a loud, angry bellow. Then: rushing footsteps on the back stairs, the slam of the front door.

Below Jean's eyes the skin turned pink, gradually darkened. Tears flowed up, found their level, overflowed.

" 'Isn't this a lovely day to take Snookums out on his lovely sled,' " I'd read. " 'Yes,' " I'd read, " 'what struck you to think of that, dear?' "

MY COMMIE FRIEND

So where'd I eat supper? At a chop suey joint, by myself. Then I dropped by the men's bar at Rosoff's, where I bumped into a guy named Joe Wein—"Red" Wein, most people called him— whom I knew from the American Fiction Guild. We had a couple of drinks, trading story-market gossip, then he talked me into going with him to a cubbyhole theater in the far west forties to see some crazy play about scumbag capitalists and saintly auto workers—no scenery but plenty of noisy cap guns. Walter Geebus would've turned apoplectic. I just got bored.

After the curtain-down, I invited Wein over to my place and we listened to some Victor Red Label recordings on the electric phonograph, the pair of us killing a bottle of vodka that he'd picked up on the walk back. Russian, of course.

You'd never think it to look at him—not with his smooth, round, guileless face—but Joe Wein was a full-blown, dedicated Communist, had his membership card and all, which I

thought was a riot, seeing as how the villains in most of the adventure stories that he wrote, under the pen names William
Race Meadows and Dexter Padgett, were humpbacked Soviet
Reds. But whenever I'd point that out, he'd just give me a little shrug and the party line, saying that survival was a comrade's most critical duty till the revolution came. He believed
in it, too. The revolution. And gave a quarter of his income
each month to the CP. He used to be a truck mechanic or a
truck driver, or a milkman, or some damn thing like that. He
was a nice enough guy, Joe was, but his politics made me tired.

So I sat there listening to Beethoven and Mozart while he
toasted Stalin or damned Trotsky to hell and then belted out
three more cheers for the Spanish Republicans at Alicante.
Three weeks after the fact, he was still celebrating the execution
of Antonio Prima de Rivera. Death to the Fascists! Yeah, sure.
I'd drink to that. I'd drink to anything. I was in a blue funk
thinking about Jewel and her screwy husband, and about them
being home alone together doing—what? Bickering maybe, or
maybe not, maybe not. And thinking so much and picturing
certain conjugal possibilities just got me drunker, and deeper in
funk.

"Hey—Alphonse! You still awake?"

"Yeah."

"What say we go out and get laid?"

"You mean to a house?"

"Unless you know some ladies that give it away. Want to?"

"No. It's Monday."

"What's that mean?"

"I go on Tuesday."

He sat up, open-eyed, and looked at me. "Are you kidding?
You only go on Tuesday? *Every* Tuesday?"

"Usually."

"Same place?"

"Usually."

"Which one's that?"

"Down on Fifteenth Street. One of Marty Planet's."

"The Sullavan girls."

"Yeah."

"Which sister?"

"What?"

"Same Sullavan? Every Tuesday?"

"No. Not really."

"Liar! So you don't want to go?"

"I don't feel like it."

"Because it's not Tuesday? You're too organized, Al. Every-thing in its place. That's spooky."

"Maybe."

"Believe me, no—it is. Every Tuesday, uh?"

"Usually."

" 'Usually.' " He giggled and sat back in his chair.

Around eleven-thirty, the telephone rang. That time of night? I assumed it would be Walter, but instead it was Jewel. "He's sorry, and wants you to come for supper tomorrow in-stead."

"He does not."

"He does."

"Where's Jimmie now?"

"In the doghouse."

"Come on."

"He's sleeping. Should I go wake him, put him on?"

"No."

"He's sorry," said Jewel. "He wants you to come for dinner tomorrow instead."

"He does not."

"He does."

There was a long pause. I looked over at Joe Wein. He was nosing around my work table, flicking through a manuscript. Then he sat down, rolled a sheet of copy paper into the Underwood, and started typing with the velocity of a private secretary at Standard Oil.

"What'd you have for dinner?" said Jewel. "Did you eat?"

"I ate, sure I ate."

"What'd you have?"

"I forget."

"Are you typing?"

"That's not me, it's Joe Wein."

"What's he doing there?"

"Typing."

"Very funny. Al, listen—whyn't you come by school again tomorrow. Will you?"

"I don't know."

"Please."

Suddenly Joe Wein ripped the first sheet from the platen, cranked another one in, resumed his attack on the keys. Ding!

"Jewel? He's right, you know."

"What do you mean, he's right?"

"To think we're maybe too, I don't know. Friendly. He's your husband, Jewel. Christ. I don't think we should talk right now. I'm a little tight."

"Al? I'm willing to admit that. We *are* a little too—what'd you say, *close?*"

"Friendly."

"But that's okay with me. Oh God. I'm going to light a cigarette. Say something, Al."

I rang off.

"What was *that* all about?" Joe Wein was staring at me over his shoulder.

"Nothing."

"But definitely a female. Who's Jewel?"

"None of your business."

"Anything you say. All right if I keep working? Inspiration strikes."

"No, it's not all right. Take it home, for Christ's sake. I don't feel so good."

"I miss a regular woman," said Joe Wein. "I mean, a woman regular, any night you want her. I was married once. I ever tell you? But you know what's strange? How this old lady you had that you couldn't stand the sight of, how she turns up in your head big as life whenever you're doing yourself."

"Go home, Joe. For crying out loud."

Since the winter of 1934, I'd been writing Ham Fisher's "Joe Palooka" Sunday page, a gig that took me all of twenty minutes once a week at the typewriter. And for which I was paid half a C. Very sweet. But in September of '36, Fisher almost sacked me—and damn near plucked out my eye with his stupid dog-head cane—when he discovered that Walter Geebus and I had introduced a bighearted prizefighter into the Dugan strip. Christ, was he ever livid! Fisher had a nasty temper, nearly as bad as Walter's. How could I do such a thing, he said, where was my loyalty, my common fucking decency, and blah blah blah. You should've heard him. It would've been funny, it would've been a riot, if it wasn't so nuts, and all the time he's yelling in my face he's waving around that antique cane. Finally I had to grab it, and he was lucky I didn't break it over his drawing table or his own thick skull. So he did "Joe Palooka"—so what? Nobody else could do a prizefighter? It wasn't like Twicey Roundabloch

was going to be a permanent fixture in "Derby Dugan," he was only a minor player in a ten-week story. Here briefly, then gone. But Fisher didn't see it that way. If you put a ring fighter in a comic strip, you'd swiped from him. That's how *he* saw it. You'd looted his house, you'd screwed his best girl, you'd cut out his heart. He was crazy as Dick's hatband, that one. He didn't write his own strip, and he didn't often draw it, either—he just signed it. Managed it and signed it. But that didn't matter. He was insanely jealous of the one good idea that he'd had in his life.

Anybody with half a brain, though, could see that Twicey Roundabloch, while he may have been as sappy as Joe Palooka, wasn't much like the champ at all. For one thing, he always lost; for another, he wasn't pro, but strictly amateur, a short-order cook who boxed light-middleweight. And for a third thing—well, as his none-too-subtle name implied, he said everything that he said twice.

Guess where I'd really got my inspiration.

And the funny part of it is, when I first dreamed up Twicey Roundabloch, he wasn't a club fighter at all, he was a competitive swimmer. "What, like Johnny Weissmuller?" Walter said, and I said, "Yeah, sort of, but with fewer brains."

"If that's possible."

"Right," I said, "if that's possible."

But Walter nixed the swimmer stuff—you couldn't, he felt, draw somebody day after day splashing around in a pool and sell any newspapers. So Twicey ended up being a boxer instead, at Walter's suggestion. I don't believe that Joe Palooka ever crossed his mind. I know that Walter never read the strip. He found it dull. And its liberal politics made him gag.

Though it caused me that grief with Ham Fisher (he cooled down finally and kept me on as writer, after I promised never to bring Twicey back), I'm glad that I made the switch. Because if

Twicey Roundabloch had been a swimmer and a double-sayer both, Jimmie Rodgers for sure would've recognized himself as the model, and, much as he loved "Derby Dugan," he wouldn't have liked it. He wouldn't have liked it. And who could have blamed him? Twicey, poor soul, was thick as a brick, and when he wasn't that, he was frisky as a Labrador retriever, and half again as goofy.

Same as Jimmie Rodgers.

Within five seconds of meeting him for the first time, I couldn't figure out for love or money how Jewel could've married the guy. He was certainly good looking enough for her; as a matter of fact, with his looks, but with another personality—with another brain!—he could easily have got himself a dishier wife. No, his looks were better than okay, it was just that he was—the word I always find myself kicking around is "crazy." Jimmie was crazy. He had a manic energy that sent off a buzz that rattled your teeth.

When he'd arrived home that Monday evening the previous March, Jewel was sitting with me on the sofa in the living room. We'd already had three highballs apiece. I didn't know about her, but I was feeling cockeyed. I sobered up quick, though, at Jimmie's entrance.

She went to the foyer and greeted him crossly. Where had he been? Didn't he know it was almost eight o'clock? He could've called if he was going to be late. I was surprised by how sharp-tongued she was. She gave him some bawling out.

Meanwhile, the guy was standing there in his still-buttoned topcoat looking hangdog. Head down, chin tucked against a shoulder. His hair was damp. He said he was sorry. He'd gone swimming, lost track of the time. He'd gone swimming. He'd lost track of the time. He'd gone swimming. He was sorry. He'd gone—

"Jimmie, I want you to meet a friend of mine. Al Bready."

He frowned for only a moment, then was polite.

"Nice to meet you. Al? Good to meet you, Al." He shook my hand with guarded pressure. "How do you know each other? Where do you know each other from, you two?" I was surprised that she'd never mentioned me to him before. After all, by that time we'd been friendly—in Clarky's office and over the occasional lunch at the Automat—for almost a year and a half.

"Al writes a lot of the stories in Mr. K's magazines. Plus some of your favorite comic strips." Jewel helped Jimmie off with his coat. "Isn't that wonderful?"

"Comic strips? No fooling! Comic strips? No fooling! Which ones?"

With each title that I mentioned, Jimmie's eyes grew wider and his laugh became a louder and louder yelp. By the time I got to "Derby Dugan" (I always mentioned that one last), he seemed positively in awe. Christ on a crutch! You would've thought I was a visitor from some exotic place, the ambassador from England or Mars. And he was so grateful that I answered his questions! "You mean you don't know how a story's going to end when you start it? You mean you don't start—"

"Let's eat," said Jewel. "Anybody need to wash their hands? Jimmie?"

When he moved past me toward the bathroom, I got my first look at the back of his head. Right below the crown, where there was a pink-and-purple bald spot an inch wide and four inches across, Jimmie's skull looked rumpled and knobby, all crushed in.

"And dry your hair, Jimmie!" Jewel called after him. She looked at me for a second, then drank some more from her glass. "Do you swim, Al?"

"Not a stroke."

"I knew there was a reason I liked you right away."

We ate in the kitchen.

"Jimmie, you sit there tonight. Al, you sit there, why don't you."

Jimmie asked what we were drinking, and fixed one for himself. But I got the feeling that he ordinarily drank something lighter, because he grimaced every time he took a swallow.

". . . so how many weeks ahead do those guys draw? I think you already told me, Al, but how many weeks ahead do they get?"

"Twelve for the Sunday, eight for the daily."

"Boy, that's far. That's pretty far ahead. Isn't it far, Jewel?"

"It is," she agreed. "Al, do you want another slice of cake? There's plenty."

"No, thanks."

"Where do you find your ideas? Where do you find your ideas, Al?"

"Oh, I don't have time to go find them. They come looking for me."

"Yeah? Really? Yeah? But what about the paper? Do you ever get ideas from reading the paper? Do you read the papers, Al?"

"I read the papers, yeah."

My head was spinning.

"Al, is Fuzzy the dog a she or a he? Is it a she or a he dog?"

"It's usually a her, but not always. Sometimes we screw it up. But she's supposed to be a girl."

"It's just that she doesn't sound like one. She doesn't sound like a girl. I'm not criticizing you, Al, but she doesn't."

"Well, it's a different species, Jim. Girl dogs talk like human Bowery boys. Nature is a funny old thing."

Jewel smiled and poked me in the arm. Then, while she cleared away the dishes, Jimmie unboxed a board game—Melvin Purvis's G-Men Game—and set it up in the living room. He put the quart of whiskey on a side table, next to his chair.

"Oh, Jimmie, I don't feel like playing." Jewel had come in and was making a face. "Let's just put on the radio and talk."

"We can play with the radio on. We can listen to the radio and still play a game. Al? What do you think? What do you think, Al?"

"It makes no difference to me what we do."

"Al's willing. Al is willing."

"Fine," said Jewel.

"I'll be green," said Jimmie. "I'll be green, if nobody else wants it." He took another distrustful swallow from his drink and read me the rules of play from a little pamphlet.

In between spinning the pointer and moving our G-man markers across a sinuous highway connecting New York, Chicago, the Dust Bowl, and Hollywood—criminal America— Jewel told me that she'd recently started doing some manuscript typewriting at home, and I got the clear impression again that Clark Kamen was in money trouble.

"Well," I said, "maybe you could do some typing for me. I've been thinking about that. I could work up twice as many stories if I never had to worry about what the manuscripts looked like." The truth? I'd never once considered using a typist. It seemed a big waste of money.

"Any time you want, Al. I'd love to."

Jimmie looked bothered by the conversation. "Don't take on too much, Jewel," he said. "You don't have to take on so much

work. You don't have to work, period. She doesn't have to work, Al. I own that lunchroom lock, stock, and barrel. Lock, stock, and barrel. She doesn't have to work. I could—"

"Let's not talk about that," said Jewel. "Al. Do you think Myrna Loy is pretty?"

"Sure. Is there any doubt?"

"I just don't think she's that pretty," said Jimmie. He spoke over the rim of his glass. "That's my opinion, I'm sorry. I just don't think that Myrna is that pretty. Shoot me."

Now, that seemed like a good idea. Problem was, my only tommy gun happened to be roughly the size of a Chiclet and currently occupied a space labeled KIDNAPPERS DEMAND RANSOM. LOSE A TURN.

Jewel and I had quit drinking highballs, but Jimmie kept pouring tots. And to hell with the ginger ale. Very gradually he turned quiet. Then he put his glass down, got up, and rushed to the bathroom.

"I better go see," said Jewel.

"Should I leave?" I didn't know if that was the right thing to say. Probably wasn't.

"It's still early, Al, but go if you want to. No, why don't you stay? I'll be right back."

She left me then, and I went and stood at the living room window. There was a good view from there of the *Daily News* building, and I just stared at it.

This Jimmie guy was a character, that's all I kept thinking. He had to be almost thirty, a guy handsome as a moving-picture cowboy, but he acted like Harold Teen. And Jewel treated him like she was his mother. Jesus Christ. Other people. What a mystery!

"Al? Could you come in here for a second? I can't lift him."

"Yeah, sure."

I gathered Jimmie up from where he knelt hugging the toilet bowl, took hold underneath both arms and dragged him to his feet. "I'm sorry about this," he said. "I'm sorry about this."

"It's all right. Why don't you rinse your mouth out, then I'll walk you to bed."

"No, Jewel can walk me. Jewel!"

"Let Al help you. If your legs go, what am I supposed to do?"

I got him out of one room and into another, then just let him fall across the mattress on his stomach.

"Jewel," he whined, "could you come in here? Could you? Jewel? Please?"

I went out as she walked in. "Al? Wait—okay?"

I took a sharp right, then loitered in the hall, listening.

"Are you going to be sick again?"

"No. Jewel? I want you to feel something. Will you feel this? Will you touch it?"

"Not now. Go to sleep."

"You mad? You mad at me?"

"I'm not mad."

"Promise? Promise you're not mad?"

"Just go to sleep, Jimmie—please? I'm not mad, but go to sleep."

I went and sat down again. Jewel wasn't long coming back. Another two, three minutes. "Should I put on a pot of coffee?"

"If it's no trouble."

"Come on." She turned off the cabinet radio in the living room, then switched on the midget set in the kitchen. Butterscotch dance music from a Long Island nightspot. I watched her grind a pot's worth of coffee. The supper dishes were stacked in the sink and on the sink counter.

All of a sudden Jewel said, "How come you never got married?"

"Never got asked."

"Do you ever stop kidding, Al? *Do* you?" I was surprised by the look she gave me; it was a little cross. But she quickly wiped it away with another world-class smile.

"I just never got married," I said. "No big heartbreak story. And now I'm just a guy who lives in a hotel."

"I lived in a hotel when I first came to New York. The Martha Washington."

"I know it, sure. Off Fourth Avenue. So you weren't married when you moved down here from—?"

"Syracuse. Well, twenty miles north of. And nope, I wasn't married. And I had no intentions of getting married, either. See? I could've ended up like you."

"I doubt that."

"No, I mean I didn't ever really *want* to be married. To anybody."

"How come?"

"Not everyone does. Want to. Look at yourself."

"Well, yeah. But women . . ."

"I don't know about 'women,' Al, I just know that I was happy with things the way they were. I was living on my own, I had a nice roommate, I had a job, I had boyfriends. Things were good. That's all."

"When did you meet Jimmie?"

"Oh, I've always known him. He grew up down the street from me. His folks owned the only restaurant in town. We played together as kids, we dated in high school. Best swimmer in Onondaga County! You should see all his medals and pins." She smiled affectionately. "Jimmie was just . . . always there. I went to college, he went to work. And he just always figured we'd get married. But then I surprised him. After I came to New York, he wrote me letters for six months. Every day, al-

most. Then he moved here himself. He just wouldn't leave me alone."

"But you liked him."

"Of course I liked him. He was a great boy. Very handsome. Well, you can see that. He still is. And he was nice—smart enough for anybody. Sure, I liked him."

Speak of the devil: Jimmie was calling her again, from the bedroom. "I'll be back," said Jewel. "Take care of the coffee? There's evaporated milk or regular."

She left, and I waited for the coffee to come to a boil, then lowered the heat, then timed it. Seven minutes. Exactly. I took the pot off the burner, put it down on a trivet, and smoked a cigarette. I smoked another. Then I pulled yesterday's *Mirror* from a pile of papers tied with string on the floor below the dumbwaiter. When Jewel came back she caught me reading "Derby Dugan."

"You're not really going to let poor Tim Topp marry that awful debutante, are you?"

"You'll have to read along and find out."

"Can't you tell a pal?"

"Not even a pal."

"Speaking of pals, I read something about your pal Walter Geebus." She was pouring our coffee.

"Yeah, I saw that. In Nosy Natwin's column? But it's not true. Walter barely knows her. And he's not my pal. How's Jimmie?"

Jewel rolled her eyes. "I'm sorry I took so long. He gets whiny when he gets sick. What were we talking about?"

"You at the Martha Washington."

"I liked it. It's a women's hotel."

"Yeah, I know. So how long did you stay single? After Jimmie came down?"

"Not long." She finally got around to sipping her coffee. "He wasn't always like this," she said after she'd put the cup back in the saucer. "But he's always like this now. You saw his head—I saw you looking."

"What happened?"

"He got beat up, and I mean *really*. Three years ago last May. Right in front of me. I have a knack for seeing people get beat up and hit by cars and fall off cliffs."

I said, "Jesus." I'd *almost* said *me too.*

"And he's been that way, the way you saw him tonight, ever since. And it's all my fault."

"How is it that?"

"If I tell you, promise you won't think poorly of me?"

"Oh, come on."

"Promise? I mean it."

"Sure I promise."

"All right, then. But remember, you promised." Jewel picked up her coffee spoon, put it down. "I guess I'd been living at the Martha Washington a little more than six months when I got a call one evening—visitor downstairs. It was Jimmie. I was so glad to see him! At first. Till he told me that he'd sold his family's restaurant and moved to New York. Just like that. Moved here! Because he'd decided that I needed to be courted. He'd got it into his head that's why I'd left Megville in the first place—that I wanted him to follow me down and court me." She tipped her head back and laughed. When she did, her breasts lifted. She looked at the ceiling and went on speaking.

Jewel kept trying to tell Jimmie Rodgers that she wasn't interested in getting married, to him or anybody else, but he just kept showing up. Night after night. She was furious, but—well, he *was* Jimmie Rodgers, from down the street. He would

always be Jimmie Rodgers from down the street. She couldn't
just chuck him out of her life, and besides, there were some
things about him that she really liked.

"Yeah?" I interrupted her right there. "Name some."

Jewel lifted her head, then sat back up straight; she looked
at me with one eyebrow arched. "He's a good dancer. He's a
good kisser."

"You can go on with your story now."

She laughed, then did.

At least once a week she went on a date with Jimmie, and
this one particular evening—in late May of 1933—they went
out with Jewel's roommate, a girl named Gladys. "Gladys was
seeing this musician," said Jewel. "Chick Bernstein. We were
going to meet him at the Savoy Ballroom. . . ."

They got to Harlem around eight, paid their twenty cents
apiece at the door, and walked in, and what a racket, what a
crush, colored and white all together on the big dance floor,
shagging to high-note bumpety-bump jazz. Soon as you came
in there you smelled reefer and saw the blue smoke drifting in
veils. It seemed like everybody was blowing the stuff—at the
bar, at the tables, while dancing, even in the gents' and in the
powder room, where you could buy it three joints for a quarter.

"Jimmie got pretty upset," said Jewel. "He'd never been to
a place like that before. Well, neither had I. And he was saying
that we should leave even before we sat down. He's always been
a straight-arrow, and seeing all that marijuana, he was terrified
the cops would come busting in. You know?" She laughed.
"But it wasn't only that. Even worse, as far as he was concerned,
was being someplace with coloreds passing you by, bumping
into you, and they weren't the help but the clientele."

Jimmie kept expecting to see a Negro man pull a knife, naturally over a woman, and he kept nudging Jewel to leave, an-

noying her, and the more that he pestered her, the more exasperated she got. Damn it, Jimmie, just relax and have a good time. But he couldn't. So he sulked.

Gladys's boyfriend was playing clarinet in the band, and when there was a break between sets, he came and sat at the table for a drink. Then he and Gladys slipped off together somewhere, and right away Jimmie started in again, wanting Jewel to leave.

"We had a little argument. Nothing so terrible, but he got the message. I was having a nice time and if he wanted to go, there was the door, but I wasn't leaving with him. Thanks, Al," she said, because I'd just refilled her coffee cup.

She offered me a brownie. I broke it in half, then ate both halves. "What happened after your little argument?"

"We stayed. But he wasn't happy about it. He wasn't happy about anything. Bad night for Jimmie Rodgers. He couldn't even catch the attention of the cigarette girl."

So he finally got up to go buy a package of smokes at the bar. Practically the moment he was gone, a young guy sat down in Jimmie's chair. He was good looking, a flashy dresser, and he pointed at Chick Bernstein's clarinet, lying on the table alongside Jewel's purse. Do you know how to play that instrument? he asked. Jewel laughed, said no, she's not musical, and besides, the clarinet's too big. If she played anything, she said, she'd play a piccolo.

The guy burst out laughing, and Jewel blushed, just then realizing that she'd innocently picked up on his double-entendre and talked back to him smutty without even knowing it. Even so, she thought it was funny. Then the guy offered her a cigarette. She declined. He asked her to dance, and she pointed out that there wasn't any music.

"You ever get the guy's name?"

"No."

"No?"

"We're talking maybe a grand total of two minutes, Al."

"All right. So what'd he do next?"

"Invited me to a party."

"And you said?"

Jewel looked at me sharply.

She told him no, of course; she was there with somebody.

The tough guy glanced again at Bernstein's clarinet, smiled at Jewel, stood up from the table. Well, he said, you can't fault a fella for trying.

"He wasn't trying very hard," I said.

"No," said Jewel, "and it was all harmless. But when Jimmie came back? I told him what happened. I'm still not sure why. But I shouldn't've."

Because Jimmie Rodgers, the Boy Scout in a sour mood, saw red—and went looking for the masher.

"They had words," said Jewel. "Then Jimmie pushed him. And the guy left. Well, he didn't really *go,* he just waited. Outside. And the minute we stepped through the front door later, he beat Jimmie over the head with a tire jack. He kept hitting him and hitting him and I thought he was going to kill him. Right there in front of me. And Jimmie's been that way, the way you saw him tonight, ever since. And it's all my fault. Think I'm awful?"

I said, "Of course not. You didn't know that Jimmie'd go so green-eyed."

"Didn't I?" She smiled sadly. "Anyhow, I married him in the hospital. I wouldn't even wait for him to get released."

Right then, Jimmie called her again.

"Excuse me," she said, and went to him.

But that time Jewel didn't return, Jimmie did—coming into the kitchen a quarter of an hour later wearing house slippers and a belted robe. He looked sweaty in the face, and pale, he was the color of buttermilk, and he was frowning. Till he put on a bright smile. A bad imitation of his wife's original.

I asked him how he felt.

"I'm feeling better. I'm feeling better, thanks." He frowned again, then laughed meaninglessly. He pinched the tip of his nose between a thumb and first finger. "It was nice meeting you, Al. Nice to meet you."

"You too."

He stuck out his hand, to shake, but when I took it, he tugged, and I came promptly to my feet. Then I got it: I was supposed to drift. Say good night and go. "Jewel's waiting," he said. "I should go put it to her. I think I'll go put it to my wife, right now." He gave me a big stupid wink, like a vaudeville comic, then turned around and shuffled off. But he stuck his head back through the kitchen doorway. "Jewel thinks she looks like Myrna Loy, that's how come I kid her about it. Myrna Loy is a peach! Myrna Loy is a real peach. Of *course* I think she's a peach. But I don't tell Jewel. I don't tell Jewel. And give her a swelled head? Give her a swelled head? Over my dead body!"

EPISODE SIX

JONES IN THE PARLOR

After Joe Wein finally rolled out, I stripped down to my union suit, brushed my teeth, and went to bed. Ten minutes later the phone rang again. Walter, that time. "Lower your thermostat," I told him, "open a window, get back under the covers, and leave me alone. You're not dying."

"That's not funny."

"I wasn't trying to be. Go to sleep."

"I can't! And you can't, either."

"Why not?"

"Because you have to come over the house, right now."

I hung up, but he called straight back, so I broke the connection and left the receiver off the cradle. Come over to his house! In the middle of the night? The guy should be committed.

I brushed my teeth again but couldn't fall asleep, so I got up and got dressed. (I've never owned a bathrobe, and if you're go-

ing to put on your pants, I figure you might as well put on everything else, even your strap watch.) By that time it was after midnight. I turned on the radio, started the electric percolator, and sat down at my typewriter. But nothing jumped. So I thought, why not? It's officially Tuesday.

Ruth let me in. She was the oldest Sullavan sister, in her middle thirties, and the plump one, but the prettiest, and she was disappointed that I hadn't brought an early edition of the *News*. Oh well, she'd just have to go buy one herself. Was it bitter out? she wanted to know. "Judy'll be free in a coupla minutes," she said.

I carried my coat and hat down the long hall, past the girls' sleeping bedrooms, their business bedrooms, and the kitchen. The unpapered walls were missing big chunks of plaster and scrawled over with phone numbers and personal messages, and thumbtacked with maps of New York, New Jersey, Connecticut, and New England. At the end of the hall was a framed tintype that hung by fish wire and showed an unidentified team of mustachioed turn-of-the-century softball players.

Sort of a dismal place, but I liked it.

The parlor was crammed with three horsehair sofas, an upholstered chair, an ottoman, a buffet, a pianola, several lamps, and a regulation poker table, where that early morning Dorothy Sullavan, the baby sister, and the one who liked Gershwin music, sat playing a board game with Clark Kamen.

"Al Bready! There was something I wanted to tell you, and now I can't . . . no! I remember! Remember that guy that stole all those stories of yours and tried to sell them? I saw him the other day and he hates your guts. If he runs into you, he's going to stab you." Kamen shook and spilled the dice cup. Then, moving his game piece—a tiny blue steamship—across the

purple continent of Africa, he said to Dorothy, "This guy typed up a bunch of stories that Al had published and tried selling them to the competition. Al got him bounced from the Fiction Guild, and now he's out for blood."

I took a seat on one of the sofas. "Don't listen to him, Dorothy. The guy he's talking about is ninety years old and lives in Queens."

"I never listen to Clarky," she said. She threw the dice for a total of eleven and hopped her biplane from the Philippines to Pago-Pago. "What, did he just say something?"

Clarky beamed at Dorothy with adoration. Then he turned his attention back to me. "So Al, how've you been?"

"Pretty good. Yourself?"

"Truth be told, not so wonderful. I've had a bit of a rough ride lately, as you know." And he looked it, too: he'd lost about twenty pounds since I'd seen him last, and his face was drawn, and his neck was scrawny and creased. "But I'm turning things around. I'm going back into business."

"That so? What with—another pulp?"

"Never! That stuff is over, Al, that stuff has had its day."

"I hadn't noticed."

"You will. No, I'm done with the pulpwoods. Those are dinosaurs. But this new thing—" He broke off, looked reflective, and was godawful hammy about it, too. Then he smiled, swiveling in his seat to lean toward me. "*You* might be interested. You might even want to do a bit of writing for me again. It's up your alley, Al."

"No, thanks."

"Say, look, I went *bust*. You weren't the only guy lost money. I lost my shirt. I lost my company! I got hurt worse than you."

"I'm not saying anything, I'm just saying no, thanks."

"Clarky? Are we playing this game, or you just want to gas?"

"Please, Dorothy, just hold your little hand steady at the controls, I'll be right with you. Al? Let me ask you something. You know a lot of comic-strip fellas. Anybody offhand you can think of might be looking for regular work?"

"Offhand? Only about nine dozen. What kind of regular work do you have in mind?"

Clarky said, "Well, I'll tell you—" then didn't, because just at that moment Judy Sullavan, the middle sister, and the one studying general nutrition at Hunter College, breezed into the parlor, preceding a slender brown-haired man dressed in a dark gray suit, a white shirt, a red tie, and a greasy black celluloid mask fastened to his face with an elastic cord. "Glory be to God, it's Jonesy! Say, Jonesy, I didn't know you were here, I thought you were still in the nuthouse."

The masked man glanced at Clark Kamen with a dim and diffident smile. He wasn't very tall, around five feet six, but he carried himself straight, and his head moved slowly from side to side. His chin was square and cleanly shaven. Mysterious Jones. He'd been a fixture around Manhattan since—well, I'm not sure since when, exactly. Sometime during the twenties, I guess. You'd see him from time to time. On the street, on the subway, in a couple of saloons down in the Village. He was scarred by acid. He had a pornographic tattoo on his face. He'd been involved in a humiliating scandal. Who knew? Nobody. And nobody would think to ask him, not even newspapermen. It was too much fun guessing.

Jonesy gathered his topcoat and fedora from a hook on the wall, and reached behind a sofa to pick up a gladstone embroidered with flowers, the kind of thing an old maid carries aboard

a train. He shook hands with Judy Sullavan, then pulled on a pair of leather gloves and disappeared down the hall.

We all listened, and once we'd heard the apartment door open and close, the Sullavan girls broke into giddy laughter. "The mysterious Mr. Jones," said Clarky. "Judy, tell us. Does he keep it on during the act?"

"You'll never know." She was wearing a pink Turkish toweling robe, and she wiped her forehead with a big sleeve, then plopped down on the sofa, lit a cigarette, and put her bare legs up on the ottoman. Both knees were red.

"Puts you through a drill, does he?"

"Ah, button it, Clarky." Then, swallowing a big yawn, she asked, "There any more takers, or can I get dressed?"

Clark Kamen gave me a slight nod. "You go ahead, I want to finish this game."

"Game. You just don't have the five bucks," said Dorothy, but not unkindly, and with a smile.

"Maybe so. But you won't be able to say that in a few more days."

"Your roll."

So I got up and followed Judy from the parlor and into the hall, and past the kitchen, where Ruth was sitting at the table, poring over *Time* magazine.

"You work for Kodak, don't you?" said Judy.

"No," I said, putting down five singles on top of the bedroom highboy, next to the pitcher and basin.

"I'm looking to buy a six-twenty."

"I don't work for Kodak," I said, feeling irked. "I can't help you."

"You're not Chet?"

"No, I'm not Chet, I'm Abe. Abe Ongo."

She looked dubious. "But we know each other."

"We do."

"Abe," she said. "Abe . . ."

When I switched off the lamp, though, she said, "Oh, *now* I remember. Sure," she said. "But you're no Abe, you're *Al.* And I'm—not supposed to say anything. Okay, Al, talk to you later. Enjoy her."

As practically anybody who followed "Derby Dugan" in that period could tell you, Abe Ongo was a tall, skinny small-town barber with a spade-shaped head—an ordinary joe with a Jewish accent who just so happened to be the most amazing person who ever lived: because he never died. He'd invented the scissors and the haircut, in biblical days, and never died. No special reason, he just never did. Never aged, either. The way that Walter drew him, Abe Ongo seemed about fifty—though when I'd made him up, I said he should look like a thirty-year-old. I was just a few years shy of thirty, myself, at the time.

Abe first appeared in the strip during the fall of 1932, in my opinion one of the best "Dugan" years ever. Maybe *the* best. It was the year we killed off Zagreb, the saintly old kite maker. A *good guy,* and we killed him off! It made the news, people sent flowers galore, there were mock funerals all across the United States, and Henry Ford, Wallace Beery, even Pablo Picasso were

said to have wept real tears. And '32 was also when Great-uncle Wondrous contracted leprosy; we couldn't actually use the word *leprosy,* the syndicate said no, but readers knew what the hell was the matter with him, all those bumps on his face, wearing that cowl, and the response was just phenomenal. Doctors wrote in, missionaries, and when Great-uncle Wondrous had to go into absolute quarantine, some lumber millionaire from Seattle wired King Features offering his private island in the Puget Sound! And the guy was serious! Oh, it was a great year, all right. Capped off with the first appearance of Abe Ongo, in a story that ran for ten Sundays throughout the autumn.

We'd always kept the daily and Sunday continuities separate, because the syndicate said that we had to, the idea being you'd never confuse or vex, and consequently lose, any reader who didn't subscribe to a paper that carried both. Except for the main two characters and the major secondaries—Ma Billions, Sheriff Pinch, Tim Topp—hardly anyone from the daily strip ever showed up on the Sunday page, or jumped from the Sunday over to the daily. To be a player in both versions, ten thousand readers had to clamor for you, in writing. At least that was the way it worked before the immortal barber came along.

Abe Ongo was a very special case. Never what you'd call a reader favorite, he nonetheless became a daily and Sunday semiregular because Walter Geebus wanted it. In fact, I think it's safe to say that Walter liked that character and what he was more than anything else I ever came up with, and that includes the magic yellow wallet, which reaped him a fortune in toy royalties.

Because of the whole color process, making separations and whatnot, we had to work three months ahead on the Sunday

pages—which means that it must have been late May, early June of 1932 when I gave Walter my rough outline and the first couple of scripts for the Ongo story. Derby is working after school at Abe Ongo's poky little Main Street barber shop when he discovers, hidden on a shelf behind scent bottles and shaving mugs, dozens of little boxes, each one containing hair clippings and labeled with the name of somebody famous: Samson, Solomon, Cleopatra, J. Caesar, G. Khan, L. DaVinci, A. Lincoln, and so on and so forth. Charlemagne. M. Antoinette. A. G. Bell. Turns out, Abe Ongo has barbered almost every famous head for the last two thousand years . . . and we're off.

I remember that I wasn't at all sure Walter would go for the idea. He wasn't especially open to what he called my "supernatural crap," which is why there never was a ghost story in the strip, though I'd pitched him several good ones. He'd say, "I want realistic stuff, Al. This is a realistic strip." And I'd say, "Oh really? Dogs talk?" He'd give me a look, maybe the finger—and out went the fantastic. Usually. When I dreamed up the magic wallet? He said no. At first he said no fucking way. But I said, "Think about it. People are broke, Walter, nobody's working—they're going to love this wallet, you'll see." Well, I was right, wasn't I? You look back on those days, what jumps into your head? Bread lines, strikes, hillbilly bank robbers. Lindbergh's baby. Gangster movies. Fred and Ginger. "Brother, Can You Spare a Dime." And Derby Dugan's magic yellow wallet, always a ten-spot there when he needed it. And Walter Geebus had been ready to bury the gimmick!

So when I came in with the first Abe Ongo script, I was all prepared to remind him about the wallet. But it wasn't necessary. He read everything I gave him and his eyes opened wide. He looked at me and pointed a finger.

Zingo.

But it wasn't till a few days later that I realized just why he was so thoroughly taken with the whole conceit. He called me up ten, ten-thirty in the morning, saying I should meet him at noon at the Union League Club; he's taking me to lunch, he says. And when I get there—to that bastion of conservative Republicanism, every peevish member a sworn Roosevelt hater, but what the hell, I'd eat anybody's roast beef—Walter's is the only smile on any face, waiters included. Look at him. He looks like the happiest guy in New York City. And as soon as I sit down, he hands me a check for a hundred bucks. What's this? "That's for Abe," he says. Then he says, "One thing, Al. I don't care what you do with the rest of the story, do what you want, just don't make it that he's bored."

"What?"

"Our friend Abe. It's not going to turn out that he's bored from living so long, right?"

"Oh, no. Right."

He sat back in his chair. "I was thinking about it last night," he says. "What an idea!"

"Yeah?" And all of a sudden I get this pang. Oh Jesus. Does he think it's an *original* idea? I mean, the damn hero pulps were full of immortals, though it's true that none of them were barbers. "So you like Abe, huh? Glad to hear it."

"Yeah, Abe's all right, he's swell. But I tell you, it didn't hit me right away, what we got here. I knew I liked it, but till last night? I couldn't tell you why."

"Now you can?"

He said, "All it takes is one."

"One?"

"One guy that doesn't croak. That's all it takes."

"Sure," I said. "Takes for what?"

"Optimism, Al. Optimism." He nodded, then our drinks came. "Here's to Abe. He's the first. I'm going to be the second. You want to be third?"

"Why not?"

"Why not!" We clinked glasses.

EPISODE SEVEN

THE BODY IN WALTER'S BATHTUB

The DeSoto's night clerk hailed me from across the lobby. "Guy's been calling for you every ten minutes."

"Let me guess. Named Walter?"

"You best ring him back, he says it's an emergency."

I nodded and started up the stairs, but got only as far as the first landing.

"Bready, it's him again!"

So I went back to the desk and took Walter's call from there. "It's two o'clock in the morning, in case you don't know it."

"Will you please shut up and listen to me? Listen! Please!" The guy sounds frantic, off his top. And he's breathing funny. Suddenly I wasn't feeling so gruff.

"What's the matter, Walter?"

"Just come over here!" And he's not asking me anymore, he's pleading. "I got a girl in the house and I think she's dead."

"What do you mean, you 'think'? Is she or not?"

"She's in the bathtub—"

"*Who* is?"

"I don't *know* her name, all right?"

"Call the cops."

"No, listen, just listen. You come over here now," he said, whispering hard, stressing each word, "and we'll get her dressed. *Then* I'll call the cops. I can say, I could say the both of you dropped by for a drink and *then* she died. Just—died. You're my witness."

"Forget it. You can just forget it, Walter, because I'm not—you hear me?—*not* coming."

When I arrived, his place was all lit up, but that was typical: Walter Geebus burned every lamp, in every room, every night. I rang the bell. Nobody answered. I started knocking. Still no Walter. So I used my key. I'd had one for years. The few times Walter had gone on vacation—always to the same place, to Ogunquit—I'd stopped by twice a day to feed and walk his dog, a big, noisy Chesapeake that he used to have. Sadie Geebus owned it now—had got it, I think mostly out of spite, as a part of their divorce.

"Walter?"

"Well, look who's here. It's Al the pal. Pull up a stair, Al, take a load off."

Dressed in chocolate flannel pajamas, the crazy bastard was seated on the carpeted stairs, halfway up the flight, and gazing at a spot in between his house slippers. A goofy, twitching smile played on his lips. His pajama top was soaked through, sticking to him.

"Why didn't you answer the door?"

He glanced up, frowning then, like I'd just popped him a tough question, a real puzzler, he'd have to rack his brain. Seeing that stupid expression—that's when I got spooked.

Because there was no dead hooker in the house. I was positive.

"You're drunk."

"Am not!"

"The hell you're not." But when I put a hand on his shoulder, leaned down, and took a sniff, I couldn't smell booze.

"Satisfied?"

"What's going on, Walter?"

"Don't shout, for Christ's sake. I got a headache."

I left him sitting there all limpsy and went on up to the second floor, then down the papered hall to look in the master bath. Like I'd figured, there was nobody—no body. And the big tub was dry.

I pushed open the connecting door to Walter's bedroom. His bed—an antique four-poster that he claimed once belonged to some New England guy who'd signed the Declaration of Independence, or refused to sign, I forget which—anyhow, the bed was still made up. No commercial activity had taken place there tonight. Jesus Christ, Walter.

I checked both guest rooms at the opposite end of the hall, along with their baths, just to be sure. No hooker. Thank God. But on the other hand: Jesus H. *Christ,* Walter.

When I returned to the front stairs, he'd got up and gone. I searched both parlors—even went out on the high stoop to look up and down the street. Then I went downstairs, through the dining room and the butler's pantry into the kitchen. And found him at the breakfast table uncapping a bottle of Jacob Ruppert.

In front of him, yesterday's *Daily Mirror* was spread open to the funnies and sprinkled with a dozen or more aspirin tablets. He picked up one from an "Ella Cinders" panel, stuck it under his tongue, and washed it down with beer. "This headache," he

said. His voice sounded better, stronger. But he was still very pale. "I woke up with this damn headache."

"Woke up where? You never went to bed."

"I fell asleep in the parlor."

"You had a headache this morning."

"That was a different one."

"Walter, you called me up—do you remember?"

"Sure, yeah." He collected three, four more tablets.

"Don't take all those."

"My head's killing me." But he swallowed only two. "It's killing me."

"See a doctor."

"They always find something wrong. No, I don't want to see any more doctors. This is all Frank's fault. He should rot."

"Don't worry about it, Walter. He's rotting."

"Yeah, him and me both. Get a beer, why don't you? Sit down. You look like the sheriff, standing there."

I didn't feel like drinking, but I sat at the table, to make him happy. "So. You remember telling me there was a dead girl in your bathtub?"

"That's what I said? I said that?"

"That's what you said."

"Holy Christ." He rubbed a fist across his cheek and pulled his mouth out of shape. "I'm cracking up. You think?"

"It's occurred to me."

"No. Wait. Something. There was something . . ."

"You were dreaming."

"Yeah. I must've been. I guess. But not about a bathtub."

"That's what you said."

"No, something else. I'll remember."

"Skip it."

"I can't believe I said that." He picked up another tablet, from "Li'l Abner," then put it down on "Desperate Desmond." "I don't know where that came from. I mean, I *do*—but why I'd think it happened to me . . ." Walter shook his head sadly. "The hooker in the bathtub. Was Ed Kellogg that happened to."

"Ed Kellogg?"

"Ed, you know Ed Kellogg."

"Sure I know him."

"I'm talking back must be seven, eight years. He drew his own strip then. Girl strip, called 'Darlin' Jane.' For the Mc-Naught Syndicate."

"I don't remember it."

"It's long gone. 'Darlin' Jane,' by Ed Kellogg. Nice signature. I always liked how he signed that strip. His double *g*'s? He did as figure eights. It looked good." Walter nodded pensively, then quick-popped another aspirin and chased it down with beer.

"He was married to this little bitty blond thing, couldn't've weighed more than ninety pounds, but Ed went in for bigger stuff. *Big* stuff." With both hands, Walter hefted and squeezed an imaginary full bosom. "Everybody kidded him for taking out these fat babies. Then one of them went and had a heart attack. In his hotel room. In the bathtub. Made the papers. Wife left him. All that. Took the kids. Well, you saw him, when he worked here. Hungover every morning."

"Jesus. That happened?"

"Really happened." Walter sat quietly for half a minute, then got up and shuffled to the sink. With his left hand, he splashed cold water quickly on his face. "But I don't know why I'd suddenly think it was happening to *me.*"

"Like you said, you were dreaming."

"No. Yeah, I was dreaming, but—I wasn't dreaming about that, exactly. Something else. But when I woke up, I guess . . . I don't know." He dried his face on the roller towel. "Did I say I was sorry?"

"Not yet."

"I'm sorry." He opened the refrigerator, took out another beer. "I'm sorry for calling you up like that. Sure you're not drinking?"

"Why not?"

"Why not." He opened two bottles and sat down. "Ed Kellogg. I don't know *where* the hell he is now."

"Working for Caniff."

That didn't seem to register. Walter just shook his head. "And Ronnie Lincoln? Drew 'Little Kit Carson'? Same thing, almost."

"Not quite. It was cocaine."

"Cocaine—and that little colored singer he was stuck on so bad."

"But he's still doing his strip."

"No, he's not. No, he is not. They got somebody else drawing it now, Ronnie's out. The man is in Arizona, last I heard, working for a paint company. And he used to have a gorgeous house in New Rochelle! Big white thing. A mansion. Now look at him. And Ed Kellogg. I could name you a dozen others, up and then down. What a happy bunch of fellas. We're all a bunch of happy fellas, aren't we, Al? All of us funnies folk?"

"Walter, you had a bad dream, forget it. You got confused."

"Yeah—enough to call up somebody in the middle of the night. 'Confused.' What's that word say to you, Al? Who gets 'confused'? Old men."

"You got a long way to go yet."

"Not at this rate. I keep doing what I did tonight—"

"You didn't do anything, Walter, it's all right."

"—I'll end up like Ed Kellogg and Ronnie Lincoln, just another guy that *used* to have a strip. I couldn't stand that, Al. They take it away, I'd shoot myself. I mean it. I'd do it."

"Like hell. And could we change the subject now?"

"Insurance companies hate cartoonists. Did you know that? We kill ourselves left and right. Billy Marriner. Gus Dirks. Rudy's brother Gus? Walt McDougall? Left and right. Bunch of happy fellas."

"Okay, let's *not* change the subject."

"That strip is all I got. Take it away—much as I hate the fucking thing most of the time—and I'm finished. But just let somebody *try.*"

"Now you sound like your old self again—so I think I should leave. And you should go to bed."

"Stay over. You can sleep in the guest room."

"Pass. I'll call a cab."

But when he reached for more aspirins, I covered his hand with mine and said, "Then let's go upstairs if I'm staying."

Going up through the house from Walter's kitchen, every lamp we'd pass, and every electrolier, each and every wall fixture, I'd turn it off. "You're not paying the bills, for Christ's sake, Al—just leave them on." He was trying to make me feel like some dotty old lady, I suppose, but it didn't take. "Leave them on! What're you doing?" He'd flopped down on a leather chesterfield in the back parlor and was shaking his head. "Leave *one* on, at least. I'll break my neck if I come down again."

"I thought you were going to sleep."

"I said if."

"It'll be daylight in two, three hours."

"Leave something on. Just humor me."

"Isn't that what I've been doing the past five years?"

"Fuck you, Bready." He laughed, though.

So I left a lamp burning. It was a little porcelain Chinese thing with a fluted shade on a table with the telephone and a small grouping of photographs in pewter frames—more of those Walter-ands, like the ones hanging from hooks on the staircase wall. Walter and the Dorsey brothers. Walter and Adele Astaire. Walter and Fred Allen. It was funny, being reminded how social the man used to be, once upon a time. "When was this, Walter?"

"What?"

"This picture." I held it out.

"If you left the goddamn lights on, I could maybe see what you're showing me."

"This picture of you with George McManus and Billy De Beck. And is it Milt Gross?"

"Milt Gross. And that's Peter Arno behind me with the noisemaker. New Year's Eve, '31, '32."

"Those were great parties, Walter. You ought to do it again."

"Never. Too much trouble." He got up and walked through the front parlor into the foyer. "You coming?"

"Right behind you." I stood the picture back on the table. And switched off the table lamp.

"Doing anything this New Year's?"

"I haven't even thought about it," he said.

"Me either." When I hit the stairs where I'd found him so dazed, I got a pang and felt uneasy again. I'd almost forgotten why I was in that house at three in the morning. "You really ought to throw another big party, Walter."

"Why, so you'll have a place to go?"

"Get your name in the paper."

"It's there every day."

"Yeah, but you'd get it in a better section."

"Fuck you again."

I smiled and went up the rest of the stairs, thinking about those parties of Walter's. Preparations started at the end of October, invitations went out the Monday following Thanksgiving. To ballplayers and theater lights, politicians, bootleggers. Prizefighters. Strip, sport, editorial, and advertising cartoonists—dozens of cartoonists. Picture stars, painters, newspapermen. You could even be a Democrat and get invited. I met Lou Gehrig there, and Babe Ruth. Freeman Gosden and Charlie Correll. I sang Auld Lang Syne alongside the mayor of New York City. Me and LaGuardia! Singing together! Me, La-Guardia—and Walter Huston! Janet Gaynor fell in my lap. Jesus, just about everybody came. James Thurber. Eddie Cantor. Rube Goldberg. James Montgomery Flagg. Even Mysterious Jones, once. They were something, all right, those parties. Nursemaids for the kids. Strolling minstrels in Derby Dugan hats. Flowers all over the damn place. Hams, turkeys, smoked oysters. Sturgeon. Caviar. French pastries. And enough champagne to float the *Normandie.* It lasted all night and you stayed for breakfast.

"When was the last one you had, Walter?"

"Last what?"

"New Year's bash."

"I forget," he said, going into his bedroom. "Ask Frank Sweeney."

Joe Wein had called me a creature of habit, and I won't deny it. How could I? Since I was a young man, I'd do a thing once, and in one particular way, and that was it—I'd do it again and always the same way. I followed the same routes—this street, not that, that shortcut, not this—and planned my days carefully, fixing schedules for work, schedules for recreation, and I stuck to them. I never changed my typewriter or my stationer. I bought a package of cigarettes, always Herbert Tareytons, from the same tobacconist every morning, and if I smoked them all, well, I smoked them all—I'd have to abstain till tomorrow morning, or else mooch. I chewed gum only on weekends. I guess that made me a creature of habit, all right. Creature of habits.

Whenever I stayed overnight at Walter's house, I always picked the same guest room. The smaller of the two, the one with dream castles on the wallpaper, and the one that Sadie

Geebus used to refer to, mockingly, as "the boy's room." And except for a large, brash oil painting of the Sixth Avenue el that hung between the windows opposite the bed, it could easily have been that. What it had, in careless abundance, was all the charm and clutter of a Woolworth's.

In there Walter kept displayed in glass showcases and on bracket-mounted shelves his pristine collection of "Derby Dugan" merchandise. For going on forty years, he'd demanded one of everything made, whether it was a picture puzzle or an air rifle, a set of gum cards, a roly-poly, the lid from an ice-cream cup, or the dozens of different, but always "official," magic yellow wallets (ten-dollar bill not included). If it had Derby pictured on it, or Fuzzy, or anybody else from the cast of characters, Walter got one, and it had to be mint—no dents, no crumpled corners, no chips off the enamel—and he put it away in that bedroom. I never counted, but there had to be three, four hundred separate items. And even though I usually pocketed a little something—a decoder badge, a club ring, or a tie clip—every time I stayed the night, he never noticed. How could he? The room was *stocked.*

The one odd and jarring element was that big oil painting—titled *Eighth Street and Sixth Avenue,* according to the small brass plate on the frame. What did a picture of the elevated station—with a pretty blond woman in the street below angrily brushing locomotive coals from a sleeve of her dark blue jacket—have to do with "Derby Dugan"? Some years back, when I'd first spent a night there, I'd asked Walter about it. "Do you see the signature?" he'd said.

"No."

"Isn't that something? You practically can't find it, if you don't know where to look. It's there," he said, pointing to the

lower left corner. "Who'd bury his own signature? Not me. But *he* does. It's right *there.*"

I looked closely and found it: *Geo. Reckage.*

"Who's George Reckage?"

Walter smiled. "He gave me my first job, when I was sixteen."

"Doing what?"

" 'Doing what?' Doing the only thing I've ever done. Drawing pictures. I was his bright young assistant. At the New York *World.* George had one of the first Sunday panels, soon as Joe Pulitzer launched the Funny Side supplement, in '95. Same time as Outcault and Opper. Even before Dirks did "Katzenjammer Kids." Wasn't a strip then, just one big picture, everything all crowded in. Took up the whole page. You had the whole page to yourself. You really never heard of Georgie Reckage, really?"

"No. Did he use a character?"

"Sure he did. Jesus. It was this one, Al, *this* one," Walter said and swept his arm past all the accumulated Derby junk. "Only the kid was called Pinfold in those days. We changed it later." He frowned. "The panel was called 'Down in Awful Alley' and the kid was called Pinfold, and George Reckage drew it, and I helped him out. Then Hearst came from California and hired George over to the *Journal,* and he started doing the same feature there. He thought I'd go with him."

"You didn't?"

"Bet your ass I didn't. Pulitzer hired me to keep drawing Pinfold for *him,* and what happened, the same character was in two different papers every Sunday. One in the *Journal* and one in the *World.* My version and his."

"How'd he feel about your staying behind?"

"Georgie? We stopped talking. Forever. After he belted me in the mouth one day on the street. The way he saw it, I'd betrayed him. And I had, I guess—but not by taking over his feature. Pulitzer had the right to keep it going. And I had the right to make my way in the world."

"You and Horatio Alger."

"No, not really. I was a doctor's son, I never said I was poor. But I taught myself to draw and I got on the Hoboken ferry and I went to New York City and I found a job, and I made my own damn life. Nobody gave it to me, is what I'm saying."

"Jesus, all right."

"You were making a crack and I didn't like it."

"I'm sorry. It wasn't a crack, it was a joke."

"It was a crack."

"All right, it was a crack. But so how *did* you betray him, Walter—this guy? If it wasn't by taking over his Sunday page."

"I slept with his wife." He looked back at the painting, then with a shrug he turned and looked at me. "I was seventeen, and it was only a few times. And he never knew about it. I don't think. What're you staring at?"

"You. You slept with the man's *wife?* Gives you a job and you commit adultery with his *wife?*"

"It was a long time ago. And I committed fornication. *She* committed adultery, for your information, Reverend Bready," he said, straightening the painting which didn't need straightening. "I don't say it's my proudest achievement."

"So what finally happened to the great rivalry?"

"Didn't last. Because George didn't stick with Hearst. Less than a year. He quit to start painting. And the *Journal* canned his feature. Mine was more popular than his, anyway. I worked at mine and he never did. It's odd, though, isn't it? How thirty years later, I ended up going over to Hearst myself?"

"And he never did another strip?"

"George? No. Just painted. What do you think of this one? You like it?"

"I think. Yeah, I do. I like the woman in the blue coat."

"I like her, too."

"The wife?"

"Joette. But the painting is twenty years old. And he painted her younger, even so." Walter took a deep sigh. "When I knew her, she looked exactly like this. She used to be on the stage. Joette Davey." He stepped back from the picture. "I'm not crazy about his stuff, but it's all right. I got another ten, eleven in the attic."

"He know it?"

"What?"

"That you're one of his collectors?"

"*One* of? The *only* one, far as I can figure. And no, he doesn't. If he knew, he probably wouldn't sell to me."

"You're a funny guy, Walter."

"Yeah?"

"Sure. You figure you're paying back this guy that got you started. Buying his stuff. But so where do you hang it?"

"What's wrong with it here?"

"And downstairs you hang the fucking cows."

"That's a good painting! It's French and it wasn't cheap. And what's wrong with hanging this one here? It looks fine."

I didn't argue with him, but every time I'd get into bed in that room, last thing I'd do before turning off the lamp was to look at that glossy ashcan-school painting by George Reckage, surrounded by the gallery of "Derby Dugan" toys and dime-store paraphernalia, and I'd wonder if Walter honestly didn't know what the hell was so wrong with hanging it in such a place. Then I'd wonder if maybe I was being too criti-

cal, too prickly. Too Bready. Maybe the guy actually thought it looked good there. Looked right. Maybe there was no meanness about it, and no smugness. I couldn't decide. I just couldn't decide.

I really hated that bedroom, but I always slept in it whenever I stayed over.

ROWBOAT, CATTAILS, MOON

"Al. *Al.* You 'sleep? Wake up."

"Jesus, Walter—what time is it?"

"Little past five. I think. Wake up."

"I'm *awake.* What is it?"

"I remembered."

"What?"

"That dream I had, before I called you. I *told* you it wasn't about a bathtub, but it was close."

I sat up, halfway, jamming a pillow behind me with one hand and shielding my eyes with the other: Walter, the electric light fiend, had turned on both the table lamp and the ceiling fixture. He'd pulled up a chair alongside the bed and was leaning over me with a hand still on my shoulder. I pushed it off. And saw him. The second I did, I was sitting erect. His damp hair was smeared to his skull, and his pallid face—even whiter

and spookier now than before—was dripping sweat. His eyes looked filmy, but like they might pop.

"Walter, I think we better call a doctor."

"It wasn't a bathtub," he said, "it was a rowboat. See, it was the *water:* that's what fooled me. The connection—see? Was the water. So write this down: Derby's in a rowboat."

"Let me call your doctor."

"I told you, get a piece of paper and write this down. It's important. We can use it. Be a good Sunday page. Now get your pencil and get your paper and let's go to work."

After wiping his face on a sleeve, he clenched a hand around the back of his neck and squeezed. "Let's *go.*" Moving slowly, almost clumping—one slippered foot coming down heavier than the other—Walter left the room. "Derby's in a rowboat," he said from the hall. "It's night."

I got up quick, put on trousers, and bolted after him, saying, "Walter, you should lie down. And let me call your doctor." Meanwhile he's still muttering about a goddamn rowboat in the dark, and "a good Sunday page." All the way down the hall and into his bedroom.

"Al. Jesus."

"You'll be fine, Walter. Just lie back. Put your feet up. Good. Take it easy."

And he did, for about half a minute. Till he leaned out of bed and opened a drawer in the night table. "Now you got a pad of paper. Even a pencil. Here. So write."

"When'd you get that?"

"What?"

There was a .22 semiautomatic pistol lying in the drawer along with the fat rubber bands, the loose pennies, and old receipts. *"That."*

"I've had it. Now shut up. I told you it was the kid and the dog in a rowboat, didn't I? Derby's in a rowboat," he says. "It's night."

"Walter. Come on."

"The whole page," Walter says, "every panel is, what do you call that—a silhouette. Are silhouettes. Color page, we don't use color. Be different. Be good. Al? Be fun. You think? All right? All right," he says, "Derby's floating through cattails. In this big rowboat. Full moon. The kid and the kid's dog, the kid's talking. About it being so quiet and peaceful, good for the soul, stars in the sky, Almighty God. And don't you dare start dialing that phone. There's nothing wrong with me."

"Walter, you got a fever or something—*something's* wrong. You're shaking."

"Hang it up. I said, hang it up."

"All right."

Then he starts in again, his voice getting hissier, less steady every second, saying, "So the kid talks, and while he's talking? We see Fuzzy get up from the floor of the boat. Her ears perk. Finally, what do we see? Exclamation mark. Above her head. Al? Above her head, an exclamation point. Size of a baseball bat. A bat and a ball. And she says. She says." Walter turned his head and looked at me. "She says, 'A girl just floated by.' "

He grinned. His face all shiny, all wet. " 'A girl just floated by.' So now Derby looks. Next-to-last panel. He reaches. Like he's leaning to fish her out. No words. Last panel now. It's last panel, he's still reaching, we see his eyes go big. Only, hey Al? Here's the kicker. The floater got tits. The silhouette? Shows points. She's floating on her back, she's built. What do you think, Al? You like that? It's not a girl, Al, it's a woman. To be continued."

Walter sat there smiling at me, openly pleased with himself, and with his bad dream—his good Sunday page. But then his jaws clamped tight. I could hear teeth snap together. His eyes rolled. He lurched forward, thrust backward, and his pillow squirted away like a wet bar of soap. Then he slumped, slumped all the way over, his top half pitching off the side of the bed.

I caught him. Another second and he would have cracked his skull on the hardwood floor.

Starting from when I found my dad and his lady friend both shot in the stomach, I'd had a proneness for being present at the scenes of medical emergencies. A girl I used to date sliced off her ring finger, washing out a pilsner glass, and went into shock. I was standing right there, right beside her. And Bobby Reid? My best friend at Bayonne High School? Broke his leg on a camping trip with me at South Mountain Reservation. One of those breaks where the bone sticks out. And when I worked for the *Graphic,* this Jewish fella, real nice guy, selling ads at the phone next to mine choked on a sandwich. He turned blue. And not too long after I'd moved back to New York from my brother's house on Staten Island, my sister Jean showed up one day burning with fever and bleeding in her underpants—she came straight to me from the abortionist's. I was stuck with her for two days. Now Walter goddamned Geebus. Now him.

Sometimes I'd think I was cursed for a bystander. The way I looked at it, though, I tried to be philosophical. If you have to be one thing or the other? Witness or victim? Be the witness. Always be the witness. You're better off. And besides, unless you're a hopeless goof, it'll teach you to look both ways before stepping off any curb in the world.

EPISODE NINE

BLUM GETS THE WORD

At the hospital, I spoke to a couple of newspaper guys, both from the tabs. They'd strolled in, checking to see if anybody famous was sick or dying, and a nurse pointed me out to them. I said yeah, it was the same Walter Geebus that did the cartoon strip, uh-huh, but identified myself only as a personal acquaintance, figuring that Walter would just get sicker if he picked up the afternoon paper (unlikely as that was, considering) and saw me labeled there as the writer of "Derby Dugan." B-R-E-A-D-Y, I said. Al *Bready*. Uh-huh. The bird from the *News* mentioned Frank Sweeney's trial, but I offered no comment about that.

After they'd gone, I curled up in a chair for a short nap. It was even shorter than I'd intended. Fifteen, twenty minutes later, one of the lobby guards starts tapping his baton against the soles of my shoes. "Ida let you sleep, but you're snoring."

"Sorry."

"No big calamity. If you want a cup of coffee, there's a cafe-
teria down this hall. But if you want breakfast, you'd do better
going around the corner. They charge you an arm and a leg in
this place."

He shuffled off, and I inquired again about Walter at the
nurses' station. He was conscious, they said, and resting. No, I
couldn't see him. Perhaps that evening. Was I a relative? No?
Well, perhaps not even then. Could I speak to his doctor? I
couldn't do that, either. Dr. Gleason was making his rounds
and wouldn't be available for another hour at least. So I left and
had breakfast in that one-arm joint around the corner. Two
eggs, toast, coffee. "And let me have one of those donuts, with
the jimmies."

At the counter where I sat, somebody had left behind a bull-
dog edition of the *News,* so I paged through it. More blather
about the king of England wanting to marry that bag from Baltimore. Will he? Won't he? Who gave a rap? I thought he
looked like a big sissy, and she was no great beauty, the Simpson dame. She looked frumpy to me. Crazy world. Anyhow, the
crossword puzzle was half done, and I finished it. Moe Levy and
Son was having a big sale. The state of Pennsylvania had sentenced a Negro postal clerk to three years in prison for sending
love letters to Greta Garbo. I had a peek at the Inquiring Photographer. Question that day was: "Abraham Lincoln once said,
'All I am, I owe to my mother.' Do you attribute what success
you have had to your mother?" Everybody answered yes.

I'd have had to say yes and no.

I was starting to read Ed Sullivan's column when I suddenly
remembered Howard Blum.

It was a quarter past eight, and I didn't know when he usually got to Walter's house in the morning. He could've been on
his way there already, though I doubted it. I took out my ad-

dress book, looked him up, then rode a Checker down to West Thirty-eighth Street. "Four-forty-one," I told the driver.

The place turned out to be a brown brick tenement, slouching and flat-roofed, off Tenth Avenue just below Schermerhorn Playground, one block north of the New York Central's railroad yards. No doorbells, no speaking tube. In the vestibule there were mailboxes, eight altogether, each pasted with a name. Howard Blum lived in 4 rear. That figured. All the way at the top. I took my time going up, and by the second landing I'd started to pray that I'd meet Blum on his way down. No such luck.

"Who is it?"

"Howard? It's me, Al Bready."

"What're you doing here?"

"Could I come in?"

"It's not locked."

I opened the door and walked in, it was the kitchen, the place cold as a meat locker and unkempt as hell. Dirty plates and bowls were stacked inside black fry pans on the stove, and stacked high in the sink, too. Milk bottles and Eichler's beer bottles and a package of shredded wheat biscuits all stood together on a windowsill. The paper shade was greasy and taped along several ragged tears. There was a garage calendar tacked to the wall, a girly calendar.

Howard Blum stood up from his plate of jelly toast. He was dressed for work in a dingy white shirt and a cheap blue suit. A necktie was draped over the back of his chair. "What're you doing here?" His breath streamed out frosty like a talk balloon. "What's the matter?"

I told him.

He listened with a glower on his face, and when I'd finished, he asked, "So is he going to make it?"

"Couldn't tell you, kid. Don't even know what's wrong with him yet, but he's awake. So that's good. I guess. And as for your *other* question—"

"What other question?"

"—I don't know if you still got a job."

When I'd said that, he looked at me for a long time. "How come you're such a prick? What'd I ever do to you?"

"Called me a prick, for starters."

"Oh, sizzle off. Don't think you can insult me and get away with it."

"All I said, I just said I don't know if you still have a job."

"I heard you the first time. So who gets it?"

"Whoever they choose. Maybe they'll choose you."

"Then you should tell me who to call, so I could find out."

"Maybe I should call first."

"Maybe you should."

"Maybe I will."

"What is it with you, Bready?"

"I thought it was Al."

He shook his head. "What hospital's he in?"

"You want to know which hospital?"

"I asked, didn't I? What's so funny?"

"Nothing. I'm just glad you want to know."

"Oh yeah? I passed some test? Well, that's great. Now, what fucking hospital is the man in, you don't mind telling me?"

"Doctor's. Eighty-seventh and East End."

"What's he doing way over there?"

"He's rich. And you'd better check before you go, see if they're letting in visitors. Or I could check, and we could go together."

"I asked you what hospital. I didn't say I was going to visit him. And if you want to check anything, check what we were just talking about. And if you find anything out, let me know."

"I'll do that. If you had a phone, I'd call right now."

"There's a candy store on the corner. I'll walk you down."

"On second thought, it's kind of early. I don't know if I'd get anybody."

"You could try."

"I could."

"So will you?"

"Whose nickel?"

"Mine—all right? Christ's sake."

He put on his overcoat and we tramped downstairs and up to the corner. Howard took a stool at the fountain and I used the booth in back to call Pete Laudermilch at King Features.

Laudermilch said pretty much what I'd expected.

I said yeah, I'd tell the kid, no problem.

"Tell the kid *what?*" said Howard Blum. He'd pulled open the bifold door soon as I hung up. "Tell him what? That he doesn't have the job?"

"Nothing's definite. But I won't bull you, Howard, it doesn't look good. Don't set your hopes too high."

"I could do it! Damn."

"You been working for Walter less than a week. At King, they don't even know who you are."

"I could do that strip!"

"I'm not saying you couldn't."

"Why can't I meet them? I could *show* them. When I lived in Chicago I ghosted a *Trib* strip for almost four years. *Damn.* Who do they want to get?"

"They said nobody was definite."

"Yeah, but they must got *some* idea—"

"Bud Lydecker."

"Lydecker? Fucking Lydecker has a cow's arm. He can't draw, he'll ruin the strip. You seen what he did on 'Radio Patrol'?"

"I thought you were just the letterer and background man. What do you care?"

"Fuck you."

"I thought you weren't even a fan."

"If I'm not working for Mr. Geebus, I don't have to put up with your lip. So *fuck* you!"

The old guy working the fountain slapped down his hand. "Hey!" When we looked at him, he seemed briefly intimidated. But then he scowled again. "You want to use that kind of language, talk it someplace else."

Howard slumped against the phone booth like air was leaking out and he was going flat.

"This mean I don't get paid? I was supposed to get paid on Friday."

"I'll see what I can do."

"Forget it. You don't have to see to anything on my account."

"Good Christ, you're touchy. What, is it true what they say about members of your tribe?"

"You want a belt in the nose? You really *are* a prick."

"Maybe so, but for what it's worth, I told Pete Laudermilch they ought to look at your stuff before they give the job to somebody else."

"You did? You really said that?"

"Yeah, I really did."

No, I really hadn't, but what the hell. What the hell. If it made the kid feel any better, what the hell.

All that Tuesday afternoon—instead of cranking out a Broadway Prowler detective story, which is what I almost always did on Tuesdays, one till six—I sat in my room going through a

package of cigarettes and wrestling with that idea of Walter's, the dream, trying to figure out just who the floater might be. Nothing came, though. Except maybe, I thought, she could have a treasure map tattooed on her scalp. Or a small earring that was actually the key to a safety-deposit box. But neither gimmick was any good. Besides, we'd used both of them last summer.

Derby's in a rowboat, it's night.

Okay.

There's a floater.

It's a woman.

Derby's in a rowboat . . .

Nothing! No matter how often I turned it around, looked it over, said it out loud—"Derby's in a rowboat"—nothing came. Any time—*any* time!—Walter Geebus had ever handed me some premise, and usually it was nothing more than a general category that he felt like drawing, a flooded town or a South American jungle, I could always pump it into a usable plot in ten, fifteen minutes, half an hour at the most. Always.

Anytime, that is, till this time. And this time, nothing. Nothing came. My head was empty as that goofy king of England's, and I began to wonder—to *worry,* why not be honest— if the jig, maybe, was up. Finally up. The well run dry.

Scary thought.

And why was I even bothering with that stupid floater plot?

Walter might be dying, I thought.

Then I thought: Derby's in a rowboat. It's night.

It's night.

Around six o'clock, I gave it up finally in disgust, took a bath, and dressed to go visit Walter at the hospital. On my way to the lobby, though, I suddenly went back. Turned out it was

a false alarm, I still didn't have an angle on the damn story. Or
if I'd had one, I forgot it by the time I sat down at the typewriter again. So I just stayed there and smoked till it got to be
seven-thirty, and I realized what I was doing, I was putting off
going out till it was too late to go. Me and hospitals. Me and
hospitals. I'd rather go to war than go to one.

From when I was thirteen till when I was fifteen, I'd practically lived at the hospital. Never as a patient, though, just visiting. Always just visiting. My grandmothers—Grandmother Brady and Nana Carroll—both died old-age deaths at the same time in the same hospital, and I'd sat bedside with each of them, every day. Sometimes I'd visit Gran first, sometimes Nana. Gran's room, Nana's. Nana, Gran.

They died within days of each other, but right afterward, two weeks later, my little sister Jean developed a big tumor on her collarbone, it was a cancer, and I spent all my afternoons, for a blur of months, playing go fish and bingo with her in the children's ward.

After a short break, I was right back again, only that time it was to visit my old man and watch him turn into a morphine addict. He wouldn't talk, though—absolutely refused to say a

word, to me or to any of the cops that kept coming by to ask, "Who shot you, Mr. Brady? Who shot you and Mrs. Meatro?" He just looked at them, and looked at me, the same penitential look, then he shook his head, but he never said a damn thing.

Then my mother ended up in the same hospital, but on a different floor, with nervous collapse.

She wouldn't talk, either.

I went back and forth, his room to hers, her room to his, then I'd run home, twelve blocks, to feed my sister, who was still recuperating. Then I'd run back to the hospital. I did a lot of running. And a lot of reading in between. That's when I got through pretty much all of Jack London. Mark Twain. Booth Tarkington. And I was never able to read anything by any of those guys ever again. Those were terrible days.

I used to smoke with the cops. They felt sorry for me, I guess. One of them, Harold Sawicki, had gone to St. Henry's grammar school with my brother, who was married by then and living in Perth Amboy and didn't come to the hospital, not even once, the whole time our parents were in there. Fuck him, fuck Donald. But I was saying about Harold Sawicki being one of the cops. I knew him, and sometimes we played checkers. Sometimes cards. He'd say, "Don't worry, kid, they're not going to do anything to your mother." And I'd say what the family was all saying; my uncles and aunts and my cousins who were old enough to understand, we were all insisting that it was Mr. Meatro, it was Mr. Meatro—*he'd* shot them. Arrest *him.* Harold said, "The man was in North Carolina, Al. I'll see your nickel and raise you a dime." Terrible days. The worst.

But one good thing, I did get friendly with a student nurse. I wasn't quite fifteen, but I looked older. Her name—actually

her nickname—was Cookie, and one night in the doctors' lounge, in the dark, she let me feel her up. No, strike that. I don't think it ever really happened. There was a nurse named Cookie, but I think I must've imagined all the rest. As a kind of relief. Made it up, then believed it. So forget Cookie. But hospitals? I hated those damn places.

SHARKEY AND LAUDERMILCH

No matter what it said in Kilgallen's "Voice of Broadway" column, Walter Geebus was neither sketching in bed nor flirting with the nurses. When I got there on that Tuesday night, he was shallow-breathing under an oxygen tent, drifting in and out of fitful sleep. His complexion? Was the color of oatmeal cold in the pot. It scared me, how ghostly the man looked. And hearing that green cylinder hiss gave me the creeps.

Practically as soon as I'd gone in and seen him, I wanted to leave, but that would've been a punk thing to do, so I pulled up a chair and read through a pile of get-well telegrams, which included ones from the mayor and the governor, and I counted baskets of flowers, sixteen altogether, and I thought, Derby's in a rowboat, he's in a goddamned rowboat . . .

A nurse came and turned off the oxygen and folded back the tent, and Walter Geebus woke up. "Al?"

"Yeah, Walter. How you feeling? Get you anything? You thirsty?"

"No. But I got pins and needles."

"Where?"

"I'm not sure." He stared at the ceiling, flicking the tip of his tongue around his lips.

"How's the headache?"

"Better. They think it was—"

"Yeah. I know. I seen your doctor."

"I'm scared shitless, Al."

"I brought you some pajamas. And I picked up your mail. Nothing looks too important, but it's here, you want to see it."

"You were at the house?" I heard a slur in his voice for the first time. Before then he'd sounded feeble, tired; now he sounded mealymouthed.

"I didn't think you'd mind. And I doused the lights. Thought I'd save you a nickel." I'll see your nickel, I thought. And raise you a dime.

"The brat?"

"I saw him. I told him. Howard knows."

"What'd he say?"

"He said—what do you mean, what'd he say? He said it was awful, what else would he say? He'll be up soon as he can."

"Sure he will." I thought Walter was going to say something else, but he didn't. He just looked at me, and I couldn't tell whether he was scared or just doped up. Then he went back to staring at the ceiling, and I read the manufacturer's plate on the oxygen cylinder. Derby's in a rowboat. I got up and opened the wardrobe and peeked in at nothing but wooden hangers. It's night, there's a full moon. Cattails. I looked out the window. The floater got tits. The floater got tits, I thought, and then,

for the first time since leaving the Sullavan girls' house, I thought about Jewel. It felt tight, suddenly, all through my chest. I could hardly breathe. Jesus. Here we go. Me and hospitals. "Walter?" I put on my hat and coat. "See you tomorrow sometime."

I spotted Sadie Geebus coming up the corridor. She stopped and waited, then gave me a buss on the cheek. "I'm afraid to go in, Al. What do you think—should I?" She was whispering.

"I thought you were on your way to Cuba."

"Oh, that was just for him—to make him jealous."

"Jealous? He *wants* you married again."

"You don't know him, Al. After all this time? You still don't know Walter. I made the man jealous, trust me."

I wasn't going to argue with Sadie. But she was wrong. And she had some gall telling Al Bready that he didn't know Walter Geebus. What nerve!

"How does he look?"

"Not so hot, but he won't scare you to death. Just almost."

"That bad?"

"He looks small," I said.

"Already?"

"Maybe I'm wrong. Maybe it's just he's pale."

"Al, would you wait for me? Please? We can share a cab."

"If you want me to, sure."

I sat on a bench across from the bank of elevators. Derby's in a rowboat. On a river? Or a lake? An *inlet?* When one of the cars opened, Pete Laudermilch stepped out, accompanied by another man, a stranger to me.

Walter's editor, Laudermilch was one of those tall guys who manage to carry fifty pounds more than they should, yet not look fat, just large. With his left hand he was clutching a dozen roses in a green florist's wrapper, and with his right, a foot-high Bake-

lite Christmas tree that dangled with crudely painted character figures, some of them cast iron, some of them tin or pot metal, and some of them solid rubber, novelties sold at five-and-dimes, and all of them characters from the Dugan strip. Tim Topp. Ma Billions. Great-uncle Wondrous. Zagreb. Yin Yi. Abe Ongo. Sheriff Pinch. Sam Sandwich. A dime-bank Fuzzy, and several different Derbys. Derby waving. Derby winking. Hitchhiker Derby. I was charmed, and touched, and wondered what Walter Geebus would think. Not what he'd *say,* what he'd think. He used to be sentimental, but I hadn't seen much evidence of that streak in recent years. Maybe he'd get misty. But maybe not.

I greeted Laudermilch and the other man, both of them murmuring just about the same things in the same tone of voice, using just about the same words: poor Walter, it's unbelievable, terrible, a real shock. Then Laudermilch said, "Al Bready, Dan Sharkey. Dan's our new properties' manager. You come from Philly, too, don't you, Al? No? Al writes Walter's strip, Dan."

I said, "Glad to know you," and shook hands with Sharkey. His palm was soft as a dinner roll. He had coppery hair and a broad, handsome face, and looked much younger than Pete Laudermilch, who was in his late forties. I put Sharkey at thirty-four, thirty-five, around my age. I bet he'd gone to a good private college and pledged a national fraternity. No wedding band. He had mouthwash on his breath.

"Well," said Laudermilch to Dan Sharkey, "shall we go in then, say hello?"

"You go," said Sharkey. "I don't know the man."

"I'll introduce you."

"No, just you go. I'll wait here."

Laudermilch looked surprised, and if I wasn't mistaken, peeved off. But since Dan Sharkey was officially his boss, he

said all right, he'd be only a minute, and walked up the corridor to Walter's room. He hesitated, then stuck his head inside—"Is the king holding court? Hiya, Walter! Hiya, Sadie!"—and finally burst in, bearing his gifts.

"Cigarette?" said Dan Sharkey, offering me one of his.

"I'm on my way out." And I was, too: I'd decided I didn't want to wait around for Sadie, if it meant talking to this guy.

"Wish you'd stay a minute. Let's sit down."

I took his cigarette and a light from his Zippo.

"It's Al, right? I guess I should've known this, Al, but I always thought Walter Geebus wrote his own stuff. That pious reputation, at least."

I looked at him. What kind of thing was that to say? Pious reputation. "Lot of strip men keep the same thing quiet, Mr. Sharkey."

"Dan. And you're right, I suppose they do. How long you been with him?"

"Since the daily. Five years."

"Do we pay you? Or does he?"

"He does."

"That explains my ignorance." Sharkey flicked ash into the sandtray. "Do you mind my asking what you make?"

"I don't know. I guess not. Thirty a week. And please don't stare at me like that, Dan, I'll blush."

With a forced laugh, Sharkey reached over and scraped the end off his cigarette. The coal lay in the sand and kept smoking. "I'm not crazy about the politics, but it's a good strip."

"Are we talking about 'Dugan' now? Well, I'm not so crazy about them, either. That's just Walter."

"Boss Rascalvelt."

"Yeah, that was low. But it never ran, so where's the harm?"

Sharkey took out his lighter again and relit his cigarette. "It's a very good strip," he said. "Most of the time."

"Thanks."

"And it's held steady at four hundred papers for the last five years. No easy thing, with new strips coming out every month. You deserve a lot of the credit."

"Some of it. But it's a good-*looking* strip, too, and it's smart. That's Walter. I don't know what makes it smart, exactly, but it's smart, and that's all Walter Geebus. And it's four-fifty."

"Four hundred."

"That's what Walter says you guys say. But he says it's four-fifty."

For a moment Sharkey looked irritated, then he closed his eyes—though not quite entirely—and gave a little shrug. "He's welcome to look at the client list."

"That's another thing Walter says you guys say. He still doesn't believe you."

"Nobody believes the boss."

"No," I said. "Nobody ever does. Or likes him much, either."

"Wait a second. Is something happening here? Did I say something wrong?"

"Yeah. Called him pious. If I don't mind him taking the credit, I don't see why you should."

"I don't."

"Good. So what do you got against him?"

"Nothing."

"You wouldn't even go in there, say hello. And you're not ten feet away."

"Look, you want me to, I'll pay my respects. If it'll get us back on track."

"What do you care if we're on track or not?"

"Al, listen. I didn't go in there because I wanted to talk to you. When I found out who you were, I thought we should have a chat. That's all."

I waited.

"And okay, you're right. I do have a grouch on. You been with him five years, so you knew Frank Sweeney. You remember the letters? That business?"

"Walter's?"

"To Frank. Yes. The letters that your friend Mr. Geebus sent to Frank Sweeney in prison. They were beauts. Weren't they, Al?"

"It doesn't matter what Frank did to him?"

"Bad enough, all that," said Dan Sharkey. "But Jesus Christ, those letters! I was in the legal department at the time, and let me tell you, we all shit bricks."

"But nothing happened."

"No, nothing did. Fortunately." He got rid of his cigarette for good; I was beginning to think he'd grown fond of it, the way he kept letting it go out, relighting it, letting it go out. "And you're right, Al. I should go in there and say hello. I'll do that."

"You should. Seeing as how he could be dead in a couple of days, which is what you want to talk to me about. Correct?"

"Are you trying to make me feel heartless? I don't think that's fair. If he can't work for a while, and that's all I'm thinking about, then we have to make some arrangements. You'd stay on, I hope."

"Why not."

"Except that Mr. Geebus wouldn't pay you, we would. Hundred a week."

"I don't want it. Thirty'll be fine."

"Al. No disrespect. You nuts?"

"You pay me that, what happens if he comes back? He won't give me a hundred, and all of a sudden I'm off the strip. Fifty. I could get Walter up to fifty."

"Anything you say."

"And what about the other part? Pete said you'd probably go with Buddy Lydecker. That right?"

"Well, it's not even certain yet that we'll need a ghost."

"It's certain. Trust me."

"Bud's available then, yes. And he's a good man. What, you don't think so?"

"He sure loused up 'Tim Tyler's Luck' for a couple of weeks. That was him, wasn't it? His men looked like women and his women looked like Martians. But other than that, oh, yeah, he's darb. Just don't tell Walter. Unless you want to make sure that Lydecker inherits the fucking strip forever."

"Thanks for your opinion, Al."

"Why not Walter's assistant?"

"The Jewish boy, you mean? This is a major property, I don't think we're likely to give it to some twenty-year-old kid who we know can use a gum eraser but besides that . . ."

"He's twenty-two. And he ghosted a *Tribune* strip."

"Which one?"

"I didn't ask."

"Well, no decisions have been made, one way or another."

"Meaning decisions have been made."

"Now I know where Derby Dugan's sarcasm really comes from."

Sharkey laughed, I didn't, the elevator came.

I took it down, thinking, Derby's in a rowboat. It's night. Full moon. The kid and the kid's dog, the kid's talking. About it being so quiet and peaceful, good for the soul, stars in the sky, Almighty God. God Almighty.

Those crazy letters that Sharkey mentioned? Walter's to Frank Sweeney at Sing Sing. They'd been stupid, all right, and Walter had been a goddamn fool. He'd started with them six months after the criminal trial, following his harebrained efforts to bring a civil suit against Frank. A civil suit, for Christ's sake. He expected to get a money judgment on Frank Sweeney? Frank didn't have a pot to piss in. Walter may've once loved the guy, but true to form, he'd always paid him peanuts. There was no point in trying to squeeze Frank Sweeney. Walter's lawyer convinced him of that finally, and that's when he started drafting those damn letters. Long typewritten letters full of threats. He even hinted in one that he intended to pay some convict—a Negro convict, said Walter—to kill Frank someday in the exercise yard.

Of course, Frank complained to the warden there, and the warden—John W. Ingall by name—wrote to Walter, caution-

ing him strongly against sending any further mail. Walter panicked, totally panicked, so what he did, he made a sketch of Derby Dugan, hand-colored it, signed it, and sent it up to Warden Ingall, along with his apology. But the warden, obviously not a comic-strip fan, refused the drawing—he saw it as a bribe, and a shitty one at that—and sent it back. Not to Walter, though, straight to King Features. Which was how the syndicate first got wind of what the hell was going on.

At the hospital, when Dan Sharkey brought up those poison-pen letters, I got a real gut pang, let me tell you. For just one second I thought—hell, I was afraid that somehow he'd found out, but obviously he hadn't. There was no way he could have. Nobody, except Walter Geebus, knew that I'd actually written them. Well, *re*written them. From the get go, Walter had demanded that I correct and polish his lousy prose, lend a bit of style to his every grievance, to every splutter of cold rage, every threat. Jesus Christ, Geebus, give it up! But he wouldn't. Not Walter. Type, Al, type! The whole thing gave me cramps, and when it all came to a crashing halt—what a relief!

I never told Walter this, but at the same time that he was writing to Frank, I was, too. Above my own signature, I wrote him three or four letters, innocuous and chatty and nonjudgmental, and I enclosed with each of them a small batch of pulp magazines, comp copies of mine. No matter what had happened, I still felt badly for the guy. Poor Frank. When he got out of prison, he wouldn't be young anymore. And God only knew what he'd do with the rest of his life. Who'd hire him? Be crazy enough to risk it? But I quit writing once I received Frank's only reply, a single terse sentence printed all in block caps, comic-strip lettering, on a penny postal card: "SHUT UP, YOU!"

EPISODE ELEVEN

THE SCOOP TUREEN

"I thought you'd stood me up," said Sadie Geebus. I hadn't noticed her come off the elevator. Too busy, I guess, watching the student nurses. There were four of them, three of them pretty, all of them blotting stencils—yule logs, camels, shepherds, and wise men—on mirrors with surgical sponges dipped in glass wax. Sadie perched sidewise, unladylike, next to me on the banquette. "But here you are, Mr. Bready."

"There was somebody upstairs I got sick of talking to."

"Larkin?"

"I think his name is Sharkey."

"From Walter's syndicate, do you mean?—that prune?"

When I mugged disgust, she touched my knee and said, "They're not taking you off the strip, are they?" She looked cross, the way I used to see her get while talking to Walter, back when they were married. When she was angry, Sadie could seem like a bona fide Amazon, you could easily imagine her

wearing a breastplate and chucking a spear. I'm not fooling, either. It surprised me when she expressed concern that maybe I'd lost my job.

"No," I said. "I can stay. With Bud Lydecker drawing. Walter ever tell you about Buddy Lydecker?"

"I don't think so, but I met his wife. She's related to Bing Crosby, or somebody like that, I forget."

"No, you're thinking of Art Leffinger's wife. Who's Jimmy Durante's first cousin. Lydecker's one of those 'confirmed bachelors,' like in Winchell's column."

"They're giving Walter's strip to a pansy?"

"I shouldn't've said that. Lydecker's not married, is all I'm saying."

Sadie lifted one shoulder, dismissing Lydecker, Sharkey, even silly old Walter Winchell. By that time we'd started walking to the mechanized exit doors. I still felt a carnival thrill every time one of them blew open ahead of me. A man of simple pleasures, that Al Bready.

We had to wait a few minutes for a taxicab, and once we'd climbed in, I told the driver to stop first at Sadie's building on West Sixty-ninth Street, then I'd be going all the way down to Broadway and Twenty-fifth.

"You've been with Walter now for how long, Al? Is it five years?" Sadie was rooting through her handbag; I thought she was digging for smokes, but she brought out a limp Kleenex instead, and a tube of lipstick.

"Going on six."

"And we never spent any time together, just you and I."

"Well, no. But why should we have?"

She redid her mouth. "Because we were both Walter's partner." Then she lipped the Kleenex.

"If you look at it like that, I guess. But so?"

Sadie laughed and touched me again, on my wrist that time; she was wearing black calf-leather gloves. Fur-lined and trimmed. "Al. You know what let's do? Let's go someplace."

"What, for a drink?"

"Or plural. Come on."

"Oh, I don't know."

Ignoring me, Sadie leaned forward and spoke to the driver.

"Change of plans. Could you drop us at the Even Twenty Club? It's by the Plaza."

"I know where it is, ma'am." He was a black-haired Irishman, and I saw him glimpse her face in the rearview mirror.

Leaning back into the upholstery, Sadie gave my kneecap a friendly squeeze. Was it my imagination, or was she flirting? I couldn't believe that she was flirting—with me? She *was* flirting.

"So how have you been, Al? Still soft on that secretarial genius with the screwy husband? With the same name as Gene Autry?"

"Jewel's a friend. That's all. And it's Jimmie Rodgers. The same name as Jimmie Rodgers. And he's not screwy—well, he is, but it's not his fault." Why the hell was I defending him, the big rabbity jerk?

"All right," said Sadie, "I'm not making fun of the man. But I thought you told Walter he was a little soft in the head. Or do I have this wrong, too?"

"No, you're right. He's a child."

"Fine, he's a child"

"Actually, he's worse than that," I said. "Mentally, the guy's a fourteen-year-old boy who gets to go to bed every night with a real live woman."

Sadie chuckled. "Well, good for her."

"Not to hear Jewel tell it. And that's enough about that."

I wouldn't let Sadie split the taxi fare; I took care of it plus the tip, and we got out under the sidewalk awning and walked past the greeter and went into the Even Twenty, which was never one of my favorite places. It was fairly fancy, with a bar that ran the length of one wall, a parquet dance floor, and a six-piece white jazz band. Harry Seltzer's Carbonated Rhythm Orchestra. I used to know the bandleader during my wild youth. A terrible lush, Harry Seltzer. But he had women all over the place, as many as three in a single big city. And that's enough about Harry.

At the Even Twenty, the waiters had good manners, but everything cost too much. It was one of those see-me night-clubs, and most of the young women there to be seen neglected to wear brassieres. That evening I didn't have to tender a bribe to get a table for Sadie and me; the hostess was a woman I'd known back when—oh, never mind, it's not important. Her name was Catherine Garlick, and she was a tall, broad-faced, pretty woman with rippling hair dyed burgundy red. She used to be a photographer's model.

Catherine greeted us like show folk and promptly got us seated. Stiff white linen cloth, a slender vase with a classy rose-bud sticking out, the cutlery all swaddled up. The menu was tall enough to change your clothes behind.

"So is it a stroke or not?" Sadie asked me once we'd ordered drinks.

"That's what the doctor told me."

"What is that, high blood pressure? Did something happen?"

"I don't know, Sadie. Really." I told her then about Walter's middle-of-the-night telephone call, and about the dream.

"The floater got *breasts?*"

"It's what he said. Well, he didn't exactly use that specific word."

"He said tits."

"Yes. He did."

"Now I can believe it." She laughed. "Did I ever tell you how I met Walter—speaking of tits?"

"No, but he did."

"He did?"

"Yeah. You fell out of your dress at some party. And later you took one out again and stuck it in a glass of champagne."

"A glass of champagne, correct. He really told you that?"

"He tells me everything."

"He does not!"

"Everything. Why, didn't he tell you everything, when you were his partner?"

She laughed again. "What, you didn't like me saying that before?"

"Not particularly."

"What bothered you about it?"

"Walter is a guy that I work for. You were married to him. It's not the same thing. It never was. And I feel funny just being out with you."

She kicked me under the table.

We both turned our heads sideways then, at the same time, to face a heavyset man who'd come and stood at the edge of our table. "Excuse me, but I just had to stop by when I seen you two. Mrs. G, Al. So how is the gentleman?"

"The *gentleman?* Do you mean Walter?"

He pretended to clip Sadie on the chin, for being impudent. "Yes," he said, "I'm talking about Walter. He on the mend?"

"We're not sure," I said. "Right now it's just fingers crossed. How are you, Marty?"

"I'm good," he said. "I'm very good."

Hardly. Marty may've been well, but he wasn't good. Marty Planet—the gangster? He'd always been very nice to me, though, starting back when I used to sell liquor at his Harlem speakies. It tickled him pink later on that I'd become a writer. Seeing as how I'd started out such a little hustler. He seemed almost proud of me, in a fatherly way. I'd told Marty some years back that I wrote "Derby Dugan," and that clinched it, I was a favorite son. He just loved that strip.

He'd once had me introduce him to Walter at the Hickory House on Fifty-second Street. Walter had been polite, but a little bit stiff, even condescending, and later he'd asked me how in hell I'd ever made the acquaintance of a moron like that. Walter was such a snob! He himself had consorted with known racketeers, but his lot dressed sharper and polished their fingernails. Marty dressed in baggy blue suits right off the truck, he was fat in the stomach and fat in the face, and he always wafted a sharp odor of perspiration.

"When you see Mr. G again, please tell him I was asking for him. Would you do that for me, Al?"

"Be glad to."

Then: "Hey Al. Would you two care to join us? I'm sitting with a guy you know, and you could maybe help me out with something." Marty gestured, and I looked, and there was Clark Kamen seated across the room at a cozy nook table. He lifted a hand and waved it like a metronome. He hadn't been smiling till he saw us looking. There was a brunette woman at the same table, sitting with her back to us. "Al? Come have a drink. Sadie?"

"Nobody's trying to bump you off this week, are they, Marty? I wouldn't want to put my life in danger."

He pointed a chiding finger. "Sadie, not even in jest." Marty made the sign of the cross, then walked away like Jimmy

Cagney. That was another thing Walter had held against him. His swagger. "Should I tell him we'd rather stay where we are?"

"No, that's all right," said Sadie. "Marty's fun. Just don't mention the mayor."

"La Guardia?"

"Just don't mention him."

Marty was standing behind his chair, waiting for us. "Sadie Geebus, may I present Miss Constance McKeever, and that mutt in the corner is Clark Kamen, who used to be in my employ."

"And hope to be again," said Clarky, too spritely, too fizzy: he vibrated desperation. And for the first time since I'd known him, he didn't let fly with one of those crazy hellos. "I'm looking forward to—"

"Would you mind waiting till I've finished the introductions?"

"Sorry, Marty."

" 'Sorry, Marty.' Just shut your mouth till I tell you to open it. Constance, Sadie Geebus. And this is Al Bready."

"Pleasure," said Constance McKeever. I'm sure that she was an eyeful, but to tell you the truth, I didn't look at her closely. It was never a great idea to look closely at anyone Marty Planet was squiring. On purpose I kept her a blur.

"Sadie? Constance? Would you two beautiful ladies care to chitchat for a minute? While Al does me a favor?"

"What kind of favor?" I said.

"Help me with a decision. Should I give this kike five grand? Or not? What do you think, Al?"

"Five grand? For what?"

"Can I speak now?" said Clarky. Then, granted permission, he said, "Comic books. I want to package them, Al. And I need a stake."

"What do you mean, comic books? You mean those magazines that reprint newspaper strips?"

"No, mine are gonna be all brand-new material. You remember I was asking you just last night about cartoonists, did you know anybody looking for work—remember that? See, what I'm putting together, trying to, is a comic book *factory*. I could make a nice piece of cash. We all could."

"How'd you get into this?"

"Through my last job, up in Waterbury. That's where I was, when I was gone, when nobody seen me around. I was in Waterbury. After Top-Drawer went bust, I went to work for the same printer that wiped me out and took my inventory. Anyhow, the plant had contracts doing comic books on their color presses—newspaper funnies cut up and rearranged. 'Mutt and Jeff,' 'Hairbreadth Harry,' 'Buck Rogers,' 'Polly and Her Pals.' For giveaways. If you bought a tube of dental magnesia, you could get one free at the drugstore."

"Or the fill-up station," said Marty Planet. "I got a few for my nephew."

"Exactly. You know what I'm talking about. The drugstore, the gas station, whatever. But free. As a premium. Then somebody had the bright idea to slap a price sticker on 'em, put a few on the newsstand, see if they sold. Al? Marty? They sold, boys. Did they ever!"

"I've seen a few of those," I said. "In with the dime magazines."

"Oh, there's a whole bunch now. I've been packaging some of them myself, for the syndicates. That's what I've been doing. King has a monthly book—'Derby' is one of the strips in it. Universal. The Tribune Syndicate. Everybody. They send me the proofs, I shoot a few 'stats, trim them to fit, paste everything up."

"Since when?"

"Since, I don't know—end of September."

"But why do you want to do *original* strips—if the market's all reprints?"

"That's just it. Who knows what the market is? A lot of pulp publishers, those guys, Fawcett and Ace, Fiction House, Timely—all those guys, now they all want to put out their own comic books, too. But there are just so many strips around. Newspaper strips, I mean. There's just so many funny sheets and they're all being used up. So what's needed? Al? Marty? Let me tell you what's needed. New stuff. Let me repeat that: *new stuff*. Which brings me to my factory idea. Can't get the license to 'Skippy'? I'll sell you 'Tippy.' Get me?"

"Knockoffs," I said.

"You got me."

"Well?" said Marty Planet.

"Loan him the dough."

"Thank you, Al. Thank you."

"Shut up." Marty turned his full attention back to me. "Will you be writing for him, Al? Because that's the condition."

"Comic books? Jeez, I don't know. Let me think about it." I put out my cigarette and picked up a menu. Not that I was ordering food. Marty's hand dropped on mine, and he spoke directly into my ear. "You're the only writer I know, Al. So you're my favorite."

"You bending my arm?"

He withdrew his hand. "I'm not touching your arm. You see me touching your arm?"

"All right. For you, Marty? I'll do it."

"That's the boy." He leaned away, but his b.o. hung around a few seconds longer. "We have a deal, Clark. See Mr. Verriest

tomorrow, he'll give you the dough. And my terms. You'll be in touch with Al, when you're ready for him?"

"I sure will."

Derby's in a rowboat, I thought. It's night.

A waiter appeared, gliding in from the side. He carried a telephone, its long black cord snaking away behind him. "Call for you, Mr. Planet." Marty picked it up, grunted, listened, frowned, rolled his eyes. "So come back here, you monkey. You gonna stay over there all night? How many blow jobs can she give you? Bullets are whizzing around my head this very second, my life is in danger." He winked at Sadie and pronged the receiver and the waiter carried the phone away.

Our conversation from that point on was never better than meandering, inconsequential, with everybody, even Miss Mc-Keever, mouthing vague, dull words about—about what? I can't remember. After Marty brought up the king of England and said, "That dame must know her business in the sack," I have no recollection of anything we said. No, wait—we talked about the ski show at Madison Square Garden. Marty thought we should all make an effort to get over there and take a look. They had artificial snow, they'd built a slope, people were skiing inside the building. Actually skiing. Or maybe that's not what we talked about at all. I guess I don't remember.

Anyhow, Clarky got up and left after a while. Then Sadie Geebus and Marty started yakking about somebody named Stephen they both knew, apparently he was a doctor and in some kind of trouble. I tuned it out. I couldn't think of anything I wanted to ask or tell Miss McKeever, and was sorry I'd agreed to come out. I was trying to figure how I might effect an escape when Diane Ozarowski stopped by the table asking if she—or rather, if Nosy Natwin—could borrow me for a couple of minutes.

"Well, well, who do we have here?" Marty Planet was such an addictive flirt that he even flirted with Diane, who was known around midtown as the Marble Girl; I had to admire him. He looked her over, top to bottom and back to the high middle, and his eyes glittered the whole time. Diane was gloriously thirty pounds overweight, and poured into a black dress. She wore a lot of white makeup, as part of her persona, but also, in my opinion, to hide a poor complexion. Marty beamed at her. "It's the loveliest dyke in New York."

She wrinkled her nose, merely irritated. "Al? Could you stop over? It won't take long." I said sure.

The face in the cameo that topped Nosy Natwin's gossip column six days a week in the *Daily Mirror* didn't, in any respect, resemble the man's real face. In the half-tone, Nosy looked like some French poet—the rumpled black hair, the open-neck shirt, a fat cigarette pasted to his lip. In person he more closely resembled a cheapskate villain from Charles Dickens. He was a scrawny guy with a high, freckled forehead, thin brown hair, and wire glasses with magnifying lenses. He wore a suit and tie. And he didn't smoke.

As usual, there was a cereal bowl, a milk pitcher, a bowl of sugar, and a box of Wheaties set out on Natwin's reserved table. Also displayed, of course, was the famous "scoop tureen."

Every single evening of the week, all evening long, Nosy Natwin held court at the Even Twenty, and while he ate bowls and bowls of breakfast cereal and pontificated ignorantly on national politics (and on Thursdays at 9:00 broadcast a program over WABC radio), disgruntled bureaucrats, plainclothes cops, and New York City press agents stopped by, paid their fawning compliments, and dropped folded slips of paper into that giant crazed ceramic bowl with fruit painted inside. Blind items,

"overheard" gags, upcoming indictments, nuptials, recent adulteries, celebrity tidbits—it all went into the big tureen, which had belonged originally to Nosy's mother. "Al," he said.

"Mr. Natwin."

Seating myself, I reached into the tureen and came out with a torn piece of canary bond: *The Jersey mob is searching for one of the flock who turned straight and ran off with their 300 G's! Plus the wife of a pal, yet. Who said—was it you, Nosy?—that sex and money is the biography of man.*

To that I would've just added: punishment. Sex, money, and punishment.

But what did I know?

"Would you like a drink, Al? Cup of coffee?"

"This must be serious."

Nosy laughed, and winked at Diane Ozarowski. She laughed, too.

"So how is Walter Geebus?"

"He's all right."

"He is like hell! He had a stroke, he's drooling!"

"Don't print that."

Smiling, Nosy reached for the box of Wheaties and emptied the last of them into his bowl. While he was pouring, a cowboy spur dropped from the carton. He saved it, flipping it into a cigar box that he kept on the floor just for premiums; the spur joined a Buck Rogers jacket patch, some Popeye decalcomanias, and Tex Ritter's Miniature Dictionary of Cowboy Words and Phrases. "Can I quote you to the effect that Bud Lydecker, heir apparent, has a cow's arm?"

My scalp crawled: maybe it was an extreme reaction, but I still felt it. How in hell did Nosy hear about that crack? There'd been just me, Howard Blum, and the old counterman.

Who could've told him? Yet *another* mystery. Life is so full of them.

"Well? Can I quote you?"

"You got the wrong guy, Nose."

"Baloney." He looked again at Diane, and whatever his expression was—I couldn't catch it from my angle—it put a deep, sympathetic crease between her eyes. She glared at me. I had no idea why they were always together, if he paid her a salary or if there was something else going on. It beat me then. It beats me now.

I took out my wallet and dropped a ten-spot into the premium box. You could always kill a tip with a tip.

Sadie was alone when I returned. She'd had a newspaper delivered to her at the table and was doing the crossword puzzle with a cartridge pen.

"Where'd everybody go?"

"Marty got another phone call." Sadie folded the paper and, leaning forward, crossed her wrists on top of it. "So. Do you want to move on? Stick around here for a while? Or we could go to my place, I'll fix a late supper."

"You cook?"

"Tread lightly, mister."

I thought, Wouldn't she be a pleasure to behold naked! But I knew that I wouldn't, I wouldn't do it. You might be saying, well, how did I know she was even available. Listen, I was there. She was available. Don't ask me why, but she was. I just couldn't, though. I couldn't do it. So I asked her for a rain check, and she capped her pen, put it away.

Marty Planet had signed for our drinks, so we just retrieved our coats and left. Outside, taxicabs kept pulling up and slid-

ing off. I put Sadie into one. She cranked down the window. "Know something, Al? You're more married to that son of a bitch than I ever was. See you."

Since it was too far and too cold to walk, I rode home. Halfway there, I flinched out of reverie and blurted to the driver, "When a dead body floats, does it always float on its back?"

The look that he gave me in the mirror, I felt stupid for asking.

W alter used to tell me the most amazing things, really *intimate* things, and I always felt I was finding out more than I ever wanted to know about the man. I'd be at his studio on a Monday or a Friday and he'd be inking figures and talking a blue streak about some Argentine beauty he'd met at a first-night party. Did I really have to know that her nipples were as brown as Hershey bars? He'd laugh when he saw me blush. "You Catholics," he'd say.

"What's that supposed to mean?"

"You're the last monogamists on earth."

"I hardly think so, Walter."

He'd tell me that his third wife had refused to go down on him, that he'd fooled around once with a band singer named Soda Wauters, that he'd met this classy dame and happened to be standing right there when she reached for her clutch bag and one of her bosoms fell out of her dress. Later she got drunk and

gave Walter another look at the same gland, when she dipped it in her champagne glass. He took her home and went to bed with her. I stopped him before he could announce the rounds.

He laughed and said, "I'll probably end up marrying her. That's my curse, Al. I fall in love at the drop of my pants."

"If you ask me, Geebus, there's entirely too much of that going on in the world."

"Catholic boy!" he said and laughed again.

I realized that he'd thought I meant entirely too much pants dropping. But I didn't correct his mistake, I just moved us on to another topic.

EPISODE TWELVE

TRICKS

Unless I was sick, and a sick hangover didn't count, every day I was out of bed, shaved, dressed, coffeed up, and typing long before eight. But when I woke up the next morning, Wednesday, it was ten minutes after ten by the clock on the stand. So right away I got this guilty feeling, then I was so disgusted by it that I went out walking. After just a few blocks, though, I felt more anxious than before. At Herald Square I turned around and practically ran back home, where I kicked off my shoes and drowned them. I disconnected the phone and tried batting out the first chapter of that Borneo novel. But it was a washout. And because I wasn't writing for the ages, just a monthly, I quit. I didn't see any point in suffering. Still don't.

I walked down to the lobby and checked if I had any telephone messages. There were three. Two from Jewel, one from Jimmie. Jewel's both said to please call her. Jimmie's said he was sorry.

"You take these?" I asked the clerk, a Mexican husky with a scarred-up face. Oscar. Oscar Garza. His girlfriend was pregnant, and he was afraid that he had a bleeding ulcer, but he wouldn't look at his stool. His mother and sister, in Union City, both saw visions of the Blessed Virgin Mary. When you lived at a hotel, you got to know the staff in a peculiar way. Not quite neighbors and not quite friends, and certainly not family, they were something else, something in between. I liked it. Whatever you'd call it.

"I didn't say you weren't answering your phone." Oscar stood on his tiptoes, grinning down at my stockinged feet. "I said you were out."

"Yeah? Thanks. This one," I said, waggling Jimmie's. "That all he said, he was sorry?"

"That's all, yeah. He didn't say you should call him."

Back in my room, I smoked cigarettes waiting for my shoes to dry on the steam radiator.

Derby's in a rowboat. It's night.

I hailed a Checker on Sixth Avenue, rode it up to Doctor's Hospital at a decent midday clip. I saw Walter, I sat with him, but he didn't know it. I'm pretty certain that he didn't. And he wasn't asleep, either. Nothing moved except his chest, and even that didn't move so much.

Although the fruit and flower baskets had multiplied, nobody else came to visit, and when I left it was going on three-thirty. Too late to meet Jewel after school. But I hadn't planned to anyway.

There was a piece of mail waiting for me at the desk, a Christmas card, unsigned but with several slices of bread, each one centered with an X, cartooned under the holiday sentiment. Jewel, of course. I thought about calling her up—she'd be home by now, and Jimmie wouldn't. But it had got funny,

and I don't mean *funny,* the whole business between her and me, and I was nervous about making false moves, I was nervous about making moves of any kind, so I cradled the phone before I'd dialed even the first letters of her exchange. I worked for a little bit, then I napped.

Early that evening I got a buzz from the front desk, and it was Joe Wein saying to come downstairs. When I did, he asked me to go out with him to celebrate the publication of his second book of parlor tricks, which he'd ghosted for a stage magician named Harry Necromein, Jr. I said I'd pass, thanks, but Joe wasn't giving up that easy: he had a pint of Ancient Age stashed in his coat pocket, and we found a couple of glasses, then sat in the lobby drinking. I rarely spent any time there— those crummy upholstered chairs and horsehair sofas, the worn carpet, and floor lamps with brittle shades almost always depressed me. I'd think, I should move. Move where, though? And why? No, I was staying.

Residents came and went, some of them stopped and had a short drink with us—Joe even sold a couple of books. He'd brought a bunch.

By nine, nine-thirty, I was half in the bag, and for a laugh tried a sleight-of-hand, as described on page 111 and utilizing two coins, two stick matches, and my handkerchief. Ended up I lost one of the coins, a dime, and managed to set fire to my shirt cuff, and while I was pressing an ice cube to a small blister on my left wrist, I happened to glance up and there was Howard Blum, standing inside the revolving doors.

"What do you want, kid?"

He looked groggy, and when he came over he seemed nervous. I pretended I didn't notice. I just asked him what was in his portfolio. As if I didn't know. He'd tentatively pushed it on me and was now untying the shoelaces that held it closed at the

top. It was a homemade cheap-cardboard thing, all scuffed up, and crumpled at the corners.

"I appreciate that you went to bat for me."

"What's in the portfolio, Howard?"

"So I figured I should have something ready to show them. Would you take a look? It's kind of a presentation strip."

"Can I see?" Joe Wein was snooping, hovering at my shoulder.

Howard laid out his samples on sofa cushions, two dailies and a Sunday drawn full-tab with color indicated. There were speech balloons, but they were all empty.

Smart kid.

And not only smart, but a phenomenal ghost. I mean it, too.

The Sunday page was so perfectly Walter Geebus it was uncanny. In the long top rectangle, the title panel (Howard had even glued down a preprinted logo), Derby Dugan is sleeping outdoors, under an overpass. Dead campfire. Scattered bean cans. Fuzzy curled up nearby. Second panel: Derby stirring in his bedroll. The dog on hind legs yapping.

First panel, second tier—BAM! a roadster blasts through the guardrail overhead. Noses down in the center panel. Crashes in the third.

Next tier, first panel: a young woman collapsed over the steering wheel. Second panel: the roadster burning. Third: Derby with his arm flung up, to cover his face.

Bottom tier. Our boy yanks open the driver's door. Fire shoots out. The auto and the kid, both in flames. Fuzzy in the foreground, a hollering silhouette.

"What do you think?" Howard leaned at me. "Al?"

Down, Rover.

I picked up one of the dailies. Right away I could tell that Howard hadn't used Walter's grade of paper, it was a thinner

ply, almost floppy. So I guess he hadn't been at the Geebus supply closet.

"This one," I said. "You should've put this guy—he's the
bad guy, right?—in the last panel. Not the first."

"You think?"

"I said so, didn't I?"

"But otherwise?"

"Very nice, Howard."

"If you wanted to script them, I'd letter it all."

I said, "That won't be necessary."

"Is this one going to run?" asked Joe Wein, lifting the Sunday page gently by a corner, like it was valuable.

"Just samples, Joe. I'll take them around to the syndicate,
and if they like them, maybe they'll give Howard the job. For a
while. Joe, I'm sorry: this is Howard Blum. Howard, my friend
Joe Wein."

"Will you do that?" said Howard. "Take my stuff to King?"

"Could. But what's it worth to you? Is it worth fifty bucks a
week? From your own pocket? If you get the job?"

"You kidding?"

"Do I look it? Do I sound like I am?"

"How much you think they'd pay me?" said Howard, still a
little thrown.

"At first? I bet you not more than two-seventy-five. Still,
that's practically a million—right? To you."

"If I get that, sure—you can take the fifty."

"You'll *give* me the fifty. I don't want to take it. I want you
to give it to me. Out of your own pocket."

"All right. I already said all right, didn't I?"

Then I asked him was there anything else that he wanted.
When he said there wasn't, I told him to just leave the portfolio, I'd see what I could do. I turned my back to him. Joe

caught my eye and frowned. A moment later, from behind us, Howard said, "Anybody drop this?"

He'd picked a dime off the carpet. "No? Well, good night again. Good to know you, Joe. And thanks, Al. I guess."

Joe left a few minutes later.

I think he was sore at me.

That episode in the hotel lobby with Howard Blum suddenly reminds me—and it's funny I never thought of this before—but that evening marked the beginning of the end of my regular acquaintanceship, actually my friendship, with Joe Wein. After that, we never got together much. Looking back, I guess he might have been appalled by my greedy ultimatum to Howard Blum, though I didn't see it as greedy then, and I don't now. And it wasn't an ultimatum, either. It was a negotiation, a verbal contract.

I don't know why I never realized before that Joe and I drifted apart after that one incident. Funny. Well, maybe not really. Things got a little crazy in my life right after the night I talked to Blum about ghosting the Dugan strip.

It's too bad, though. About Joe, I mean. He and I had a lot of fun together, we used to go bowling and hang out in the amusement arcades on Times Square. And he introduced me to

some people I enjoyed knowing. Mostly Joe's Moscow-smitten intellectuals, but still they could be good company. I went to parties in Greenwich Village. Everybody chain-smoked. They had to leave all the windows wide open—one time they even had to leave them open during a blizzard. People paired off and there was a lot of public fondling, and serial occupation of the bedrooms. I met Dashiell Hammett at one of those parties, I even helped him find the bathroom. He was blind drunk. Of course, the girls in the American Communist movement were big on free love, and you could pretty much count on getting laid at or after one of those parties, just as long as your standard of beauty wasn't long-stemmed society blonds.

There was this one special girl I met at a party. Anne Goodman, the daughter of two union organizers, a black-haired, zaftig girl—really big headlights—who was humorless and asexual till she'd had something to drink. Then she acted like a Tenderloin streetwalker. But as soon as we'd finished copulating our brains out—usually at her squalid apartment on Twelfth Street—Anne jumped right back to being a serious revolutionary. She lost interest in sex exactly like a man, as soon as she'd had her climax.

We started seeing each other regularly, and pretty soon she announced that she'd quit being promiscuous. She was only going to sleep with me. Well, it's not like I minded that, it was just that along with her self-imposed monogamy came all the personal questions. What was my childhood like? What did my father do? Did I read books? Was my mother a housewife? She was fascinated by the Catholic Mass and wanted to hear about it, and she wanted to know all the big and little things that happened to me along the way. One evening she said, "I wish I had a picture of you as a little boy," and I said, "We didn't have our portraits taken, there was never enough money."

Saying that was a big mistake, because Anne was then even more charmed that I'd grown up poor. She'd just assumed I came from a fairly well-off family. I said no, we were broke a lot. My father, I said, was a delivery man for the Hibernian Coal Company, but kept getting laid off every spring. Then I distracted her; I can't remember exactly what I did, maybe started playing with her body again, or maybe not, but I know for sure that I changed the subject.

Eventually Anne and I drifted apart, and she took up with a married literary critic. Not too long ago I read the guy's memoirs, just to see if Anne got a mention. Did she ever! According to the book, she was the best lay of his life, but a little crazy. I'd never seen any sign of that, and it boiled me to hear him talk about Anne Goodman like that. But at least I found out what happened to her. She got a job on *Time* magazine and married a rich man, turned Republican, and had seven children.

Joe Wein had introduced us. I guess that's all I'm saying, and that I'm sorry Joe and I drifted apart after he must've decided I'd put the squeeze on poor young Howard Blum.

Which wasn't what I'd done at all.

EPISODE THIRTEEN

LYDECKER GRABS HIS HAT

King Features had its offices in the Daily Mirror building on West Fifty-ninth Street. My appointment Thursday was for eleven o'clock, but when I got off the subway at Columbus Circle it was only a scratch past ten-thirty. Ordinarily I would've walked around the block till it was time, but I didn't feel like dragging along Howard's cheesy-looking portfolio, so I went straight up to Pete Laudermilch's floor. It turned out he wasn't busy and could see me early.

His eyes jumped when I showed him the Sunday page.

"Did Walter do layouts?"

"Nope. And I didn't do the scenario."

"Christ." He sat down and wheeled his chair back against the wall. "But I can't, Al. I can't let Blum have it. As it is, there's a lot of hurt feelings around here." He slowly rolled his head around his shoulders. "Some of the bullpen guys think I

should've made a contest out of this. But I didn't want to. It seemed disrespectful."

That kind of remark was how come I'd always liked Pete. He could talk in those terms, in terms of respect and disrespect, even when he was talking about a cartoon strip or a recipe column. A lot of syndicate managers were prep-school brats and Yalies, or else they acted like it, and were inclined to treat the company talent like citrus pickers. Well, Dan Sharkey was the perfect example.

"But why does it have to be Lydecker, Pete? What do you guys owe him?"

"He's been around forever."

"Oh, for crying out loud."

"He wants to work at home. He lives with his mother, and she's not well."

"Poor woman."

"Al, come on."

"No, you come on. His mother's not well? Jesus Christ, Pete, that's very goddamn kind of you to worry about her, but—"

"It's not only that. The other guys in the art room can't stand Buddy. I'm getting rid of him as much as anything else, you know what I'm saying?"

"Dan Sharkey picked him, didn't he?"

"All right, so I'm a coward. Bud's old lady really is sick, though."

"Is Sharkey around? Maybe he'd like to see what Howard could do."

"Don't waste your time. He thought you were a shit."

"He said that? He really called me that? Little prick."

"Listen, what I'll do. Send Blum to see me, I could put him to work here."

That was that. And to indicate it was, Pete Laudermilch stood up and slid Howard's strips back into the portfolio. But I wouldn't let him tie the strings. I did that myself.

"Buddy around?"

"Sure."

"Maybe I'll go talk to him."

"Al. Before you leave. Have you seen Walter again?"

"Yesterday afternoon."

"Is he paralyzed?"

"Who said he was paralyzed?"

"Nosy Natwin."

"I haven't heard anything about it."

King's art department was on a different floor, higher up. Although a few strips and gag panels, some very minor things, were produced there, most of the work consisted of cleaning up syndicate product and turning out character drawings for toy packaging. The pillars and walls were covered with insulting caricatures, and the wastebaskets were enormous. At eleven o'clock in the morning they were all stuffed full of wadded paper. Twenty guys sat on stools at tilted boards or huddled in packs around pasteup tables. Guys in shirtsleeves, baggy trousers, slack braces.

When I found Bud Lydecker he was standing over his board using a razor blade to slice a tiny rectangle out of a "Barney Baxter" daily. He was a pale blond man in his late forties with a weakling's curved posture and a slight pot belly. Bud. Buddy. What a stupid name. The stupidest! And the seat of his woolen trousers was full of pills. His shoes needed heels. I waited while he fitted down the pasteover: a relettered speech balloon. He finally jerked, like I'd sneaked up behind him. "Al! Why didn't you say something?"

"No hurry. How are you, Bud? Congratulations."

"Oh, for that. Yeah. Thanks. Danny Sharkey mentioned I ought to phone you. And I probably would have, tonight."

Danny?

"Look. Bud. Could you take an early lunch? I'm up here to-day, maybe we should talk now. Do you need to ask permission to leave?"

I'd said that just to irk him. He was sensitive at his age about being a wage slave, a clock puncher, still having a super-visor. Everybody knew that he'd never done a strip under his own signature; for a long time he'd tried, but nothing that he pitched ever sold, and he just gave up. Bud filled in whenever strip men fell behind on their deadlines, or got sick, or went off on a toot, or the wife died. A week here, a week there. A Sun-day page for several months. And he always did a lazy job, never a decent copy, not even close. Bud. He *did* have a cow's arm. Established guys, guys with their own strips, scorned him, and so did the guys who'd had their own strips but lost them and were back in harness, and the young hopefuls all stayed clear of him, like they were afraid of being infected.

I couldn't believe that Bud Lydecker had just inherited "Derby Dugan." I felt as heartsick about it suddenly as—well, as Joe Wein felt about comrade Stalin turning out so blood-thirsty. The world shouldn't work this way.

"Let me just grab my hat, Al."

While he did that, I picked up his razor blade, sticky with glue and bristling with trimmed-off snippets of paper. Take it, something told me. Take it. What compelled that klepto part of me I couldn't say. It seemed I'd always done it—at least ever since I was a boy and started pinching coins from my parents' bureau, never so many at a time that they'd no-tice, and keeping them all in a cigar box that I kept in my bottom dresser drawer. Eventually I accumulated, along with

several more cigar boxes, almost thirty bucks in pennies and nickels and the occasional dime, but I never spent any of it. Never.

I decided to put down Buddy's razor blade, to put it back, and I did.

We had sandwiches in a lunchroom nearby, sitting at the counter. Bud asked me if I typed up a full script, and I said, "Of course," and he said, well, not every guy did that, some guys were pretty loose, some of them just wanted to talk to you on the telephone. You could tell that he didn't have much use for writers.

I said, "I'll give you pages. Panel one, panel two, this is the setup, here's who's there, here's what they say."

"Okay. Do you mail me your stuff?"

"I could. Or I could drop it off at your place once a week."

"No, you don't have to do that. Just mail it." He looked at me, and his expression wasn't entirely friendly. Don't bother me, it said, and I won't bother you. Fair enough, I thought, and wanted to kill him.

At the rear of the lunchroom, in an el-shaped alcove, were four pinball machines, none of them in play, and after we'd taken care of our separate checks, Buddy drifted over to one of them. I followed. Two of the machines were one-ball payouts with a five-dollar jackpot, the other two were just novelty types, seven balls for a penny. Buddy stepped up to one of those, a game called Traffic. He batted the spring plunger with the heel of his fist, then attacked the cabinet with hip, pelvis, and banging hands. The steel ball caromed off pins, fell into a circuit hole, popped out, jumped around the playfield, rico-cheted off a peg, was lost down the run-out slot.

"Al?" He fired another ball, but without so much as a bump he let it roll straight down the middle. "I need to ask you some-

thing. Could you lay off the New Deal cracks while I'm draw-ing this thing? I'm for Roosevelt."

"We've been good boys lately. Haven't you noticed?"

"To be honest, I haven't read the strip in years."

He fired another ball and I watched him play it, slapping the cabinet sides with his palms, then pounding the top glass. It exploded, and a razor-sharp piece slit his wrist, cut an artery. Then he started jiggling around like he'd touched a live electric wire. His blood squirted everywhere.

No, it didn't. I made that up. It was just something that I thought about. He never cut himself. It never happened. The world doesn't work that way.

I took out my notepad and said, "Let me get your address, Bud, while I'm here."

Way back—way, way back when I was ten or eleven, definitely when I was not yet in my teens—I used to play this secret rainy day game with my little sister. She must have been six or seven—the cutest girl! Jeannie had a very high, squeaky voice and a head of blond curls that looked as rich as caramel, and we'd hide ourselves in the attic or under my bed, and sometimes we'd ask each other catechism questions, and sometimes we'd play hangman or checkers, but sometimes, especially during those endless dreary housebound hours when Dad was at work or visiting Mrs. Meatro and Mom was drinking in her bedroom, we'd pass the time telling each other how we thought the world should work.

Our dad actually gave us the idea for the game; he was always telling us, "I'm sorry, but the world don't work that way." "You can't stop going to school—the world don't work that way." "We can't strap your mother to a chair and throw her out

the window, much as we'd all like to—the world don't work that way." Dad really said that to my brother and sister and me one time. Of course, he was three sheets to the wind. But still, he said it.

I was saying, though, about the game that Jeannie and I played.

She'd always start. "We should be able to live in the forest, if we felt like it. Just you and me, Alfred. The world should work that way."

And when it was my turn I'd maybe tell Jeannie, "People should grow up faster. The world should work that way." Or maybe I'd say, "People should be able to make themselves invisible." Or maybe I'd say, "There should be color funnies seven days a week. The world should work that way."

Donald never joined us whenever we played that game. For one thing, I guess he was too old by then—he would already have been fifteen or sixteen. But for another thing, he was the realist among the Brady children. He didn't give a rap how the world *should* work. He turned religious and married the first girl he dated.

I remember Jean saying once, "Children should live in big houses all by themselves," and I said, "Yeah, the world should work that way."

EPISODE FOURTEEN

CLARKY RECRUITS

I'd been loafing across the street from St. Joseph's for ten minutes before I realized who I was looking at through the school yard fence. I'd thought maybe it was a dope peddler, but it was Clark Kamen, in a camel's hair coat and a winter fedora. He was pacing in front of three shabbily dressed teenage boys seated on a bench.

"Al! You following me around?" he bellowed when he spotted me coming. "But do you think you should be seen in broad daylight?" As I passed through the school yard gate, he addressed his next remark to the boys. "My friend Al, here, is being pursued by J. Edgar Hoover himself. He strangled a federal judge."

As I shook hands with Kamen, I took a peek at the boys. They hadn't reacted in the slightest way to Clarky's nonsense. Hunched over lapboards, they sat writing—no, drawing, in pencil on sheets of cheap yellow paper. Two very dark Italians

flanking a slender kid with fine blond hair, blue eyes, and clear skin pulled tight across cheekbones that stuck out. German. Or a Swede. Both Italian boys were drawing Dick Tracy in profile, the other kid was doing Flash Gordon firing a ray gun. "Finish it up, fellas," said Clarky. "Hurry it up. Two minutes." He rested a hand on my shoulder.

"Recruiting," he said, strolling us away.

"I already figured that out. Watch you don't have the truant officer showing up at your office."

He chuckled, then turned serious; he removed his hat and held it over his heart. "Al. I want to thank you again, for helping me out with Marty. You're a good guy. And I swear I'm going to pay you soon as I get your paper. You give me a script, I give you a check. That's how it's going to work."

Before I could get in a word, he'd turned swiftly and strode back to the boys. "Time," he announced, then collected the lapboards. Almost right away Clarky returned the Dick Tracys, but he kept the Flash Gordon, telling the blond kid who'd drawn it, "I like your work, son, it's very good. What's your name?"

"Olsen, mister. Floyd Olsen."

"So, Floyd, you want to be an artist?"

"It's the only thing I'm interested in, mister. You going to hire me?"

"Hold your horses," said Clarky. Then he addressed the other boys. "Any time you fellas want to try again, you just come see me." He passed them each a business card; I couldn't read what it said. "All right? You promise? Thanks, fellas. And keep practicing." He reminded me of my high-school baseball coach on cut day.

As they rose, sulkily, to go—one of them had already crumpled his drawing into a ball, the second was jamming his into

his pocket—Clarky gave them each an encouraging pat. Their eyes slid to me, and I rolled mine.

"I'm paying two dollars, fifty cents a page," Clarky told Floyd Olsen.

"I'm interested." None of the buttons on his pea coat matched, and the left sleeve glistened where he'd wiped his nose. "When do I start?"

"Wait a second. That's two dollars, fifty cents a page—penciled, inked, *and* lettered. Still interested?"

"Still interested."

Clarky ruffled his hair, gave him a card, and said to show up next Monday morning any time after nine, he'd put him straight to work. "No, keep the pencil, Floyd, that's yours. It's a gift. But bring it on Monday."

We both watched him walk away. Floyd didn't look back at us, but he did glance sidewise at the school building.

I said to Clarky, "So what do you do, you just roam the streets looking for cartoonists?"

"Practically. I found somebody this morning at a tattoo shop. I suppose you could say I roam the streets. At the moment I can't afford Rube Goldberg. So. Is this really a coincidence, Al, or did you come looking to find me?"

"Jewel teaches here."

"Our Jewel? Teaches here?" Clarky spun around and faced the school, smiling as though he could actually see her, pinpoint her, through brick. I could see her myself. She'd be teaching her seniors. Forty pupils. Room 215. Last period. Arithmetic for Business. I knew Jewel's schedule. Her different classrooms. Her problem students—I knew their names. And I knew the names of all the nuns she taught with every day. Sister Rose Bernadette. Sister Gertrude Louise. Sister Michael Marguerite. Sister Maureen Immaculate. I knew that the school nurse was a

grass widow and the geography textbooks were out of date. I knew everything. "So you've stayed in touch, you two."

"Oh yeah. Jewel and me? Oh sure. What?"

"Nothing," said Clarky.

"Why are you looking at me like that?"

"Like what?"

"Like that. What's that smile supposed to mean?"

"Nothing. Jeez. How's the goof?"

"Jimmie? Fine."

"He makes a good sandwich, I'll say that for him."

I'd been trying to set fire to a cigarette, but the breeze kept blowing out every match. Finally Clark Kamen loaned me his Zippo, then school let out, then we spotted Jewel and she gave Clarky a big hug, but she barely looked at me. And what with one thing and another, I ended up pocketing the lighter. I still have it.

Clarky was right about Jimmie Rodgers making a good sandwich. He never skimped on the lunchmeat, he sliced it paper-thin and piled it thick, and his rolls and bread were always fresh. The guy even mixed up his own special mayonnaise.

The first time I had one of his creations was a month or so after I met Jewel. By then I'd started dropping in on her at Clarky's office without any pretext, and if she wasn't busy trafficking pasteups, I'd stay for an hour, just shooting the breeze. Twice already we'd gone out together for a stroll around the block. Christ, I liked walking with her! I loved it! I could feel the smile on my face. I used to pretend it was another city full of blind people and I could take Jewel's hand and hold it.

But I was telling you about the first time I ate one of Jimmie's sandwiches. Until then, Jewel had never mentioned her husband. I don't think I even knew his name yet. I remember that she unwrapped a glazed-ham-and-mustard on white bread

and put half of it on a paper napkin for me. I was seated on a chair drawn up beside her desk. She said, "Jimmie made this."

"Jimmie?"

"My husband."

So there. I really *didn't* know his name till then.

"He packs you a sandwich every day?"

Jewel smiled that beautiful smile. "He owns a lunchroom in the bus station. Around eleven, I usually take a break, go check on him, and he'll make me something."

While she was telling me that, I mechanically reached for my package of cigarettes. But my fingers started shaking, so I put it back rather than call attention to my sudden case of nerves. I wondered why she'd used the phrase "go check on him." *Check* on him? That sounded a little funny.

When I finally picked up the sandwich, my hands seemed perfectly steady.

"His dad owned a lunchroom, and poor Jimmie's been making sandwiches since he was nine years old. Lord, he hates it."

"Yeah, well, I can understand that."

Then, clear out of the blue, Jewel asked me, "What did your father do?"

I took a bite and made a little interrogative grunt, as if I hadn't heard the question.

"Your father," said Jewel. "When you were growing up, what did he do?"

"Oh, he just worked at a coal company," I said talking with my mouth full. "This is good! Your husband makes a very good sandwich!"

And before you knew it, we were talking about something else.

EPISODE FIFTEEN

JEWEL'S BIG NEWS

Clarky drove a Dodge car, registered in Connecticut, with an electric clock and a radio. He was taking Jewel and me to a commercial building west of Times Square. He'd been so eager to show off his new joint that we hadn't had the heart to decline, despite there being some better things to do. Well, I can only speak for myself. Perhaps Jewel really wanted to see the place. "It's full of press agents," he told us, "but there's a couple of publishers. There's a guy puts out a nudie book. But he's on a different floor."

Stopped for a red light, Clarky turned from the wheel and beamed at Jewel. She was sitting up front. I felt a mile away in back. There was plenty of rear leg room in that automobile. "You're looking prettier than ever, honey. I didn't mean to gyp you, by the way. And I'm going to pay you that last check I still owe you, soon as things get rolling."

"Don't worry about it, Mr. K. And I never thought you'd gypped me. Is that what Al told you I said?"

"I didn't say anything!"

"He didn't, hon. I guess I just felt like a gyp. I don't know."
We drove some more. When "Pepper Young's Family" came on
the radio, Jewel switched to music. "And will you look at this!"
said Clarky. "A parking spot in front. Must be an omen."

We took a self-service elevator to the fifth floor. Clarky
steered, jiggling the lever with a mariner's authority. He flung
open the folding grate. "I'm right there. People step off the car
and right through my door. They won't get lost!"

"And that's important when all your employees are high-
school boys."

Jewel actually cracked a smile; on the ride over, Clarky had
told her about his hiring strategy. I nudged her a little, then
nudged her again, while Clarky unlocked the door. She
wouldn't look at me, though. Boy! was I ever getting the freeze
out. She was giving me what I'd seen her give to Jimmie a
dozen times, and I didn't like it.

"What do you think?" Clarky pointed at the lettered glass.
THE KAMEN STUDIOS, it read.

"Congratulations, Mr. K. And good luck."

I said, "Very pretty."

With a flourish, he opened the door.

"What do you think?"

What did I think? I thought it was an empty office, a long,
empty rental space with electrical wires dangling from the ceiling, cheap brown linoleum, water puddles at every radiator,
and an old-fashioned candlestick telephone on the floor that began to ring as soon as we'd stepped inside. "Excuse me." Clarky
lifted off the receiver. "The Kamen Studios." His face bright-
ened. "Mr. Cutler! Thanks for returning my call." He turned
his back to us and started murmuring; I heard some dollar figures and a few dates, then I walked farther down the floor. I

looked over my shoulder to see if Jewel was following me. She was, but her face seemed tight as a mask, and her eyes cut elsewhere whenever they met mine.

"You're angry."

"Oh? Have you noticed? I don't like people hanging up in my ear. For your information, Mr. Bready. And I haven't heard from you in days."

And don't think I didn't know it. It was four—almost four whole days. I hadn't spoken with Jewel since late Monday when Joe Wein was drinking with me up in my room. I'd thought about her, though. A lot. "Thanks for the Christmas card," I said.

" 'Thanks for the Christmas card.' " She breathed noisily through her nose. "Thanks for the toaster!"

"Jewel . . ."

"I'm just very disappointed, I guess."

"Well, I guess. But you heard about Walter?"

"I heard he was in the hospital."

"He had a stroke."

"Well, of course I'm very sorry to hear it, and I suppose you've been going to see him and all that, but I've been going crazy, Al. Not because of you, so don't flatter yourself. It just would've been nice to've had a friend I could talk to."

Clarky joined us. "I had to take that call. Al? You know Leon Cutler—Diamond Publishing? No? I thought you did cowboys and Indians for him. Anyhow, that was Leon, and I think he wants me to do his new line of comic books. Six titles!" He was all wound up, talking more to himself than to me, and he kept glancing around the big room, no doubt envisioning it in full operation. Then he said to Jewel, "I'm waiting to hear about some used drafting tables, but if I don't hear something today, we'll have to—" He slapped his hands to-

gether. "Listen to me! *'We'll'!* Next thing you know, sugar, I'll start bossing you around again, just like old times. What do you think, doll? Would you ever consider coming back?"

I was two seconds behind—and by the time it clicked that he'd just offered her a job, she'd refused it.

"Don't worry about the school," said Clarky. "If that's what's bothering you. Work till Christmas vacation, that's fair. They'll find somebody else for the winter."

Jewel smiled. "I'm not worried about that. No, if I wasn't moving, I'd be tempted, Mr. K. Honest. But Jimmie and I are moving back upstate."

The only place to collapse was on a windowsill, and I took it. I had to sit down. "What do you mean, you're moving?"

"What do I *mean?* I'm moving, is what I mean. I'm putting everything into large boxes and I'm moving away. I'm breaking the lease. I'm walking into the freezer and closing the door. Does that clear up your confusion?"

"No. I talked to you Monday."

"And today is Friday."

Jewel was gazing down the length of the empty room. I looked out the window.

She said, "He found a buyer."

"Jimmie did?"

"It happened suddenly."

"Christ. It must've."

"You didn't call me back. If you'd called me back, I would've told you."

Straight down below I noticed a kid loitering by a trash barrel on the corner of Tenth Avenue. It was Floyd Olsen, from the parochial school yard. The successful job candidate. I hoped he wasn't planning to stand there till Monday morning. Not that I gave a hoot.

The morning that Frank Sweeney was to begin helping out on the Dugan strip, I arrived at Walter's house before eight-thirty. Sadie answered the door and looked surprised to see me. Well, it's true, I usually never got there before ten. "You want some breakfast? We're still downstairs."

I told her sure and followed her to the kitchen, admiring the roll of her buttocks under a mint green wrapper. "It's Al, Walter," she called ahead.

The great man had a rumpled scowl on his face when I came in and sat down. "Am I supposed to gather from this early-bird visit that you're here to give my first brat the Al Bready once over?" He glanced to Sadie, who was sliding a cup of coffee in front of me. "Al's very annoyed that I hired what's-his-name—"

"Frank Sweeney," replied Sadie with an edge.

"Al's annoyed that I hired Frank without consulting him first."

"As usual, he's got it wrong," I said. "I've been telling him for months to hire some help—well, you have, too, Sadie. No, my only beef is that he never told me he'd decided to go ahead and do it."

"Do you want some cold cereal, Al? A piece of toast?"

"No, thank you, Sadie. Walter can hire whoever he likes. And it's about time! I'm just surprised he didn't tell me, that's all."

"I hurt Al's feelings."

"Will you two quit talking to *me?*" Sadie refilled the milk pitcher, put the milk bottle back into the icebox, and went upstairs.

"I hurt your feelings. Admit it. I hurt your little feelings."

"You should know by now that's impossible."

Walter smiled, finished his coffee, and put his cup and saucer in the sink.

We went up to the studio together, and while he did his morning rituals—untied his shoes, unnotched his belt buckle, selected the day's cigar, opened a fresh package of cigarettes—I stood at the window. Finally I saw a young man hurrying down Seventy-seventh Street with an artist's portfolio pressed under an arm, and I said, "Frank's here."

I looked to Walter, and he was staring back. For just a second, he looked frantic. Then he said, "If this works out, I think I may take up golf. You play, Al?"

"You couldn't get me on a golf course with a bayonet."

"I didn't ask you to play with me, I just asked you if you played."

"No."

There were moments when I really hated that son of a bitch, and one of them happened that morning, a few minutes before nine o'clock, just as the doorbell rang.

EPISODE SIXTEEN

VISITING HOUR

On Friday evening Walter Geebus had such a crowd of visitors that I had to wait in the lobby till some of them left. I saw Bob Hope go out, and Harry Hershfield and Cliff Sterrett; I used Hershfield's floor pass. Upstairs in Walter's ritzy wing of the hospital, I saw the judge who'd burned Ruth Brown Snyder and Henry Judd Gray, and a couple of sports writers, and Ed Sullivan, and if I wasn't mistaken, two of Walter's previous wives. One of them had really packed on the weight. And I saw Sadie Geebus again, too. We nodded from ten feet. Everybody was jammed together in the hall, and you could tell that the nurses were impressed by the turnout. I spotted one of them get an autograph from somebody I think used to play second base for the Dodgers. King, king of England, Edward, Mrs. Simpson. The same business was on everybody's lips. I was sick of it. Who cared? So he quit. His choice. At least the man had one to make.

Nobody actually went in to see Walter. When I got there, I thought nobody was *supposed* to, that there were medical reasons or something, doctor's orders, but that wasn't the case. People just stood around outside and socialized. Edward. Queen Mother. Simpson. England. Baltimore. King of England . . . great blow jobs?

I opened the door and went in.

He was awake and gazing at the ceiling with such a familiar expression of pique that I knew for certain he was clearheaded.

"How're you feeling, Walt?"

His forehead started to wrinkle, then stopped. His left eye rolled wildly. It finally centered itself, held steady. I think he said, "Shit." Or maybe, "Shitty." It didn't come out clear. His hand moved under the blanket. He started thumping the bed with his left fist, in a rage.

"Walter, you crazy? Stop that! You want to blow another fuse? Crying out loud!" I almost biffed him, I was so mad. Instead I scolded him some more. "All right," I said. "That's better. Listen. Walter. You can't get so angry. You can't do that. Listen, you can't. That's what's wrong with you, Walt. You're always so mad. Quit it! If you have to think about something, and you start to think about Frank, whyn't you think about this. You got the best job in the world. No, wait. You do. I seen you once—I saw you. This was pretty far back, not too long after we got going. You were sitting at your board, you'd moved it to the window, and out the window it was getting dark and you could see the top of that big tree out there. Not a leaf on it. It was cold out there, almost dark. Inside, it was great."

Walter had shut his eyes again, the big pain in the ass.

"The ink was still wet. On the daily. And Walter? You looked happy, Walt. Your face looked twenty years old. You had

on a plaid flannel shirt. Walter? You have to get better, and do it again."

"Very nice, but I don't think he heard you."

"Hello, Howard. And he heard me all right. He's not asleep, he's just pretending. He doesn't want to hear my crap. He wants to stay unhappy. Walter! So stay unhappy, who's stopping you? Just don't get so mad!"

Nothing. No response.

"Where should I put these?" Howard had brought a wrapper of yellow flowers. Before I could answer, he did what I would've suggested—stuck them in a vase with some mums. Then he perched on the windowsill. His shirt was clean, his red-speckled blue necktie held a carefully symmetrical knot. I picked a fleck of paper off his suit coat sleeve. "Any word?" he asked me. "About . . . you know. Work."

"Nothing yet."

He made a grimace, then sent that look packing. And put on a high-hat face. "So. Al. Surprised I came?"

"No. Yes. No."

He laughed. "Which is it?"

"Yes and no. But I'm glad you're here."

"Uh-huh. Jeez. He looks so . . ."

"Small?"

"Pale. I was going to say pale." He stepped over to the bed. "Mr. Geebus? Mr. Geebus? It's Howard Blum."

"Don't wake him."

"Then what's the point of visiting?"

"All right. So wake him."

"Never mind."

"No, wake him up. Go ahead."

"Would you quit it?"

A woman's voice over the public address system announced
that only five minutes remained till the end of visiting hour.
Visitors should please leave the building promptly at nine.

Howard Blum said, "Do you think I could use Mr. Geebus's
studio? There's no heat all day at my place. If I get the job."

"Why don't you worry about it then?"

"I guess." Then he changed the subject: "I've never been this
far uptown before. I wasn't really sure where I was going. If I'd
even find this place."

"How long have you been in New York?"

"Not long. Last month, that's all. I got here from Chicago
four weeks ago last Monday."

I put on my hat. "You feel like going to a picture?"

"What?"

"The pictures. You feel like going?"

"What's playing?"

"I don't know. We could check."

"I'm broke. I think maybe not."

"I'll spring for your ticket."

"Thanks anyway."

I turned back to Walter. "Did he just say something?"

Howard looked. "I don't know—maybe."

"Walter? You say something?"

His eyes were open to slits.

"Walter? You said something?"

He nodded, then said it again.

I turned to Howard Blum. "He said, 'Go to the fucking
movies already.' "

"I didn't hear that, Al. You're making it up. He probably
said, 'Fuck you, Bready.' "

"Howard? Trust me. I heard him right."

I can still remember the strip that was tacked to Walter's drawing table on that late fall afternoon, years earlier, when I'd found him looking so damned happy, sitting there in his buffalo-plaid flannel shirt. It was a daily from the second or third week of the first Ma Billions story—the fat old broad smacking Derby Dugan in the head with a long-barreled revolver. Walter had just finished inking all the figures with his pen; he'd laid it down on the taboret but hadn't selected a brush yet. He had jars and jars, mason jars, crammed with good red sables. Maybe the radio was playing, but I can't recall for certain. There was, I'm sure, the ever-present smoldering cigarette. The ever-present cup of cold black coffee. A shot glass full of inky water. And Walter, smiling off into space. I didn't want to move—it was like when you chance upon a couple of deer out in the woods or you see a bird you've never seen before. That sounds stupid, but I'll stick with it. It's how I

felt. I didn't want to startle him, I didn't want his mood to flinch and disappear.

But then he noticed me.

"What are you staring at, Bready? My handsome face?"

"Of course."

He laughed and got out of his swivel chair, threw his arms up, then bent over and touched his toes. His vertebrae popped. He straightened up again, tucking in his shirttail. Then he looked down at the strip. He shook his head. "You're a strange guy, Al."

"What's that supposed to mean?"

"You're strange, that's all. The stuff you dream up. This witch is hitting a ten-year-old kid! Is that a product of *my* imagination?"

"It's your signature. And he's fourteen. I thought we agreed on that."

"Fuck he is not fourteen. He's ten."

"He's fourteen. And what's wrong with Ma Billions?"

"Nothing is wrong, Al. Did you hear me say wrong? *Strange.* That's all I said. Like you." He laughed. "How does she look, anyway? Does she live up to your mental picture? Have I captured her essence? Have I pleased you, Alfie?"

"She's great."

"She is."

We both stood there looking at her pistol-whip our boy.

Then Walter said, "I was up to King last year for something, and there was a leak in the ceiling—and do you know what? They'd used about a month of 'Krazy Kats' to soak up the flood. The original art!"

"I never understand that strip."

"Well, I don't either, but the thing is beautiful. It's beautifully drawn. And they used it to soak up dirty water!" He sat

down again at the board. "Did you ever draw? When you were a kid, I mean. Did you?"

"Doesn't everybody?"

Walter said, "I don't know. Do they? I can't imagine not drawing. But it's nutty, when you think about it. What the hell am I doing, drawing these stupid pictures day after day? You ever get that feeling? About your own life? What you do?"

"Of course."

"Not really, right? Is that what you're telling me?"

"No, no, I get that feeling, Walter. Sometimes."

"But I'm not too worried about it. Yeah, it's a crazy occupation for a grown man, but what else could I do? I always say that, don't I?"

I watched him resume inking, but he botched the brushwork, spoiling Ma's face in the second panel with a heavy smear of ink. He had to wait till it dried, then he glued down a pasteover and redrew the face. The second version wasn't half as good as the first.

By then it was completely dark outside the window.

When he noticed that I was still hanging around, Walter asked me to find something good on the radio. I fiddled with the dial and tuned in a spooky melodrama. "Something else, Al, please."

Sadie trudged up to the studio in her bathrobe and coolly said good night to us both. Walter and I were drinking straight whiskey by then. I couldn't believe that it was after eleven o'clock. I'd been there since the middle of the afternoon. He held out his glass and I refilled it.

I had to watch him like a hawk—by then the man kept dropping cigarette coals into his lap or onto the carpet.

I slept over that night, in the boy's room.

Frank Sweeney hadn't yet come into our lives.

THE BLUMS OF WOODSTOWN

We saw *Charge of the Light Brigade.* The Blum kid loved it, I thought it was bunkum. When we came out of the show it was past eleven o'clock, we were in Times Square, and I invited Howard Blum for a drink. I remembered an Irish bar on Forty-first Street, so that's where we ended up. It had a steam table, but neither of us felt hungry. We got ourselves settled behind glasses of beer and talked a little about the picture. Howard wanted to know if it had really ever happened, if there'd ever been a real Charge of the Light Brigade. So right there he tells me everything I need to know about his education. I said, "You're from Chicago?"

"No. I just lived there. I'm from New Jersey."

"So am I. Bayonne. And Walter's from Hoboken."

"Ah, that's practically New York, both of you guys," said Howard Blum. "I'm from way down. Woodstown. Salem County?"

"Is that right? Not too many Jews there, I wouldn't think."

He tightened for a moment, then lifted one shoulder and re-laxed. "No, not many. We were the only ones in a Quaker vil-lage—not counting the greenhorns from Poland that worked for my father."

"Doing what?"

"Making chairs, highboys, all that stuff." He opened his coat and removed a package of Old Golds from his shirt pocket. I pointed, and he shook one up for me. I had Clarky's Zippo, and lighted both our cigarettes.

"He still alive?"

"The old man? Oh yeah. So's my old lady."

"Ever go see them?"

"No. No, never."

"Because you don't have a car or because you don't want to?"

Instead of answering, he turned his face and scanned the bar-room. For a couple of seconds he followed a dart game. I looked around myself. A party of six, four men and two bottle blonds, were talking quietly with their heads bent close together, al-most touching, at a booth across the barroom. And seated by himself at another booth was Mysterious Jones. He was paging through a two-dollar book. I recognized the cover. It was *101 New Magic Tricks,* by Harry Necromein, Jr.

When I looked back to Howard, he was staring at me. "You sure ask a lot of questions."

I laughed. "I'm just curious, Howard. We're colleagues. Practically family."

"Yeah? We are? How do we know that? How long do they need to make up their minds? You'd tell me if you heard some-thing, wouldn't you, Al?"

"I'd tell you, sure. But you tell me about Woodstown."

"Nothing to say. You got your cattle, you got your Tuesday auction, you got your fishing in the creek. Go read *Tom Sawyer.*"

"Get along with your mother?"

"Did *you?*"

"Sure." Not precisely the truth. Like Ma Billions, Mary Catherine Brady knew a dozen different ways to clobber a little boy, but telling Blum that would've changed the conversation, and I liked it fine the way it was.

"My mother was all right," said Howard.

"But not happy."

He frowned. "No. Why did you say that?"

"They never are—are they?"

"Who, mothers?"

"Females. In general."

"I wouldn't know," said Howard Blum.

He drained his glass. I quickly refilled it from the pitcher, we clinked another toast, he drank some more. Then he really started talking. No big surprise—I'd had that kid figured since I first met him for a two-beer drunk. I sat back and just listened.

oward's mother, the unhappy Esther Blum, was addicted to milk chocolates and fruit pies, but especially to the colored funnies in the Philadelphia newspapers—she loved the "Katzenjammer Kids" and "Boob McNutt," but her favorite was "The Gumps." Although Howard, an only child, could never convince her to buy him a pair of skates or a new kite or tickets to the circus by throwing himself on the parlor rug and kicking his feet—by having a tantrum—he could always, every time, get whatever he wanted merely by sitting down and drawing, then coloring with crayons, a funny sheet just for her. The poor woman would give anything for a good laugh.

Isaiah Blum, the father, was an utterly humorless man; sober and strict, and though only middling religious, as proudly moral as Abraham in the Bible. Howard didn't describe him to me, but I saw him this way: a crabby face clouded by cigar smoke. Owner and president, taskmaster and paymaster at

Blum's Fine Furniture Company. Where he never missed a day, including Saturdays. Or made an error. Or cracked a smile. Chairs were serious. Tables were serious. Life was serious. He told young Howard. Who just rolled his eyes, then carried his tricycle through an attic window and pedaled it around the roof gutters. Who stretched a wire between two elms, then walked it. Who once let some farm boys tie cement weights to his legs and throw him into a creek. The escape artist!

In 1930, when he was sixteen, Howard Blum made his greatest escape: he convinced his mother who convinced his father to send him to Philadelphia to study mechanical drawing. But he hated school (he always had), and six months later, when his father's company failed, Howard was only too happy to quit. Instead of returning to Woodstown, though, he stayed living where he was and found a job across the river in Camden designing light fixtures. Torture! Thank God he was soon fired for doodling tramps and submarines on the margins of his technical drawings. Apparently there were those who could resist, who were naturally immune to, the charms of cartooning. A lesson.

In Philadelphia, Howard fell in with a group of young art students, and whenever he could afford it—he sporadically found work jerking sodas or parking cars or selling tickets at miniature golf—he took figure-drawing classes at the Pennsylvania Academy. The models were skinny or flabby, but still it was good, and it was time, to see a few women in the flesh.

After a year he became skillful enough at illustrative drawing that he could freelance for an advertising company. Then he worked for a mail-order house, drawing shoes and hats and furs and corsetry for its seasonal catalogs. Then he worked in a department store. Then he got an Irish girl pregnant. So she claimed. And then he moved to Chicago.

By that time Howard was eighteen and it was 1932, rock-bottom year of the Great Depression. He had a few bad months, so bad that he ended up eating at soup kitchens and sleeping in tabernacles, where they made you listen to a thumping sermon before they'd let you have a cot. But his luck turned, not entirely around but far enough that he could feed himself and rent a basement room: he landed a job drawing spot-pictures that went on toy packaging. The Dick Tracy Police Station, the Moon Mullins Paddy Wagon, the Mutt and Jeff Camera, the Orphan Annie Skipping Rope, the Buck Rogers Battlecruiser. Then, through the older brother of a girl he'd started dating—the guy was a news photographer with the Chicago *Tribune*—Howard learned about a cartoonist named Clarence "D. C." Gast, who was looking for an assistant to help on an aviation strip that he'd recently sold called "Sky Legion."

Howard applied for the job and got it. It came with a table, a chair, and a couch in a warm studio on the fourteenth floor of the Tribune Tower. From the window he could look down into the swank Medinah Club. This was in 1933, I believe. Howard confused me a little with his dates, but I think he started working for Gast sometime early in the winter of 1933.

D. C. Gast turned out to be a kook, dressing often in a goggled helmet and a Lindbergh jacket and always grinning from ear to ear, making his little sleazy mustache wiggle. And he was a great talker, a big yak, but the only things he talked about were barnstorming airplanes and flopping showgirls. He was also an amiable fraud: "the flying cartoonist," as he was dubbed by the Trib Syndicate's publicity department, couldn't draw. Not a bit. He'd paid a pal of his one hundred bucks to work up the presentation strips, and he paid Howard Blum a ten-dollar salary to do the strips that actually went into syndication.

Gast appeared at the studio just twice a week, on Tuesday mornings to bring in his "script"—always a page torn from a dimestore notepad and jotted with piddling directions: "Blizzard/Iceberg/Big Crash/Cute Eskimo Girls"—and then again on Friday afternoons to sign the six dailies and the Sunday half-tab. The rest of the time he was off somewhere in the clouds. Literally. He'd bought his own two-cylinder Aeronca.

And what did Howard Blum think about all this? He thought it was great. So what if the hours were long? Once he got the hang of drawing biplanes, the job was a breeze, it was great. And the studio was great, too. It was small but it was great, and guys on a scaffold washed the window every two weeks. Howard felt like a hot dog, waving to them. And being left alone, no boss to breathe down his neck—that wasn't great? It was. Everything was. It was all great.

Till it was terrible. Till Mascot Pictures bought rights to "Sky Legion" for a thirteen-episode chapter play to star John Wayne and Ruth Hall. Till "Sky Legion" aviator pins started coming free in specially marked packages of Wheaties, sponsor of the popular new "Sky Legion" afternoon radio program. Till there were "Sky Legion" Big-Little Books, gasoline station giveaway glasses, footed pajamas in the Sears Roebuck catalog, and pot-metal toy planes from the Louis Marx Company. Jesus Christ. Till "Sky Legion" was a roaring success.

And what did Howard Blum have to show for it? A twenty-dollar raise. Meanwhile, D. C. Gast, that no-talent son of a bitch, bought a dairy farm in Woodstock, Illinois, and traded in his second-hand Aeronca for a brand-new Cub Coupe.

"D. C." What did *that* stand for—Dirty Chiseler? That lousy Dirty Chiseler, thought Howard Blum—I hope he crashes. Into a goddamn cornfield. Into one of his goddamn *cows!*

Although he swore every day that he was going to quit, Howard Blum ended up ghosting Clarence Gast for nearly four years. Unfair as it was, it still was a job. It kept him off the dole. It did something else, too. Decided him once and for all that he was a comic-strip man.

Before "Sky Legion," he hadn't been sure whether or not he wanted to spend the rest of his life drawing little pictures under scalloped word balloons; now, by God, he was positive that he did. It was *exactly* what he wanted to do. This was the way to get filthy rich. But first, of course, he'd have to cook up a strip of his own.

Most evenings Howard didn't bother going home. He'd finish up the day's salaried work at around five, then order out a sandwich and a container of coffee. Following a short break— he did calisthenics—he'd take out some clean illustration board, and with the radio playing orchestra music, sit back down and draw for himself, and keep on drawing till midnight, one o'clock in the morning. Then he'd curl up on the couch and sleep till seven. Get up and start drawing "Sky Legion" again. His social life spluttered and his sex life died, but he did generate, one after the other, five original comic strips. A month's worth of each. He even colored the Sundays by hand, to make them look really fine.

But none of them sold.

So he took a short break, then doggedly tried yet another strip. This time a crime strip—fast, lots of gunplay. "Butch Sanderson," about a gruff, big-hearted drifter moving from town to town, finding trouble, doing good. And the McClure Syndicate was interested. Howard even signed a contract. Proofs were pulled, ads were taken. Then reps went out—but returned with a measly three sales. Three stinking papers.

Toledo *Blade,* Richmond *News-Leader,* Trenton *Times.* That
killed the deal. And when Clarence Gast read about it in *Editor
and Publisher,* he was so furious at Howard for being disloyal
that he swooped down from the sky one afternoon and fired
him. On his twenty-second birthday, no less. November the
sixth, 1936.

Three days later, Howard Blum left Chicago on a Yellow
Way bus to New York City.

MORE BAD NEWS FOR HOWARD BLUM

". . . and a week later, not even a week, I found that job at the *Daily News.*"

"And met Ray Catlow."

"Who told me about Mr. Geebus. Yeah."

By that time, Howard Blum and I were hoofing it down Broadway; it was half past one in the morning.

He laughed suddenly.

"What?"

"Just thinking."

"About what?"

"Never mind," said Howard. Then he said, "From Gast to Geebus—lucky me," and gave a stagy, self-pitying gesture and almost lost his balance; I grabbed him by an elbow. Christ, you'd think he'd been swallowing martinis. But it wasn't even four beers. Three and a sip. I let go, and one of his knees buckled. He swooped. I caught him again, but he jerked away.

"What about you, Al?"

"What *about* me?"

"I told you all about me, what about you? Do you like every-thing you see? What *don't* you like? Ever been persecuted?" He started weaving drunkenly all over the pavement, and talking the same way, in a lot of zigzag. "D. C. Gast!" he said. "Fuck him!" Then he said, "Fan mail! When I was doing 'Sky Legion,' I got fan letters! Couple dozen every week! Every. Single. Week." And then he said, "You ever read it, Al?"

" 'Sky Legion'? Sure."

"What did you think?"

We were approaching Thirty-eighth Street, where Howard Blum would be turning off to go west.

"I asked you what you thought of 'Sky Legion,' Al. And don't tell me it was no fucking good, because it was fucking gorgeous!"

"Did I say it wasn't?"

"But Al? I'm sick of drawing airplanes, so no airplane stuff in 'Dugan,' all right?"

I said, "You didn't get the job."

"What?"

"Bud Lydecker did."

Howard took the news physically. He stopped short, his left hand clutching his stomach.

"I'm sorry."

"Wait a minute! You knew? You knew about this? But I kept *asking!*"

"I felt shitty having to break the news."

"A lot of pull you had. If you even tried at all."

"I tried."

"Yeah, so you could squeeze an extra fifty bucks a week out of me. I hope Lydecker don't give you a dime."

"I wouldn't think of asking him. You think I care about fifty bucks? I'm a rich man."

Howard laughed. Well, laughed and sneered. "A rich man—you?"

"Relatively speaking, I'm rich."

" 'Relatively speaking.' Fuck you, relatively speaking."

"Howard, listen to me. I don't write for King Features, I write for Walter. Walter pays me. So I wanted you to pay me."

"I really believe that, Al. And I believe in leprechauns, too. Hey, look! Over there! Is that one?"

"I don't care what you believe, Howard. It's true. I wish you were doing the strip."

"Go to hell."

"But you're not. So you need something else. All right. You still listening to me? There's a guy that I know—"

"Straight to hell."

"—starting up a comic-book company. All new strips. He'll give you as much work as you can handle."

"Comic books!" Howard Blum looked like I'd told him to go play right field when he'd expected to pitch. "This is a comic-book place?" He was very suddenly sober. "I seen some of those things—they're crap! It's nothing but crap."

I took out one of Clarky's business cards and my cartridge pen. "I'm going to write a little note, you can show it to this guy. That's his name, right there. I'm writing it down that you're to get five bucks a page."

"Inked?"

"And lettered."

"Holy Jesus."

"What's the matter?"

"Five bucks?"

"Just till you find something better, then."

"Think I could get six?"

"No way. You could do all right if you work fast. But if you—"

"I can work fast, don't think that I can't! This is guaranteed? I'll definitely get some paying work?"

"Guaranteed."

"Comic books, though. Christ."

"Think what you want, Howard. Do what you want. I'm just telling you. If you decide to go up there, I'll probably see you around once in awhile."

"Gee, Al, that'll be swell."

He went and stood under a streetlight, held the card in front of his face. Scowled at it. I thought for a second that he intended to rip it all to pieces. But he didn't. He took out his wallet and stuck it in the money fold.

"How much was Walter supposed to pay you today?"

He saw me taking out my own wallet. "Forget it."

"How much?"

"Thirty-five."

We both grinned.

I gave him a couple of tens.

And don't think that I forgot to tell him about Pete Laudermilch's offer. I hadn't mentioned it on purpose. I didn't think he should go to work for King after the way they'd treated him. And who was I to decide for Howard Blum what he should or shouldn't do? Nobody. But I did it anyway.

Fan letters? "Sky Legion" got a couple dozen fan letters a week? Big deal. "Derby Dugan" got a hundred. More, sometimes. On every second Friday, after he'd messengered over to King a parcel of strips, Walter Geebus would sit at that picnic table he kept in the studio and go through the fan mail, jotting down on a pad those things that his readers liked, or didn't, or wanted to see, or worried about. ("We are all concerned that Fuzzy is crippled for life. Please find her a good vet—please!")

Walter's policy was to answer every single letter, and for a couple of years he had a freelance secretary named Min Callen who came to the house on alternate Fridays. Mostly, of course, Walter sent back a standard thank-you note, a form letter that he personally signed. But if somebody famous wrote to him— Elsa Maxwell or Fred Allen or George M. Cohan—he took the time to respond with a handwritten note. The only time he didn't was the time John Dillinger—I swear!—dropped him a

line from the jail in Lima, Ohio, suggesting that Walter slen-
derize Ma Billions ("If she was fifty pounds less, I could go for
her myself!") and banish Yin Yi from the strip because he had
no tolerance for yellow men. Though it irked Walter to dis-
cover that a notorious public enemy was a faithful reader, what
really infuriated him was that ugly slap at our kindhearted Chinese master of the martial arts. For all of his faults, Walter Geebus was no racialist.

If some correspondent asked him a specific question, no matter how dumb it was, Walter would patiently dictate a reply and
Min would type it up. Anyone who asked for a drawing of Derby
Dugan got one. I was amazed by how quickly the man could
make a sketch; he didn't even have to look at the sheet of paper—
he could be talking to you and drawing at the same time.

And Walter, who'd never had any children, was a real sucker
for his kid readers. He never let a form letter go out to a child,
and often he sent along an original strip, inscribed. Even when
he was feeling most miserable and acting his grouchiest—
throughout the entire Frank Sweeney ordeal, even—Walter took
great pains to be considerate of his youngest fans. He boasted
about that, pompously comparing himself to other strip men
who never paid the slightest attention to their juvenile readers.

Sometime in late 1935, Min Callen (who'd had a brief, mu-
tually meaningless affair with Walter; I know because he told
me) got married and moved away, and I ended up volunteering
to help with the correspondence. Every other Friday I'd show
up at the house at around three, put on a fresh pot of coffee,
then we'd just plow through all the mail. Later, I'd alphabetize
and file it.

On this one particular Friday afternoon that I'm thinking
about, it must've been early in 1936, Walter was patting himself on the back once again for being such a thoughtful guy, a

guy who took a special interest in his kid fans even though they
didn't buy newspapers. I guess I'd had my fill of it, because
suddenly I told him, "You never answered *my* letter."

"What do you mean—what letter?"

"When I was kid. I wrote you a letter."

"Get out of here! You?"

"Sure. I wrote you a nice letter but you never wrote me back."

"You're making this up, Al." Then he looked at me queerly,
and I wondered if perhaps he didn't much like being reminded
that he'd been drawing the "Dugan" strip so long that I'd read
it as a little boy. "You never sent me any fan letter."

"Did so!"

"What'd you say?"

"How the hell can I remember?"

He snorted, gave me another suspect glance, then went back
to reading letters.

Well, the following Monday when I showed up to deliver
the week's scripts, Walter greeted me with an apology the moment I walked in.

"You *did* write, you son of a bitch!"

He picked up a sheet of lined cheap paper, the kind flecked
with coarse wood chips, and waved it in my face. It was the ac-
tual letter I'd sent him years before! Over the weekend he'd
gone and dug it out from one of the four-drawer filing cases in
a storage room behind the studio.

When I reached for it, he snatched it back. Then he put on
his glasses and cleared his throat like an after-dinner speaker.
"Dated October 14, 1915. How old were you, Al?"

"Eleven."

"Eleven! Jesus!" He scowled, then read, " 'Dear Mr. Geebus,
I like Derby Dugan very much. I like Fuzzy, too. They are my
favorites.' Even then you had a way with words."

"You don't have to read this out loud, you know."

"Yeah," Walter said, "I do." Then he resumed: " 'I live in Bayonne, New Jersey. My big brother likes Derby Dugan too. His name is Donald. So does my little sister but she is too young to read it by herself. Her name is Jean. Would you answer a question? Is Fuzzy a girl dog or a boy dog? I hope he is a boy!' " Walter looked up. "You added an exclamation point."

"Uh-huh."

" 'I hope he is a boy,' exclamation point. And then you go on to say, 'I am sick a lot with bad headaches, but whenever I read Derby Dugan on Sunday I feel good. I thought I would tell you.' Thanks for telling me, Al!"

"Screw you, Geebus."

He laughed. "Any of this ringing a bell?"

"No."

"Really?"

"Let me have it, huh?"

"Bad headaches?"

"It was a noisy household."

Walter glanced back to my letter. " 'Do you have any helpers? If you do, I would like to be one of them when I am older. It would be fun!' Another exclamation point. 'I do not have a dog, but if I did I would name him Fuzzy.' And it's signed 'Your friend, Alfred O. Brady.' " Walter smiled as he read the letter again to himself, then he lifted his eyes, met mine, and said, "Know something, Al? You wrote *better* when you were eleven."

I grabbed for the letter, and that time he let me have it. Jesus. Seeing it, seeing that extinct handwriting, gave me the willies. And that line about headaches. Bad headaches. Oh yeah. I'd had them for years, real killers, so blinding that I used to vomit.

Mine had been a very goddamned noisy household, indeed.

"Sorry I didn't reply," said Walter.

"You broke my heart."

"Did I?"

"I hardly think so."

"Yeah, but you remembered that I never answered."

"It hasn't been plaguing me, Walter. I promise."

"I was going through my second divorce that fall. I must've been negligent."

"That must've been it."

"Sorry."

"It's okay."

But that wasn't the end of the episode. Later that same week, I came back to my hotel and there was a large parcel waiting for me at the desk. I took it upstairs and unwrapped it, and inside was an original "Derby Dugan" Sunday page, dated October 17, 1915. Mid-slapstick era. Inscribed: "To My Good Pal Alfred O. Brady."

And there was a handwritten note:

"Dear Alfred" (it said), "Thank you for writing to me. It was nice of you to do that, and I want you to know how much I appreciate it. I was sorry to hear about your headaches, but trust they will disappear when you grow up. Childhood is rough, as our mutual friend Derby Dugan knows only too well. If you still want to be my helper when you grow up, I would like that very much, too. Best wishes, Walter Geebus."

Naturally, there was a P.S.: "But I warn you, little boy. I'll never pay you more than 30 bucks a week."

EPISODE NINETEEN

NIGHT CALL

After Howard Blum and I parted company on Broadway, I went home and took a bath. Derby's in a rowboat. It's night. Night on the river. Derby's in a rowboat on the river. While I soaked in the tub, I forced myself to keep taking drinks from a bottle of Old Granddad.

It was going on three in the morning by the time I climbed out, dried off, put on pajamas. Then I telephoned Jewel.

"Al? What's the matter? Are you ill?"

"Yeah." She was always worrying, bless her heart, that I'd get sick in my room and nobody would know. "I'm dying, Jewel."

"Al Bready! You are not, you're drunk. I don't think this is very funny. You don't call me all week, then you call me up in the middle of the night. I hate night calls!"

I heard Jimmie ask if everything was all right. Jewel said yeah, then covered the mouthpiece so I couldn't hear what else

she told him. "Still there, Al? What's the matter with you? You never get drunk."

"That's not exactly true. But I don't get drunk very often. And I don't get very drunk often at all. Once in a blue moon. What'd you just tell Jimmie? Who'd you say you were talking to?"

"You."

"He standing there?"

"No, he isn't. Now, what's this all about?"

"I don't want you to go."

She was silent.

"Jewel?"

"I'm here. But what am I supposed to answer? I don't want to go, either. So what? He's my husband. I'm the wife. I could show you the piece of paper. But it's sweet your saying that. I appreciate it."

"That mean we're friends again?"

"You coming next Monday for supper?"

"We'll see."

"Al! If you were here right now, I'd club you with this telephone."

We laughed, and for the first time since I'd dialed, I relaxed. I heard Jewel light a cigarette. I lighted one myself.

"So. Did you find a new typist?"

"You know I wouldn't do that. But now I guess I'll have to." Fat chance in real life. I'd just start typing my own final copy again. Save myself a bundle. "Jewel, tell me. How did this all happen?"

"With the restaurant? Totally by chance. Jimmie was talking to some customer, and the customer's uncle is looking to buy a business. It all took about three hours. The deal, I mean."

"When was this?"

"Wednesday morning. I must've called your hotel six times."

That was an exaggeration—she'd called only twice—but I didn't correct her. "Jimmie called me, too. To say he was sorry."

"I know he did. I made him." She excused herself and put the phone down. She came right back. "I was just putting on a lamp. I hate being in the dark."

"Do you really?"

"You didn't know that? I mean, I hate being in the dark by myself. Oh sure. I hate it." She struck another match, fired another cigarette. Or relighted the first one. "So tell me about Walter. Is he going to be okay?"

As I brought her up to date, she clucked and tutted at all the right places—even pretended to recollect Bud Lydecker's brief stints on "Radio Patrol" and "Tim Tyler's Luck." Jewel didn't follow many comic strips: except for "Derby Dugan," she read only "Winnie Winkle" in the *News* and "Tiller the Toiler" and "Ella Cinders" in the *Mirror.* Well, nobody's perfect.

"I can't believe they'd give your strip to that awful man," she said.

"It's not my strip, it's Walter's. But no, I can't believe it either."

"*You* should decide. It ought to be up to you. If Walter's out of the picture. I think you should go back there and make them change their minds. Say they have to give it to Howard Blum, if he's so good. Say you don't want it looking like something the cat dragged in."

"Mrs. Rodgers, let me tell you something I thought you knew already. Walter's strip is just one of several that I write, and besides—"

"Yeah, yeah, yeah."

"What's that supposed to mean?"

"It's supposed to mean tell it to Kelsey, but don't kid me. And why don't you want me to leave New York?"

"Because I couldn't stand living here without you. Didn't think I'd say something like that, did you?"

"No."

"Do you want me to go on? I could go on and on."

She laughed. "I don't think so, Al. But thanks for the offer."

She must've pressed a finger to the disconnect toggle because, just like that, the line went dead.

I went into a sort of hibernation for the rest of that December, staying in my room except to visit Walter and to make the occasional trip out for coffee, groceries, newspapers, and fresh ribbons. I didn't even bother with the Sullavan sisters. I read a lot, instead. I read *Hearst: Lord of San Simeon* and was surprised to find Walter's old nemesis George Reckage (but spelled with a "W"—Wreckage) mentioned briefly in the section about the Old Man's newspapering days in New York City. Reckage, or Wreckage, was lumped in with a group of Sunday supplement cartoonists from the turn of the century—Richard Outcault, Rudy Dirks, Fred Opper, Gus Mager. Those guys. Walter's name wasn't included.

One night, a few nights before Christmas, I felt so choked from being indoors—I'd spent the day reading and writing, the evening visiting Walter—that I took a long hike south from the hospital and then all around midtown. It was cold, snowing

a little, and I finally ducked into an amusement arcade just to thaw out my nose and forehead. And who did I find there— carefully working a game lever, trying to scoop up some junky prize with a mechanical shovel—but Mysterious Jones.

I watched him for a while, he kept plugging pennies into the coin slot, sliding the lever, positioning the shovel, punching the red drop button—and missing the snatch, every time. He looked at me and said, "Would you mind not lurking? I can't concentrate."

"I'm lurking?"

"Please," he said.

"Did you make that yourself, or did you find a haberdasher?" I was pointing to his mask, of course.

He didn't think I was funny, and bent to pick up his glad-stone bag from the floor under the shovel machine. I was supposed to cave in and walk away, naturally. But I didn't.

"Do you have a license to wear that thing? Is it hot under there? Does your face sweat? It must. Do you have a disfigurement? Port-wine stain?"

Jones said, "Buddy, you got diarrhea of the mouth."

"I'll give you twenty bucks for that mask."

"Get your own."

"I already got my own, but I kind of like yours."

He became so disgusted that he shoved past me and went straight through the arcade and out to the sidewalk. He'd left behind, on the rim of the shovel table, a couple of pennies and a package of Black Jack chewing gum with two slices left. I took the gum, then I changed a quarter into pennies and played that shovel game myself, but I never got a prize.

Anyhow, December went past. The king of England quit, they got his brother. Joe Wein left for Detroit to help the auto workers stage a sit-down strike. I kept busy with all the usual

things, all the strips I did, the radio show, the marriage novels, that Borneo job, and then of course I'd started turning out comic-book stories for Clark Kamen. Scripts for eight-page action stories.

Clarky had given me a list of widely syndicated strips that he wanted imitated, the knockoffs to be as close to the originals as I could make them without getting him and his clients sued for copyright infringement. "Mandrake the Magician"? I did "Samarkind the Sorcerer." "Flash Gordon"? My guy was called "Streak Dawson." "Dick Tracy"? "Jack Slooth, Plainclothes Cop." "Tarzan of the Jungle"? "Jun-Gull of Darkest Africa." "Terry and the Pirates"? "Young China Joe." "Alley Oop"? "Dan Small, Neanderthal."

I ran into Howard Blum at Clarky's shop a couple of times late in the month, but we only said hello in passing. I was there delivering paper, he was hunched over a board in a room full of pool-hall types and truant high-school boys with bad teeth and cheap smokes and wet sandwiches they'd brought from home to eat at their tables. I got the impression that Howard had quickly become the studio's darling. Well, from what I could see, he was the only joker there who knew anything at all about drawing pictures. There was no doubt he was prospering. I'd heard he'd even got a telephone installed in his flat.

On Christmas Eve, Jimmie Rodgers and I met for the first time since he'd appeared in my hotel lobby. At Jewel's insistence, I went over to their place in Tudor City for a couple of hours, to help decorate the tree with tinsel and balls and drink a little boozed-up eggnog. Jimmie pretended that he'd never banished me. Acted as though I'd stayed away through sheer busyness. And he asked me—several times, twice each time— to resume having supper with them again on Monday evenings, since they wouldn't be in town for too many more. He was def-

initely rubbing it in. I thanked him and said I'd try like crazy
to come, but my weekly meals with the Rodgers were a thing
of the past. A dead ritual. I didn't go back for a single one. And
Jewel didn't seem to begrudge me my stubbornness. Which
was disappointing.

Every day, either in the afternoon or at night, I popped in on
Walter Geebus at the hospital. Sadie and I were the constants as
far as visitors went. We kept running into each other, and sitting there together, but after the first few times we didn't have
much to say to each other.

The year drew to a close, the new one started, and Walter's
condition stayed precarious; he'd have hours of lucidity followed by days of twilight comas. He'd lost a lot of motor skills,
and his tongue was floppy in his mouth.

But by the end of January, he'd stabilized. He was out of
danger, the doctors thought. He couldn't feed himself, but
fairly soon there'd be no medical reason to keep him at the hospital. He'd just have to hire a visiting nurse.

Meanwhile, I'd been sending my "Dugan" scripts to Bud Lydecker, and I guessed everything was all right. I hadn't heard
anything to the contrary. I hadn't heard anything, period. Not
even one phone call from old Bud. And I'd be damned if I was
going to call *him!*

EPISODE TWENTY

WALTER COMES HOME

In the first week of February 1937, Walter Geebus was released from the hospital. He went home in a taxicab. Sadie called me up shortly before noon, saying that he was settled in and everything seemed jake. I asked her if the private nurse had arrived yet. "That's all been arranged for," she told me.

Around three that afternoon, anxious to see him again in his own surroundings, I rode up to Walter's house. But when I rang the doorbell, nobody answered. I couldn't believe that he'd been left alone. I let myself in and went straight upstairs to the master bedroom.

The bed was empty, still made.

Going back down the hallway, I flung open every door, linen closet door included, and so barged in finally on Walter in the boy's room. For some reason, he'd ensconced himself there amid all the "Dugan" paraphernalia. And at the moment I blundered through the doorway, he was getting a vigorous hand job. Sadie

grimaced, then let go. She jumped up from the side of the bed. "What the hell are you doing here?" She didn't seem embarrassed, just furious.

"I'm sorry. But nobody answered the bell."

"For a good reason." She looked down at Walter's penis, then stepped away from the bedstead. "Do you want to finish this, Al?"

"Shut up."

"It's just that I've always wondered."

I slapped her face.

Soon as I did it, I was sorry. But there's no taking back your violence, is there? She screwed up her mouth and glared at me. Then she grabbed my hand, yanked it to her lips, and bit it.

"Will you two shitheads cut it out and kindly cover me up?" That came out of Walter, and sounded perfectly fluent.

While Sadie brusquely drew the covers over him, I apologized to her. She didn't say anything. At least she didn't until I'd asked her again about the nurse.

"Will you shut up about the nurse? *I'm* the nurse."

"You're moving back in?"

"For the time being."

"With Walter's permission?"

"Fuck you, Al." She sailed out of the room and didn't come back.

I sat on the bed, but closer to the foot than Sadie had been. "So. Walter. Was she trying to kill you or was that true love?"

He smiled, and it made me blue to see the raggedy way that his lips drooped.

"Any improvement, Walt? In general?"

I believe he shrugged. Then his cheeks ballooned out, and he sighed. He definitely sighed. I sat there racking my brain for something to say. Ask him if he wanted the radio turned on?

Needed another blanket? I said, "You want me to read you the paper?" I'd picked up the *Mirror* in the back of the cab coming uptown. There was plenty of flood news from the Midwest.

He turned his head, lifted his chin.

I think he said, "Let's see our boy."

I'd already had a look at the strip. It was Bud Lydecker's third day. His third published daily. And so far the kindest thing you could say about his tenure on "Derby Dugan" was— funny, I've drawn a complete blank. Give me a century, though, I'll think of something.

When I found the comics page, I creased it flat and laid it on Walter's lap. "There."

For a long time he just stared at the deformity. Then he lifted his eyes and gaped at the wall. Well, not at the wall, ex-actly—at that big gilt-framed oil painting that hung on the wall.

Eventually Walter mumbled something.

I said, "What?"

He repeated himself, and I'm pretty sure, I'm almost posi-tive, that he said, "Did the cops take all of Frank's arsenic or is there some still left in the studio?"

I laughed, and so did he, but his yawning mouth was so badly twisted, so out of control, that it made me think of half-wits; it made me think of Jimmie Rodgers.

M ore than once Frank Sweeney had asked me—practically begged me—to write a comic strip for him to draw. I always turned him down. Sorry, I'd tell him—too busy. But that wasn't the reason. That was baloney. I didn't want Frank to go out on his own, that's why I said no. When Walter Geebus had first hired him, I'd been nervous about it, afraid that our smooth little operation—the way that we clicked, Walter and I—would somehow be damaged, even go all to smash with somebody new in the picture. But just the opposite happened. Freed up by an assistant, Walter planned his compositions more carefully, and it showed. If you look at "Dugan" strips from 1933 and the first half of 1934, especially the Sunday pages, you'll see what I'm talking about. The figures are simpler, but denser, and the crosshatching is atmospheric and very creepy. It's a dangerous world, Derby Dugan's. The strip never

looked better than it did during those eighteen, nineteen months.

During the early Sweeney period, Walter seemed full of pep, every time I saw him. He was always joking with me, teasing Frank about his bummy shoes, talking about last night's big adventure sans wife at the Stork Club. And taking delight in the day's board work. Anticipating tomorrow's. I'd never seen him in higher spirits, or looking healthier, and whenever Frank suggested—always out of Walter's earshot—that he and I should huddle together sometime and cook up a strip that he could draw on his own, I wouldn't cooperate. I refused. Nothing doing. Never happen. I wanted things to remain exactly the way they were.

One evening, at his invite, I met Frank Sweeney for drinks at a gin mill near my hotel, a little place where the clientele was almost exclusively guys who worked at the wholesale flower market. It was late May, so by then Frank had been assisting Walter Geebus for almost six months.

"Gosh, is this the first time I've seen you outside the studio? I think it is."

"I think it is, too, Frank."

"Hope it's not the last time."

"It shouldn't be," I said. "But that all depends."

He seemed taken by surprise. "On what?"

"On whether you keep pestering me to do something with just you. You were planning to ask me that again now, weren't you?"

"Not really."

"Oh no?"

"Look. Al. You write for everybody else, why not for me?"

"I do write for you."

"It's Walter's."

"It's ours."

"Balls. I don't want to sound like I'm complaining, but Christ, I've never even inked anybody's head! That's just him, how he is. But what is it with you? You don't like me?"

"I like you fine. And so does Walter."

"But I want my own strip."

"So do one, nobody's stopping you."

"But if a guy like you were to write it—"

"No."

He looked at me for a moment, then shrugged. "If it's no, it's no. But I had in mind a baseball strip. A good baseball strip. What d'you think of this for a title: 'Centerfield Smith'?"

I didn't give him any encouragement. I liked it, though. "Centerfield Smith." Yeah. I liked it.

"A baseball strip, Al."

"I heard you. But I'm passing."

"Jesus. All right, okay." He folded his forearms on the bar top and leaned over them, staring at a little puddle of spilled beer. "Okay."

"Frank. I'll see if maybe I can get you a raise."

"That's not the point."

"No?"

"No! I want my own strip. Look." He yanked open his wallet, then filched out a tabbed-up sheet of tracing paper from the money fold. He carefully opened it and showed me. It was covered with at least a dozen, all different, Frank Sweeney professional signatures, some in boxes, others in ovals, a couple in bubbles, and one inside an isosceles triangle. All caps. All lowercase. Block printing. Swooping script. Dingbats. Curlicues. "I'm ready," said Frank. "Do you see what I'm telling you? I want my own damn strip to sign."

I was astounded by the signatures, all that practice, and when he moved to pull the paper away, I reached over and grabbed it. Studied it some more. Finally I said, "I like this one," pointing to the plainest, mostly because it looked like something you'd write endorsing a check. The other ones looked goofy.

"I could use that one," said Frank. "Sure. But how about this one?" He took out a pen and scribbled my name above the signature I'd preferred, then jotted an ampersand in between them. "How about that? 'Centerfield Smith' by Bready and Sweeney. I don't mind your taking top billing."

"Frank, the only strip that you and I are ever going to do together is the one we're doing right now."

"But—"

"Shut up and listen. It works, Frank. You and me and Walter, it works. It clicks. Everything is balanced, nothing's wobbly, no big surprises. I like that. God knows I like that. But say I write a strip for you and we sell it? What happens then?"

"Walter could find somebody else. Another assistant."

"I'm not talking about Walter, I'm talking about the Dugan strip. The 'Derby Dugan' strip. It wouldn't be the same. You'd be off it, I'd be off it, and I don't—"

"You could still write it."

"Like hell. After I'd been the cause of your striking out for greener pastures? Like hell. He wouldn't talk to me again. Ever."

Frank lit a cigarette and sulked.

I said, "You know 'The Gumps'? You know that strip, right?"

"Sure."

"Walter told me this story. Sidney Smith, the guy who drew it? Knew this jeweler in Chicago named Sol Hess, and this Sol guy was a great, great storyteller, a terrific joke man. So when

Smith sold 'The Gumps' to the Chicago *Tribune,* he went and asked Sol Hess to write the continuities. And he paid him just a few token bucks, but the jeweler didn't care because he got to tell everybody that came into his store that he was making up all those stories they read every day in the newspaper. So a couple years pass, and 'The Gumps' is now the biggest strip going. Remember when Mary Gold died? They closed down the stock exchange for ten minutes so everybody could read it."

"Yeah? So?"

"So I'm getting to the point, Frank. What do you think Sol Hess feels about all this now? He doesn't feel so good, Frank. Especially not when he reads in the paper that Sidney Smith is making more dough than everybody in the United States of America except for maybe five or six oil barons. So he thinks— and I can't blame him—he thinks that it's him that made 'The Gumps' so popular, so he quits and finds a cartoonist and then he comes out with another strip that's almost identical, called 'The Nebbs.' You know it, Frank?"

"No."

"Right. Because it stinks. And you know what? So does 'The Gumps.' Ever since. Sidney and Sol: it worked. It clicked. Equilibrium. Sid without Sol, Sol without Sid: nothing. Dead space. Hot air. It's easy to wreck, Frank. It's not easy to find, but it's very fucking easy to wreck."

Frank Sweeney stared at me. "But that Sol Hess guy was right. Al, for sure you can see that yourself. Why should he write the damn thing for a few bucks and the other guy pockets a million? He *should've* left!"

"Well, he did."

"Well, he should've!"

" 'The Gumps' was a great strip, Frank. And the man wrecked it."

"Jesus Christ, so what? It's just a goddamn comic strip."

I took out a buck and threw it on the bar, then I slid off my stool. "Stick around. We'd hate to lose you."

"Yeah, yeah." Frank noticed his page of practice signatures still lying there, and quickly folded it back up, put it away.

"And if you stick around long enough, Frank, you *will* have your own strip. Think about it. Walter's getting up there, you know?"

"He'll never retire."

"No, but a man his age. God forbid, but you never know."

I've wondered, of course. Whether or not I put the idea into Frank Sweeney's head. I've had my share of bad nights. Whenever I have a dream about sitting at my typewriter typing, I'm always writing a story about a baseball player named Center-field Smith. It's crazy, but there you go. Every time I have that dream. Six or seven times a year. And in the dream, I'm racing against a drop-dead deadline, I have to get the story finished, it's crucial, but I can't come up with a single idea. Because I don't know anything about baseball. Because I don't know any-thing about baseball players. Because I don't know anything about anything.

EPISODE TWENTY-ONE

TO BAYONNE AND BACK

When I returned to the DeSoto after visiting Walter on his first day home from the hospital, there were several telephone messages waiting for me, a sheaf of them. My heart jumped at the sight—I was certain they were all from Jewel. None of them was. "Call Dan," they said. Each and every one of them. "Call Dan." "Call Dan." The young guy at the front desk that late afternoon was Dick Barthorne, an athletic, eager-to-please twenty-five-year-old from the Virginia Tidewater who'd only recently quit answering open calls for chorus boys. I asked him if he'd taken the messages.

"No, sir, Mr. Bready. I just came on twenty minutes ago, sir. Oscar must've taken those."

I thanked him and hiked upstairs, then dialed King Features, asked for Dan Sharkey. What other Dans did I know? But I couldn't imagine why Dan Sharkey would be calling, unless it was to bounce me from the Dugan strip. I got angry even

before I knew the real story. Good thing Sharkey was occupied in a conference, I would've screamed in his ear if he'd come on the line just then.

"I'm returning his call," I told the secretary, and she made me spell my last name.

Ten minutes later the telephone bell rang. It was Sharkey. "What do you mean, returning my call? I never called you."

"I got several messages from somebody named Dan."

"Not me."

"Sorry."

"No harm done. Funny enough, though, I had it in mind that we should talk. I heard from Pete that you're not too happy with Bud Lydecker. I hate to hear things like that, Al. I happen to think he's doing a great job. What? No comment?"

"Is one required?"

"Do you want off the strip?"

"You got somebody else in mind?"

"Excuse me?"

"Who wants to write 'Derby'? Somebody you know?"

"Al? It's amazing. But you always manage to irritate me."

"You want me to quit?"

"I'm not asking you to do anything. But if you're so damned unhappy, we can make other arrangements."

"I'm praying for Walter's speedy recovery, that's all, Mr. Sharkey."

"Dan. Please."

Around seven o'clock that evening, I got a call from my brother.

"Don't you ever pick up your messages, Alfred?"

"That was you? It said Dan."

"He must've written Don and you misread it. But I distinctly told him Donald. He seemed foreign."

"What do you want, Donald?"

"I have some bad news. It's Jean. She won't go to work and she hasn't left the house for two weeks. God knows what's going on in there."

"You haven't been to see her?"

"I just got a call from Benny Safford this morning."

"The Saffords still live next door?"

"Still do, Alfred. And why shouldn't they?"

"Just asking."

"Benny telephoned me and now I'm telling you, in case you want to go check on her."

"It's easier for you to go. You own a Ford, it's twenty minutes across the Bayonne Bridge."

"Benny Safford called me and now I'm telling you, in case you want to go check on Jean. I'm just passing it along, Alfred."

"You know I don't go to Bayonne."

"And I do?"

"Did you try calling her up?"

"Of course."

"Really?"

"She won't answer the phone, Alfred."

"All right. How about this? Do you want to meet me at the house?"

"No, I don't. Benny called me and—"

"All right, okay. Thanks for telling me."

"Don't ring off angry. So. You're still living in that hotel. Still working?"

"Oh sure."

"Still in the ad department?"

"Afraid so." I guess Donald hadn't noticed that the *Graphic* had folded several years ago.

"Be glad you have something, Alfred. In these times. Well. Mary and I always remember you in our prayers."

I'll tell you: nothing is more worthless than to be remembered in somebody's prayers. Remember me in your will or don't remember me at all.

After we'd said our good-byes, I sat on the bed thinking. Trying to decide whether or not I felt guilty enough to go see Jean.

Ten minutes later I was crossing Twenty-fifth Street, angling toward the corner of Sixth Avenue, when a voice hollered my name. I turned, and there was Jewel standing outside the De-Soto, at the foot of the steps with her hand on the railing. Flicker from the hotel sign animated her face. She was wearing a black leatherette coat, snugly belted, and a black hat on sideways.

"He doesn't only write fast, he walks fast," she said. "Where're you going in such a hurry?"

I started back toward her, and she met me in the street, slipping an arm through mine. "Can I walk with you, Al? I can walk fast."

"No real rush."

"Where are we headed, just by the way?"

"Tube station on Twenty-third."

"Happy to see me?"

"Very. But surprised."

"Over the last six months I've walked by your hotel a dozen times, I bet."

"On purpose?"

She laughed. "Of course on purpose. I walked by always thinking I'd stop in and call you from the lobby. But I always chickened out."

"Tonight, though."

"Tonight, though. I finally get up the nerve to come see you tonight, and what happens? You're running off to New Jersey."

"Why'd you need to get up any nerve at all?"

"Can I come with you?"

"To Bayonne? I'd rather you didn't. I have to see somebody."

"Family matter?"

"You could call it that."

"Is everything all right?"

"Oh sure. Oh yeah."

"And everybody?"

"They're all fine. I just need to run over there. It's nothing. But you wouldn't want to come."

We stopped talking at the corner of Twenty-fourth, to look both ways and cross.

"You were going to tell me why you needed any nerve at all, just to come see me."

"I was? All right. Because I was planning to suggest, Mr. Bready, that we sit around in your room and smoke cigarettes and drink a little bit and talk about—oh! I don't know. Anything. Like we used to when we used to go to the Automat, when I worked for Mr. K."

Before I could say anything in response, Jewel nervously blurted, "Do you ever think about buying an automobile?"

I guess I was distracted (smoke cigarettes? drink a little bit? talk? in my *room*?), because at first I didn't realize why she'd asked me such a funny question. "Where would I drive a car?" I said. But then it hit me, and I tried to fix things. "Besides to Albany, of course."

"Syracuse."

"Twenty miles north."

"Twenty miles north," Jewel said with an edgy little smile. "And it even has a name."

I said, "Megville. See? I didn't forget. And when I visit, I'll take the bus."

"You won't come."

"Sure I will."

Syracuse! I never left the island of Manhattan. Well, hardly ever.

We'd reached Twenty-third Street, and Jewel unhooked her arm from my elbow. "I should let you get on your way." When she stepped back, I started down the stairs to the Hudson Tube station. I turned to wave, and she called, "I guess we're never going to talk about this." I waved.

In Jersey City, I caught an interurban bus that ran south on Hudson County Boulevard. It took forty minutes to reach Thirty-second Street in Bayonne. Then I walked across town to Avenue A, passing a dozen saloons and breathing that famous local air that smelled like rotten eggs—from the oil refineries along Constable Hook. That city could make you dizzy and cranky, just breathing. Saloons, churches, bad air, a dramatic bridge to Staten Island, and plenty of crowded-together houses full of Polish, Italian, Czech, Russian, and Irish families; the alleys in between the houses and tenements were barely wide enough for the coal man to squeeze down with a sack on his back. Bayonne! Birthplace of Alfred O. Brady.

My sister was still living in our parents' house. After our mother died—she'd gone into the hospital diagnosed with nervous collapse, but they discovered a cancer—after Mother died, the house came to my brother, my sister, and me. Donald wanted to sell it, Jean wanted to live in it. I gave her my share. I was glad to be rid of it! She paid Donald rent. At least she used to pay him some rent. My guess was that she no longer gave him anything. And naturally, he wouldn't quarrel with

her about it. He wouldn't demand it. He'd just cut her off. That had always been Donald's way. I wasn't much different, I suppose. American Irishmen are fairly simple. Either we shout and swing our fists, walk around all day bloody and scabby, or else we close up like clams.

Anyhow, Jean lived in the old homestead by herself. I probably still had a house key somewhere in my possession, but I hadn't thought to look for it before I left the hotel. When Benny Safford, the old guy who lived next door, came outside in his undershirt, I was standing on the front porch still ringing the bell. "She won't answer, I've tried. It's like what I told you this morning when I called you, Donald."

"It's Alfred, Benny."

"Alfred! Did your brother tell you?"

"Yes, he did. What's this all about? I thought Jean was working a job at Standard Oil."

"She was, Alfie, and for a long time she was doing just great. Me and Peg even seen her at the pictures every once in awhile. Over at the Lyceum. She was doing good, Alf. I don't know what happened. Peggy thinks it's another bad romance. Jean and her romances, we all know about them, don't we? The poor kid. But if it was that again, Alfie, I didn't see her with any regular fella. You know what you might do? Seeing as how you're family, why don't you break in? Go through the coal bin, that's the smallest window. Cheapest to replace."

I said, "Geez, I don't know."

Then lo and behold! the porch light came on, and Jean opened the front door. But she didn't unlock the storm door right away.

"It's me, sweetheart. Alfred."

"Alfred?" she said, peering at me. "I can't believe it!"

Then she unlocked it. I guess Benny Safford went back into his house; I didn't see him again.

Standing in the long downstairs hallway was strange for me: it was so terribly familiar! The same wallpaper, the same mahogany half-moon table under the same convex American eagle mirror, the same threadbare carpet runner. The twenty-volume encyclopedia that Dad had bought—impulsively and to his sorrow—from a door-to-door salesman was still where it had always been, in the same cheap bookcase. Seeing those red-spined books certainly brought back some horrible memories. The quarrels they'd had, our mom and dad, over those goddamned encylopedias!

"It's good to see you, Jean."

"And you, too, Alfred! Goodness! I can't believe that you're here. Imagine that! My big brother Alfred actually came to visit me."

"All right," I said, "knock it off. Donald called me and said you'd gone crazy again."

"Again! I like that."

"So I thought I'd check up on you. Since you won't answer the telephone."

"Did you try calling?"

"Donald tried. So what's going on?"

"Nothing."

"What happened to your job?"

"Nothing. It's the same crappy job it always was."

"And since when did you start using language like that?"

She laughed, and there it was: the odor of Four Roses. Turning around, Jean walked down the hall and into the living room. She had on Mother's pajamas and a robe of Father's and thick woolen socks. I'm sure she'd knitted those herself. Jean was a grand knitter.

She flopped down on the sofa. There were dozens and dozens of our dad's old *National Geographic* magazines splashed open on the floor and on every chair and table, even on the mantel, on practically everything in the room except for the lampshades. It was smoky. Several ashtrays were filled. I looked around for bottles. Nope. She was a discreet drunk, Jean was; even alone. I wondered if she used Mother's old hiding places. I bet she did. Even living alone, she probably hid the booze.

Jean asked if I wanted some coffee.

"No." I parked myself in the big wing chair. "Are you eating? You don't leave the house at all? Not at all? What's going on, kiddo?"

She picked up a Chesterfield package, made a disgusted face when she discovered it was empty. Then she crumpled it up and shot it away from her with an index finger. "I got plenty to eat. I get it delivered." Her eyes looked bright in the pupils, and her skin was pale. Her bobbed hair didn't look especially clean.

She insisted that I go look in the icebox, see for myself that she had food. That done, she then insisted we both have cups of tea with cinnamon toast and apple sauce.

"So you're a hermit now?" I asked her. "You sleeping okay? You going to the bathroom regular?"

"*Al*-fred! Gee whiz. I'm *fine.*"

"How are you paying all your bills?"

"I'm not."

"Oh, great."

"Are you going to stay overnight, Alfred?"

"Would you mind?"

"No! That would be wonderful! Can I sleep in Donald's bed? We could talk like we used to! Stay up late? Could we?" She leaped from a kitchen chair, laughing, and pulled me to my

feet. "Why don't you get ready for bed, Alfred? Then we can have a long conversation in the dark, just like we used to."

Bed sounded good. It sounded terrific. But conversation? I didn't know about conversation. I suddenly wanted nothing more than to go to sleep. And sleep for three days.

I found a baggy pair of pajamas in my parents' bedroom, and used their bathroom to wash; I'd always loved the green tile in there. I looked in their hamper. It was empty, of course. On the way out, I glanced over at their dresser, to the dish where my father had always deposited loose change at night. Still there. And that was cold comfort. Even so, you take comfort wherever you find it, and of whatever degree.

When I came into the room that I'd shared with Donald, my sister was already in one of the twin beds, under the counterpane. It was actually my bed, but I didn't care. I climbed into Donald's. Two identical crucifixes, with secret compartments that held candles and crism for the Sacrament of Extreme Unction, still hung centered above each of the beds. Jean turned off the lamp.

We didn't say anything for a couple of minutes.

"It was nice of you to come."

"It's good seeing you. I mean it. I don't know why we don't see each other more."

"You don't?" she said. "I do."

"Does that old radio still work?"

"I don't know. But don't play it. How old are we now, Alfred?"

"I'm thirty-two, you're twenty-eight. And please tell me you already knew that."

"I did. Of course I did. I was just . . . I'm so unhappy, Alfred."

"I know, honey."

"And I can't kill myself because it's a mortal sin."

"Don't talk like that."

"Do you hate me?"

"No, of course I don't hate you."

"Donald hates me. He still thinks I told Mommy—"

"Donald. Forget Donald."

"How do you forget Donald? How can you forget anything?"

"I guess you can't."

"You don't think I told on Daddy, do you?"

"Jean, that's enough."

"You're right. I'm sorry. This isn't what we're supposed to be talking about! Do you remember when you got some tobacco from Huey Kerr and we all smoked it up here with the windows open? Alfred, do you?"

"I remember, yes. I taught you how to roll your own."

"You did. You were always the nice brother, Alfred. When I was in the hospital that time. And all."

We were silent again.

Then Jean asked, "Are you still doing that telephone work?"

"Oh sure."

"I bet you're very good. I bet you're very effective. I bet you sell a lot of ads. Do you?"

"Enough to get by."

"I bet you're much better than that." Then after the briefest pause, she said, "Alfred, do you remember how we used to make up stories, all three of us? How you'd start and I'd have to pick up the story and then Donald picked it up from me? And we kept trying to make it crazier, to make the story crazier so it was harder for the next person to think up something? Do you remember that?"

"Sure."

"Let's do it."

"What? Now?"

"Come on!"

"I'm pretty tired."

"Oh, come on, Alfred. If you play with me, I promise I'll get dressed tomorrow and go out. You start."

"Jean, no."

"Please?"

"All right."

"You go first."

I folded my hands in back of my head.

"Alfred? You go first. You start."

"All right."

"We had fun when we were all little. Didn't we?"

"I thought you wanted me to start."

"Sorry. Sorry. I'll shut up."

"All right. There's a boy in a rowboat. He's fishing. It's dark. He's night fishing. There's a dog with him."

"What kind of a dog?"

"A talking dog."

Jean laughed. "Already you're making it hard for me. No fair."

How come she didn't immediately think of Fuzzy when I mentioned a talking dog? Didn't she read "Derby Dugan"? It ran in the Bayonne *Times,* for crying out loud. Everybody in the *world* read "Derby Dugan." Everybody except Jean. I lay there fuming a little, wondering if I should tell her that I wrote the fucking thing.

"Alfred? Aren't you going to go on?"

"So they're drifting along, just the kid and his dog, it's night, when all of a sudden—"

"You're not going to say anything scary are you? Please don't."

"Then forget it. You can't have a story without something scary."

"All right. I'm sorry. Go on."

"Forget it."

"No, I don't want to."

"Jean."

"I don't want to forget it. This is good! So they're drifting along and all of a sudden . . . what?"

"A body floats by. It's a woman. Your turn."

"My turn?"

"Your turn."

"Not fair!"

"It's your turn, Jean, if you want to play."

"Okay," she said and laughed softly. "Okay. Um. The dog jumps into the water and, um, tries to catch the woman by the hair. Um. But she's too heavy. So then. Um. The dog starts to go down. So the little boy jumps in. He wants to save the dog, his beautiful talking dog, but he can't. And they both sink. Um. To the bottom. And they drown. And the woman's body just floats away. The end. Oops! I wasn't supposed to do that. *Not* the end. Your turn."

"No, that's all right, sweetheart. Let's just leave it right there. The end."

Then I must've fallen asleep. Because next thing it's morning, and Jean's shaking me, asking if I have to get back to New York and go to my job. Job? Then I remember, it's my sister, I'm in Bayonne, and I ask her what time is it.

"Little after six."

"Let me sleep till seven."

While I was dozing off again, I heard pipes thumping in the wall. Jean was taking a shower.

She'd put on makeup and brushed her hair, and dressed in a clean blouse and skirt, and she was fixing waffles for our breakfast—pouring gooey batter into the iron—when I came down-

stairs at seven-thirty. The coffee was ready. "I'll walk you to your bus, Alfred."

"Glad to have the company."

"Syrup or jam?"

"Syrup."

We ate quickly, then got on our hats and coats and started for the boulevard. It was a cold, pretty day. Big white clouds, a pale blue sky. But the petroleum stink was enough that I couldn't breathe through my nose. Jesus!

"Alfred? Do you think we should sell the house?"

"That's up to you and Donald. I gave you my share, remember?"

"I get scared being cooped up in there. But whenever that happens, that's when I just stay inside and never go out. It's crazy, I know. Donald's right. But if I *couldn't* live there, then maybe that would be better. I'd have to go someplace else. But I don't know where to go, Alfred. And I don't know what I'd do."

At Hudson County Boulevard, Jean stepped off the curb and peered south at the traffic moving in our direction. "I see your bus. Do you have your fare?"

"All set."

"Thanks for coming, Alfred. And I'll be fine. I'll be good. I promise. And tell Donald, if you talk to him."

"Answer your phone, Jean."

"I will."

"And pay your bills." I gave her fifty bucks.

The bus pulled over, the brakes wheezed, the accordion door buckled open. I kissed my little sister on the cheek, gave her a squeezing hug.

"We had fun, didn't we? When we were little?"

"For a long time, yeah. We did."

"And then it just stopped. Alfred, I didn't want our family to stop! It just stopped, that was so unfair!"

The bus driver was getting impatient. I had one foot through the open door, I finally let go of Jean.

"Find another," I said.

"Another what?"

I was inside the bus by then, dropping my nickel into the coin box. The door thumped shut, the bus started moving.

I knew that Jean couldn't hear me, and I didn't want the other riders to hear me, so I didn't answer.

Another what? Another family, of course.

Sadie Geebus seemed glad when I called at the house, and she talked a regular blue streak following me up the stairs. Was it as nice a day out as it looked from inside? Did I want a little lunch? Be careful of the carpet there, she'd have to snip off that loose thread before it tripped somebody. Was it as nice a day outside as it looked? On the landing I turned and smiled at her. "Not good, huh?"

"Today he just lies there, Al. He won't even *try* to talk."

"You seem all in."

"Well, I am! But it's not like he's demanding, he doesn't demand anything, it's just . . . he's not there. I could swear that he's not, but then I'm not sure. Yesterday he was so much better. But after you left . . . oh, don't listen to me, I'm sorry."

"Whyn't you take a nap? I'll sit with him for a while."

And I did. Sadie was right, though. Walter just lay there under the covers, eyes open but unblinking. Yesterday's *Mirror* was tucked under his pillow. I pulled it free and dropped it into the wastebasket. Even the slight clunk that it made didn't catch his attention.

I stayed close to two hours, and we never spoke a word. He didn't look at me once. Before I left to go home, I snooped around in one of the display cases, finally picked out a pair of Abe Ongo safety scissors. But I didn't have the heart, and I put them back.

Later that afternoon I called Pete Laudermilch and quit the Dugan strip.

Derby Dugan" was the first comic strip that I wrote, and I'd been doing it for only a short while, a few months, when I got a phone call late one Thursday morning from somebody telling me his name was Leonard Duveen. I didn't know him.

"I write 'Streaky and Son' for the Tribune Syndicate. It runs in the *News*."

"Yeah sure, I know it. Jack Crane's strip. What can I do for you, Leonard?"

He said he'd like to invite me to have lunch with him and some friends. I asked him, "What friends are these?" but Duveen said why don't I just meet him at noon in the lobby downstairs and he'd walk me over to Cavenaugh's. That was a workingman's speak a little south of the DeSoto in Chelsea.

"How about another day?" I said.

"Oh, come along, Bready, come along. I'll see you at noon."

Duveen was the most anonymous-looking man I'd ever seen—he could've been twenty-five, he could've been forty, a brown-haired blank, medium height, medium build, dressed in a cheap blue suit, a white shirt, and a necktie.

"Al? Lenny Duveen." He shook my hand. He had the same calluses that I did, from speed typing. "Should we head on over there?"

"Hold on a second, Lenny. How'd you get my name? What's this all about?"

"Ron Geary told me about you. You remember Ron."

"Yeah sure." Ron Geary was a pulp-fiction writer I knew from the guild; he did some radio work, too, and scripted "Blondie" and "Barney Google" from time to time. "How's Ron doing?"

"You can ask him yourself. He'll be at Cavenaugh's."

I guess I hadn't been paying much attention, because suddenly I discovered that we'd left the DeSoto together and were trotting down the front steps.

"Mr. Duveen? This is some kind of . . . what—a club?"

"You could call it that." He grinned widely, and for the first time I saw his teeth. They were yellow, and speckled with cheap fillings.

"You're being very mysterious."

"I'm taking you to a public place, Al! Relax."

The entrance to Cavenaugh's was below pavement level, and inside it was hot and stuffy, packed solid. As Duveen shouldered his way nimbly through the crowd, I followed him—past the table area, past the long bar, through a door marked PRIVATE, and into a back room with sawdust on the floor. I heard a loud snapping sound, then a bedsheet draped me from head to foot. There were eyeholes, and through them I saw fifteen or twenty men of various ages circle me like a wolf pack, then

douse me with schooners of gangland beer. Thus was I impressed into the New York chapter of the national fraternity of comic-strip ghost artists and writers—the Purgatory Club.

After I'd blotted myself dry, I shook hands with everybody, all the frat brothers. Then Leonard Duveen handed me a crude little sock doll, the label strung around its neck lettered "Walter Geebus." Once I'd driven the doll full of needles, as directed, and then been applauded, baloney sandwiches were served. I thought it was all a joke. It wasn't.

After lunch, the agenda turned to character assassination, one guy there talking about the Hearst cartoonist, kid strip in three hundred papers, who'd had his wife committed to a looney bin so he could shack up with an actress; another guy saying yeah, and did you know he couldn't manage a hard-on till he whipped her first with his belt? Bad enough about him—what about the asshole, said somebody else, who'd just got a plaque from Boys Town and he hadn't drawn a panel since 1928. Or the son of a bitch who didn't know that his hobo strip had been changed to an exotic adventure strip, and retitled, till it was time for him to put his John Hancock on a huge new contract. And not only that! Same son of a bitch spent half his dough publishing anti-Negro pamphlets and the rest of it on dope. Everybody seemed outraged. And exploited. These were the guys who worked for those bastards, who wrote the scripts, who drew the pictures.

With schooners thumping and spittle flying, they'd harangue and moan and freely gripe, saying why in hell should each and every one of them—at weekly salaries of ten, fifteen, twenty-five bucks—entertain the entire fucking American public every morning while the cartoonists of record, doing nothing, got filthy rich. Well, fuck those slavers! They're all Republicans anyway—so fuck 'em! Fuck every one! There

ought to be a law! Law, hell, there ought to be a revolution! That's right, a revolution. Expose all those lousy pricks, those bloodsucking phonies, those frauds, papering their penthouse apartments with goddamn stocks and bonds while the real strip workers sweated and bled India ink, and for what? For peanuts. And no credit. No byline. Jesus, they got fussed up!

Well, I could understand, and I could sympathize, but I couldn't pretend to feel what they did. I felt too lucky to complain. Scripting "Derby Dugan" was easy for me, there was nothing to it; it was fun. But seeing it every day in the newspaper, that was heroin. I can't explain it. It wasn't sex, but it was sex. I didn't care about Walter's money, it had nothing to do with his money. "Derby Dugan" may've been a cheap little comic strip, but I loved making it. Call me a class traitor and a fool, but I loved making it! And since I couldn't say things like that at the Purgatory Club, I never attended another luncheon.

HOWARD'S CHOICE

I was at The Kamen Studios.

"Al Bready! I see you're walking again without that crutch. And you hardly seem gimp at all!"

"Hiya Clarky. Is Howard around?"

"Someplace. Ike, where's Howie?"

Ike was a pipe-stem teenager with thick eyeglasses and a crisp part in his black hair. He was seated at a drafting table, one of fourteen that jammed the big room, two across and seven deep with an aisle down the middle. The place was set up like a galley ship. All of the tables except Howard Blum's were currently occupied. "I think he went to the gents'," said Ike.

One of the other boys confirmed that.

"I wasn't expecting you today, Al."

"I'm here to see Howard."

"Oh. That's right." He looked a little hurt, a little suspicious, but then he smiled. "Excuse me, will you?" Clarky

turned his attention back to young Ike, or rather to several of Ike's penciled boards.

Every page that left the shop had to have Clarky's initials on them, and he was a finick; to my surprise, I'd discovered that he was a goddamn finick. He'd never been nearly that scrupulous when he published the pulp magazines. I was struck by how serious he was about the crap that he published now—and crap it truly was; most of those kids couldn't draw their way out of a paper bag. But Clarky was always serious, every time I was up there, and I was impressed. Good for him. He'd brush away some erasure flecks, or pick at the glue still edging a pasteover, grunting as he did, and he examined faces and sabers and costumes and rocketships for consistency. He made certain that balloon tails pointed to the right speakers and checked all of the pagination bubbles. He sniffed and he hummed, and he took his sweet time—searching for tiny mistakes, and for glaring ones, plainly expecting to find both sorts.

"Ike," he was saying now. "Where's the earring?"

"What?"

"Where's the earring? Look." He pointed to a panel on one of the boards. "Pirate has an earring over here. But over here? It's gone. What'd he do, he lose it?"

"It's a different pirate."

"What?"

"It's a different pirate, Mr. Clark."

"Says you."

"It is!"

"What are they, twin brothers?" Clarky laughed, and so did the kid, who grabbed his pencil and scalloped in a teensy earring. "You have to keep an eye on these guys, Al. Some of the crazy stuff they'll pull! Just for instance. The other day? Hymie Sayer? Yes, you, Hymie, I'm talking about you! Are your ears

burning? Anyhow, he's doing a vampire story, Al. You remember this, fellas?" Clarky said, raising his voice. "Hymie's vampire?" Some of the boys smiled. "He brings me a page, Al, I look it over, I'm flabbergasted. I said, 'Hymie, it's stupid to show his fangs when his mouth is closed. What is he, a walrus? He's a vampire, Hymie.' Stuff like that, Al."

What do you say to a speech? I didn't say anything.

"Nice ship," Clarky said then, about a brigantine plowing through a splash panel. "Where'd you swipe it?"

"I forget," said Ike.

"Trace it?"

"No!"

With a quick wink at me, Clarky resumed his examination.

I looked around and noticed Floyd Olsen. I went over there, took a peek at his board. He was drawing page three of a Jack Slooth adventure—one of my scripts. Well, almost all of the scripts were mine.

"Very nice," I said. But it wasn't, it was ugly and all over the place. Olsen kept letting his characters violate panel borders, crashing through one and falling into another. I hated it. "Nice job," I said.

"Thanks."

"Were you ever in any of Mrs. Rodgers' classes?"

He looked confused for a moment, then refocused and nodded. "Yeah! Sure! You know her? She was real nice. When you see her, tell her Floyd Olsen said hi. Yeah, she was a real nice lady."

"She's leaving New York pretty soon, moving away."

"Is that right? Well, good for her. If you see her before she goes, tell her I said hi."

"Oh, I'll see her."

Then Howard Blum walked back in, spotted me, and looked surprised when I waved. He was dressing a lot better lately; had

bought a few Arrow shirts, even a couple of striped ones, and a pair of good woolen trousers. That day he wore a deep red tie over a white shirt. New shoes. Florsheims, if I wasn't mistaken.

"Howard, could you spare me ten minutes? I wanted to ask you something."

"What?"

"Could we use Clarky's office?"

He seemed interested then, as if some intrigue were involved. "Sure," he said. And he didn't ask permission, either. We just went in there. The kid had perks. Clark Kamen knew what he'd found in Howard Blum. He had quickly gotten over being so angry at me for insisting back in December that he pay Howard five dollars a finished page. In two months Howard had become Clarky's right-hand man and for all practical purposes the studio manager. He also gave on-the-job art lessons.

"What do you want, Al?"

"You want to do a strip together?"

He looked around, then sat down on the old sofa that Clarky had probably scavenged off the street and dragged up on the service elevator. "I thought about asking you that a couple times myself."

"So why didn't you?"

He shrugged. "I didn't like you. I thought you'd turn me down. I didn't like you." Howard grinned. "You don't have enough work already?"

"I'm off the Dugan strip."

"Get out."

"I quit. Yesterday."

"I don't believe it. I mean, I do, but—how come?"

"Have you seen it lately?"

"Sure. But what did anybody expect?"

"Exactly. You know it was deliberate, don't you? Dan Sharkey has it in for Walter, and he did this on purpose. I know he did."

"Let's kill him," said Howard.

"So I was thinking about a crime strip, but our guy is kind of a drifter. He's not official, he's not even a private op. Maybe he's looking for somebody, he's moving from town to town looking, and he keeps running into trouble."

"Derby with hair on his balls."

"All right," I said. "It could be."

"He could be looking for a girl. His girlfriend."

"He could. But why'd she run off on our guy?"

Howard Blum said, "Maybe she didn't. Maybe our guy ran off on *her*. But then he came back, see, but now she's gone."

"Maybe your Mr. Gast knew what he was doing."

"What?"

"You were a guy he could say 'Eskimo' to and 'plane crash' and know you'd take it from there. It's a thought."

"He was a prick."

"I'm sure that he was. Anyway, there's an editor at NEA's been calling me up ten times a year wanting me to do a new strip for them. I don't think we'd have any problem selling this one, Howard. You want to do your own strip, don't you?"

"Maybe."

I'd expected "sure."

"What do you mean, 'maybe'?"

"Yeah, what do you mean?" Clarky had opened the door and stepped in. "What's up, you two?"

"Al wants me to do a presentation strip with him."

"And you're 'maybe' what? Interested? You got to be kidding!" He closed the door finally, and firmly. Then he crossed to his desk, glaring at me. "Well, are you?" he asked Howard Blum.

"I'm considering it."

"Don't be stupid. Newspaper strips! I want to vomit on newspaper strips! Bunch of Protestants! All those strip guys come from Indiana! You didn't know that? Missouri!"

"Illinois," said Howard with a bitter smile.

"Exactly! Some damn place with farms. They're not people like you, Howard. Or me."

I said, "Oh cut it out, Clarky. What's Al Capp? Lutheran? I don't think so."

"The exception that proves the rule."

"Harry Hirshfield. Bud Fisher. Jesus Christ, Clark."

"Jesus Christ yourself," he said, then turned back to Howard. "I'm asking you to stay with me, Howie. I'm thinking in a couple of months' time to quit the middle-man stuff and start up my own line of books. Top-Drawer Comics Inc. I'll make you my partner. I swear. And till then I'll pay you seventy bucks a week above and beyond what you make drawing. To supervise the boys, improve their stuff, show 'em how it's done."

"I'm doing that already."

"So now I'm paying you for it. Do we have a deal?"

It hit me suddenly how desperate Clarky sounded, how pale he'd gotten. And I wished that I hadn't come, or said anything to Howard Blum. But like I'd told my sister . . .

"Please," said Clarky. "Don't. You'd be making a big mistake, Howard. This is the future right here. This is your fortune."

Howard smiled apologetically at Clark Kamen, then asked me, "How far have you got? You got any script?"

I hadn't really expected Sadie to give her permission, but she did. Of course, she said, of course Howard Blum could use the studio. On one condition. That he take care of Walter for a little while every day. Just a few hours, that's all. Keep an eye on him, see if he needed something, and come running whenever he knocked on the boy's room wall with an Official Great-uncle Wondrous Walking Stick. So that's what happened. Sadie got some relief, and Howard, after finishing up a few odds and ends at Clarky's shop, went back to his drawing table in the heated attic.

We all decided to keep the arrangement our little secret, though. Sadie was afraid that Walter would nix it, and I didn't want him to know that Blum and I were developing a strip together. I felt disloyal. I hadn't told him that I'd quit as the Dugan writer. What was the point? Besides, he never mentioned "Derby Dugan." He never mentioned anything. Except

to ask for help getting to the bathroom and to refuse most of his meals, he no longer spoke at all.

Sitting at Walter's bedside that early February, sometimes I had the weird feeling that I was back visiting my dad at Bayonne Hospital. Whenever that happened, I'd get up and leave. Walter's eyes would follow me to the door, just as my dad's had always done. And Walter's expressions—Christ, they were identical to my dad's. There were only two of them. One was terror, and the other was fury.

THE ADVENTURES OF BUTCH BURLAP

The morning Howard and I got started, I picked him up at his tenement and we rode to West Seventy-seventh Street together in a taxicab. I used my key to get in. We tiptoed up through the house.

While he fixed a pot of coffee, I raided the supply closet for Walter's best Strathmore paper.

First thing we did—while I sat at the picnic table and Howard used a straight-edge and a razor blade to cut the heavy paper into five-and-a-half-by-twenty-inch boards—was to wrangle over our strip's title, which would also be the name of our guy. The hero. Howard wanted to go with Butch again, but with a different last name. I said we didn't want to remind any features editor of the hapless "Butch Sanderson," and suggested we call our guy Billy something. Something rugged sounding. Something that suggested hard traveling.

"Drifter," said Howard Blum. "Billy Drifter. Bill on the Bum. Driftin' Billy. Come on, Al. Something rugged? Billy Stoner. Billy Boulder. Billy Backroads. Backroads Bailey."

"Backroads Bailey?"

"I'm just . . . come on, you're the writer. Billy. Joe. Bob. Jack. Jim."

"Jim?"

"Jim Boulder. Jim Bailey. Butch Bailey."

"No Butch."

"Burlap!"

"What?"

"It's rough. Jim Burlap. Bob Burlap. Joe Burlap."

"Butch Burlap?"

Howard looked at me. "I thought you said . . ."

"Like it?"

"Maybe. Let me drive it around the block."

"Go ahead." I went and poured our coffee. "There's no milk. If you need it, you'll have to go downstairs."

"I drink it brunette," said Howard. Then he said, "Butch Burlap. Yeah. Okay. It's Butch Burlap. Now what?"

I sat back down on the bench at the picnic table, crossed one leg over the other, and said, "We start with a bus. It's coming down a road, there's a marker. A sign. Midvale. Or Midville. Someplace fairly small town, even cozy—it's coming up in five miles. Now our guy. Second panel. He's sitting inside the bus, he's talking to a lady wearing a hat. Church-lady type. She's asking him if he's getting off in Midville."

"Or Midvale," said Howard. "You making all this up off the top of your head?"

"Maybe you should get a pad, write it down."

"You always gave Walter full scripts."

"And I'll give you the same. Later. All right? All right," I said. "Our guy Butch is saying yeah, he's headed home, he's going back to see his girlfriend, to ask her to get married. He mentions the girl's name. It's third panel now. He mentions her name, and the hat lady reacts, very surprised. She repeats the girl's name. Exclamation point with a couple of question marks."

"What is it? The girlfriend's name?"

"We'll think about that," I said. "Last panel. We're up ahead, we've jumped up the road, to a bunch of land pirates set to waylay the bus. Which we can see in the distance, coming at us."

"Land pirates?"

"Highwaymen."

"In 1937?"

"Howard. You worry about the pictures. So. You want to get started?"

"But what happens next? That's all you're going to tell me?"

"You interested?"

"Yeah . . ."

"Then that's all I'm going to tell you."

I left him and went down to the second floor, knocked at Walter's bedroom door, waited, then slowly opened it and stuck my head in. He was on his side, hugging a pillow. I stood there till I was certain he was still breathing. When I stepped back into the hallway, Sadie hollered to me in a whisper from Walter's office. I walked down and met her coming out, then I walked her back in. The top of the desk was covered with legal documents, insurance policies, savings books, a pile of bills.

"I heard you boys up there," she said, taking her seat in the big recliner. "But I figured I wouldn't bother you." She had on

a white satin dressing gown, like the glamour girls all wore in MGM pictures, but her hair wasn't brushed and her eyes looked bald without cosmetics. Her full bosom sagged. She laughed when she caught me giving her the once over. "It's amazing to me, too, Al. I'll be fifty-two in a little over three weeks. The number seems impossible."

"You still look great. He's sleeping, by the way."

"Well, good. He was up most of the night."

"You too?"

"Yeah, me too."

"Been to bed at all yourself?"

"I caught a few hours, but then I was just, I was wide awake and scared I'd go back in there and find him . . . well, you know."

"Sadie, you could still hire some help. If it's wearing you thin."

"Thin I'll never be. But I could. I still might." She pointed to a chair, though I wasn't sure that I wanted to sit and chat with her. "If you hadn't asked me for the studio, I might've broken down and called the visiting nurses. I might've cleared out and gone home entirely. So thanks, Al. I think this ought to work out fine. With Howard here to help a little bit."

I took a seat.

"And thanks for asking *me* if you could use the studio. And not Walter. That was good of you."

I said, "Well, here we are, spending time together, just you and me."

Sadie laughed. "I'm sorry I made that crack the other day."

"I was wondering if we'd ever talk about it again."

"It was low and stupid. I didn't mean it."

"I don't even much like him. I don't consider Walter a good friend. But even if I did, I'm still no pansy."

"Of course you're his friend. What a thing to say."

"How? I never liked him."

"I did."

"Well, I should hope so. You were married to him."

"But I didn't like him all the time. How could I? He was always upstairs working, and when he wasn't, he was out screwing around. But he had his qualities."

"Name one."

Her eyebrows arched. She grinned. "He was hell at canasta."

"And still you divorced him? You must've been crazy."

"I know, I know. I guess I forgot I wasn't still twenty-five."

She got up, walked around the room, found a full package of Camels on a bookcase shelf. Breaking it open, she went and stood behind Walter's desk. She lighted a smoke and put it in the tray, then never picked it up again. She was antsy, exhausted. Pretty soon she'd collapse. I watched her scoop all the papers up from the desk and stuff them into a big string envelope. She opened a drawer, took out Walter's checkbook, and threw that into the envelope, too. "Phil Aron called last night. He was very sweet, but he wanted to make sure that I knew my place."

Phil Aron was Walter's lawyer.

"I told him I wasn't planning on cleaning out the bank accounts, I'd be only too happy to let him do that."

"Did he laugh?"

"Oh sure. But I could tell he doesn't know what to make of me. He must've asked me six times if I was really living here again. Finally I said, 'Phil, do you want me to pay some rent, is that it?' "

"And did he laugh?"

"Not that time. Al. What do you think? You think I'm wrong to move back in, to make believe that we're still married? Remarried? Whatever. You think it's stupid, right?"

"Why stupid? No. If you think you can put something back together and make it work, go ahead and try."

Sadie nodded, but her expression was uncertain, a little wary. Then she cocked her head, looked to the doorway. "Is that him knocking?"

"I don't hear anything, but I'll go check." I stood to leave.

"I'm feeling too old to start over. The last couple of years? I'm telling you. I've never felt so lonesome. I don't think I've ever *been* lonesome before, not really."

"I should get back upstairs."

"Walter," she said, winding the red string around and around the envelope's button, "really *was* hell at canasta."

When I came back into the studio, Howard Blum showed me several sketches that he'd made of Butch Burlap. I said I liked the blond version best; he liked the black-haired one. So we compromised: made him blond with a zigzag black streak on the side. We both agreed that he looked good with a busted nose.

Then Howard said, "Cathy. Susan. Mary. Helen."

"The girlfriend?"

Howard nodded. "Jenny. Sara. Myra. Nancy."

"Running through all your memories, kid?"

He grinned. "I wish."

"Know what you mean. Let's make it . . . Myrna."

"Myrna? Myrna Powers? Myrna Johnson? Myrna Jones? Myrna Smith? Myrna . . . should I get out the telephone directory? Myrna? You like that name?"

"Myrna Powers sounds good."

"Myrna Powers. Myrna Powers. Myrna Powers. Okay."

I stayed past noon, and by the time I left Walter's house, Howard Blum was busy penciling the first daily, and I'd left him a handwritten script for eleven more and one twelve-panel Sunday.

It went as smoothly as that. Even so, I went home with a splitting headache.

The first symptoms of arsenic poisoning that Walter exhibited were migraines. He'd get violently ill and have to go to bed, and if you went by his bedroom door you'd hear him groaning and thrashing around. One week he was in torment from Tuesday afternoon on. Thursday morning I got a call from Frank Sweeney, asking my advice. "We're way behind schedule, but he won't let me ghost him. What should I do?"

"If there's no work, go home."

"We can't just let everything fall behind. You want to talk to him?"

I didn't promise that I would, but later that same day I dropped uptown, bringing Walter a cardboard twist filled with a druggist's headache medicine. I found him in the studio looking bleary and wearing his bathrobe. There was a blank daily tacked to his board.

"I haven't heard of headache powders in twenty years!" he said. "They got Bayer now, Bready, in case you don't know." He reached over and plucked a bottle of five hundred from the picnic table.

"This stuff always worked for me," I said. "That's all. If you don't want it, don't take it."

"I'll take it," he said. "I'll try anything!" He filled a glass with water, poured in the powder, stirred it with his finger. He swallowed it all. While his head was thrown back, I glanced at Frank. He gave a hopeless shrug.

I said, "Walter, have you been able to do any work? Maybe you should—"

"I'll get caught up," he said. "Don't worry about it!" He sat down and put his head between his knees.

Frank never ghosted even one day of the Dugan strip. Somehow Walter Geebus always managed to cram in a heroic amount of catch-up work during his occasional well hours.

I remember Frank telling me how much he admired Walter for that, for showing guts and self-discipline in the face of adversity, talking about Walter like the man could walk on water.

I've always wondered what Frank was thinking about when he was saying all that crap.

EPISODE TWENTY-FOUR

THE PRESENTATION STRIP

Two mornings later, when I saw Walter Geebus again, he said, "More, Al, more! This kid is gonna *suffer*"—but in that garbled, growling way that he had now. I'd got into the habit of not looking directly at him anymore, I'd shift my gaze a tad to the left or to the right. That day, though, I couldn't help but look at him. Stare at him. He was sitting up straight in bed with a serving tray straddling his lap and angled to be a drawing surface. And he was talking! "More, Al," he said, "more!"

He seemed chipper, but there was a funny light in his eyes. It was like a bouncing ball in a sing-along cartoon, but tiny; a tiny bouncing light. It made Walter seem antic, feverish. I guess I should've felt heartened that he was talking and thinking about work again, but I didn't. I felt anything but heartened.

Howard Blum was there—he'd been sitting at Walter's bedside when I came in.

"Mr. Geebus," he told me, "feels like drawing today."

"Yeah? Great."

"He wants some paper and things." Howard looked at me with deep significance. "Should I get it?"

"Why not?"

Walter said, "This kid is gonna suffer, Al!"

I followed Howard out into the hallway. "Did you prop him up?"

"No, when I went in to check on him, he was already sitting like that. What do you think? He's talking funny, but he looks a little better."

"You sound worried."

"Don't start with me, Al. I've been awake for three days. You got to come see, though. It's all ready."

"What? Everything?"

"I'm fast. I told you that."

"Yeah, but is it any good?"

Blum's nostrils quivered; they always did when he took umbrage at something. I'd been noticing that since the beginning. "I think it's good, yeah. You want to come take a look?"

"No, you go on and get Walter what he wants. Let me sit with his nibs for a couple of minutes. Make it five."

"But what should I do about the ink? He wants a bottle of ink. And pens and brushes. He can't handle all that stuff."

"Get him what he wants."

"Yeah sure, and if he spills a whole bottle?"

"Just do it, please."

Walter's head turned when I walked back in. He was definitely alert, but his bottom lip hung down like a flap and his eyes had those glints.

I took a seat. Then I bent toward him, asking, "What?"

But he just said that same damn thing again.

"Lord, you're a pain in the ass! Shut up about the kid. He'll suffer, don't worry. Soon as you get better and we're back in business. So. Is there anything I can—*what?*"

That time when I bent close to understand him better, he tugged at my sleeve. "Yeah, all right," I said. *"What?"*

"I'm just vaudeville," he said with a good deal of saliva in his mouth. "I need a good story man." When he tried to wink, his eyelid drooped and stayed down.

"Walter."

"My two little orphan boys," he said.

"Walter. Don't do this, you're scaring me."

He kept talking, but I understood less and less, fewer words, and finally it wasn't any sounds that I recognized.

By the time Howard returned—it was more like ten minutes than five, and it felt like sixty—I was well past eager to get out of there. Howard looked chagrined, embarrassed—flush in the face—as he taped a sheet of paper to the breakfast tray, and helped Walter, like you would a year-old baby, to close his fingers around a pencil. The pencil kept falling, clicking as it rolled down the board. I had to get out of there. I told Walter I needed to make a phone call.

I know that we're supposed to visit the sick—they taught us that in Catholic school. It's one of the corporal works of mercy. Feed the hungry. Give drink to the thirsty. Clothe the naked. Visit the imprisoned. Shelter the homeless. Visit the sick. Bury the dead.

Well, anyhow, I'd always done my share of visiting the sick. More than my fair share. But I didn't know how much longer I could keep on visiting Walter Geebus. It was driving me nuts. I was back on a regular diet of aspirin, and my dreams had turned bad. In them I became Walter, or he was still Walter but I was the one sick in bed. Or I was going from Walter's

room to my dad's, my dad's back to Walter's. It was all driving me crazy.

But I was saying about slipping out of the boy's room. I didn't have to make any telephone call, that was just my lame excuse. I went straight up to the studio. The place was fumy as a railroad smoking car. I was on my way to open a window to let in some fresh air when I noticed the person working at Walter's table. A blond boy, in shirtsleeves.

"Floyd. What're you doing here?"

"Oh, hello, Mr. Bready. Howard needed somebody to spot for him."

"Is he paying you?"

"No, it's more like a swap. I do this, maybe later on he can help me out. I hope it's okay for me to be here."

"Oh jeez, I don't care. I just didn't expect to find anybody." I pushed up the window, but it wouldn't stay; it slipped all the way back down, except for two or three inches.

"What do you think?" said Floyd. He'd got off his stool and was pointing to the wall, where the first twelve "Butch Burlap" dailies were tacked in three descending rows of four. "I think you guys got yourself a real good strip, Mr. Bready."

From across the room the samples looked strong. But on closer inspection, they bothered me. It was good work, but troubling. The balloons, for starters. Howard had copied Walter's lettering style exactly. And the panel compositions. There was a lot of "Derby Dugan" in the figure work, too, in how the characters were placed, their proportions and their postures, and the backgrounds had all been rendered in broken horizontal lines: pure Geebus. But it wasn't a total swipe—Walter never drew faces in close-up; Howard did, quite often, then filled in the surrounding air with ink. No, the presentation strip wasn't a cold swipe, it just looked enough like the Dugan

strip to give me the blues. I felt another headache start behind my left eyeball.

"You know what I like about it best?"

"What? I'm sorry, Floyd, what?"

"What I like best about your strip? How your guy Butch? After two weeks, you still don't know anything about him. Is he a good guy or a bad guy?"

"He's the hero, Floyd. Of course he's a good guy."

"Yeah, but." He jabbed the fourth daily, where the modern-day highwaymen board the bus with tommy guns and start looting passengers. "The leader of the gang? How come he looks so happy to see Butch? It's like they're old pals. And this Myrna dame." He pointed to the seventh daily. "She's packing up a suitcase and slipping out the back door, and we already know that she got a letter from Butch saying he's coming." Floyd glanced up to the fifth daily, tapped the second panel. "She's reading his letter. And she don't look too pleased. And next time we see her, there, she's packing, she's leaving. She's *gone*. What's with this guy Butch anyhow? You see? Bad guys know him, his girlfriend takes off. You got to wonder."

"That's the idea."

"What's the idea?"

"Keep it a mystery as long as you can."

"Yeah? But you know, right? *You* know what's going on."

"Floyd, I don't have the faintest idea. But then I always think of something."

He looked at me. "Is that how you do it?"

"That's how it's done."

"I couldn't work like that."

"Work? Are we talking about work?" When he frowned, I smiled and clipped him on the shoulder. "Forget it, I'm just be-

ing a wiseguy. Butch is definitely a hero. Don't worry about it. You bet he is, Floyd. But he's coming home from prison."

"Really?"

"Sound good to you?"

"Yeah!"

"Then he's coming home from prison. But it was a bum rap."

"Only his girlfriend thinks . . . yeah! I get it! And those bad guys, I bet they met him in jail. Pretty good there, Mr. Bready. You know your stuff."

"Floyd, I didn't get to the pinnacle of my profession without knowing my stuff."

"I'll bet."

"I was only kidding again. Pinnacle. What pinnacle?"

Floyd looked at me like I was nuts—of *course* I'd reached the pinnacle; I was getting *paid* for turning out this junk, wasn't I?—then he shrugged and climbed back on his stool. He picked up his brush, dipped it in a jar of Chinese white, whittled it to a point, and resumed correcting the sample Sunday page. I watched him cover several bleed areas, then had a peek at Howard's title-logo.

The stark, flat letters were textured like clothespin sacks. Burlap. I gave the kid points for that. It looked good, what he'd done, and best of all it didn't at all resemble the logo—the trademark logo—that Walter Geebus had designed when I came along in '31 and "Derby Dugan" changed format.

Howard had boxed the credits below the title.

By Bready and Blum.

But wait a second.

It didn't read "By Bready and Blum." It read "By Bready and *Blaine.*" I said "Blaine" out loud, with a question mark.

"That's Howard's professional name," said Floyd.

"Since when?"

"Since about four this morning. Mr. Clark is always saying they hold it against you when you have a Jewish name."

"But Blaine is Irish. Catholic. That's almost as bad."

"You won't get any argument from me."

I said, "Blaine. Is there any first name? Mike Blaine? Joe Blaine? *Huck* Blaine?"

"I think it's still Howard." Floyd picked up an art-gum eraser and obliterated a pencil line. With his lips puckered, he carefully blew away the erasure. "Where are you guys taking the strip, if I can ask?"

"NEA."

"Yeah? They were interested in my strip, but they turned it down anyway. Same as everybody else."

"You worked up a strip?"

"Oh yeah. Sure. 'Mr. Z.' I could show it to you sometime."

"No, that's all right."

"It wouldn't be any trouble. 'Mr. Z,' you're prolly saying, 'what's that about?' It's Zorro, you know Zorro? Douglas Fairbanks? Only it's today, it's Zorro in today's New York. Only I don't call it New York, I call it Bigburg."

"Bigburg?"

"You like that? Bigburg. But it's really New York. And it's Zorro in New York, only I call him Mr. Z. I did a whole month of strips."

"He walk around with a sword?"

"No. How could you? I got rid of the hat, too. And the horse. No, he's got a couple of forty-fives that he's packing, and he's dressed all in black, he's got a black mask."

"Nobody nibbled?"

"NEA, I already told you. But nobody else. I could show it to you, next time you're up at the shop. Howard thinks I should do it as a comic book instead."

"Just watch out what you give to Clarky."

"So you think I should bring it to somebody else?"

"I'm not saying anything. Except watch out what you give to Clarky. He'll own it."

Then Floyd Olsen said, "Excuse me," and I leaned away from the Sunday page so that he could untape it from the board. He pinned it on the wall beside the daily strips.

We both were still standing there looking everything over when Howard came in. He was very pale and went directly to the picnic table, sat down hard.

"You know what just happened?" He swung around, straddling the bench, and looked at us. "Mr. Geebus had me rough out twelve panels. I said, 'Let me go get a straight-edge,' but he wouldn't let me leave. I thought he was going to hit me with that stupid walking stick that he keeps on the bed. So he makes me sketch out four tiers, and he acts like he's going to start drawing, and I swear to God, he's been sitting like that for the past ten minutes. He's got the pencil in his hand and he's got the point on the paper, and he hasn't moved, I swear, in ten minutes. I thought he'd died, but when I got up from the chair, he yelled at me. I think I'm clearing out of here today. I'm sorry, Al. If you want, I'll tell Sadie myself."

"Is she back?"

"Yeah, she's back."

"Let me tell her," I said, then I told Howard I thought he'd done a great job on the samples.

"You can take them with you, if you want," he said. He seemed ready to collapse with fatigue; his eyeballs looked raw,

bloodshot, and his hair was disarranged. He touched his shirt pocket for his cigarettes; they weren't there. "Floyd? You got any smokes left?"

I told him, here, take one of mine.

But Howard ignored my offer and accepted a Camel from the Olsen boy. After he'd lighted up, he rolled his head, stretching his neck, as he approached the wall of strips. "Don't you think it's a little talky, though? Al?"

"Talky?"

"Too many words." He flicked his fingertip from balloon to balloon to balloon. "Maybe if you cut down some on the talk, I could make the pictures say a little more."

"Nobody ever complained about the talk in 'Derby Dugan.' "

"Yeah," said Howard Blum, "but we're not doing that. We're doing this. Anyhow, I'm not complaining. Don't get so defensive, Al." He picked up the electric percolator—it was un-plugged—and shook it, then poured a trickle of cold, bitter-looking coffee into a used cup. "So. Are you going to take them with you?"

"Sure. And I'll mail them tomorrow."

"You couldn't do that today?"

"First I have to write a letter. Then I have to look up the ad-dress. Then I have to get a map and find out where there's a post office. This could all take hours."

He smiled at the crack about looking for a map, but I could see that he didn't feel I was doing my fifty percent. Well, he could just go straight to hell. Too much talk in the strips! What a prick! I'll give him too much talk. I'll give him a shot in the head! Too much talk! I could've pointed out that there was too much Geebus in the strips, as well. And that when he lettered, he bounced every verb that Walter would've. But I didn't say any of that. And I even gave in, I even told Howard

that I'd see what I could do. Maybe I really would be able to get the package into the mail today.

"Yeah, well, don't break your back or anything."

From there, from that remark, it probably would've escalated; I don't think I would've taken that sort of lip from Howard Blum, no matter how little sleep the brat had had—I'm sure I would've said something needling after his last remark, except that Floyd Olsen called, "Hey fellas? Hey you—fellas?"

We looked, and he pointed.

In pajamas, bathrobe, and slippers, Walter Geebus had just come in, braced against Sadie. "Here's the boss," she said, "everybody look busy!" I wanted to throttle her. Not just because she'd brought Walter up there—we'd had an agreement!—but also because, especially because, of her chirpy, kindergarten-teacher inflection. "He just *insisted* on making a little visit. Just a short one today, though—all right, Walter?" All right, children?

She tried directing him to a chair, but he'd noticed the presentation strips and now insisted on continuing across the floor, shuffling toward them.

I glared at Sadie and she crossly shook her head, denying responsibility.

Walter stood two or three feet back from the wall display and just stared, like he was at a museum. He didn't say anything, didn't croak a single word. Then he must've given Sadie a nudge, because she turned him around gently and he let himself be turned. Walter moved his head till he spotted me. After he'd made a brief sound in my direction, Sadie walked him out.

"What'd he say to you, Al?"

"Was that him? Was that Walter Geebus?"

"Shut up, Floyd." Howard looked at me again. "What'd he say?"

"I didn't catch it."

"I can't believe she brought him up here!" Howard slapped the wall with his open hand. "For Christ's sake!"

"What's the matter with him, anyhow?" said Floyd Olsen.

I told Howard, "Stick all the samples in a big envelope," then I went out and started down the attic stairs. Walter and Sadie hadn't reached the bottom yet. I couldn't think of what to say, if there was anything that I *could* say, so I kept my big mouth shut. I thought of Jean.

And then it just stopped, she'd said.

That was so unfair.

At the boy's room, Walter refused to go in. With his chin, he pointed toward the far end of the hall, down to the master bedroom.

Sadie took him there.

I waited till they'd gone in and closed the door, then I sat on a stair and crossed my arms on my knees and put my head down. Sitting perfectly still, I felt like I was swooping.

"Al?" It was Howard Blum, behind me. "You okay?"

"I'm fine."

"You sure?"

"I'm sure."

"Forget what I told you about leaving. Don't say anything to Sadie. I just got spooked for a second, I guess. Okay? But I'm not going to run."

"Just go make that parcel, all right? So I can take the strips and get out of here. Would you please just do that for me, Mr. Blaine?"

Howard went away. I stayed where I was. About a minute later, Sadie came out of Walter's bedroom. She sat on a lower stair, with her back to a railing spindle.

"I wouldn't worry about it," she said.

"Worry about what?"

"Him suing you."

"Suing me?"

"Isn't that what he said, up in the studio? 'I'll be suing you'?"

"No." I laughed. "But he probably should've."

"So what did he say?"

" 'I'll be seeing you.' That's what he said. 'I'll be seeing you.' "

By early spring of 1934, Walter's doctors had been telling him for months that his chronic fatigue and growing mental confusion were strictly the result of overwork. But what about the blisters on his tongue, he kept saying, what about those? And they'd tell him that it was psychosomatic, or possibly a yeast infection. Had he performed oral love recently on a prostitute? We'd both had a good laugh about that one. It was one of the few laughs we'd had together lately. He almost always felt nauseous that spring, and a lot of the time he felt woozy. He'd lost weight, he'd stopped going out, his temper had grown ever shorter, and he and Sadie could often be heard arguing somewhere in the house. Frank and I would exchange glances and raised eyebrows. I finally told Walter that perhaps he really ought to consider taking a vacation. Go up to Maine. Do some oil painting. Frank could handle the strip for a couple of weeks.

Walter said, "I don't do oil painting and I don't need a vacation." I think he was scared that he had a cancer.

Two things caused me to get suspicious of Frank. The first was something that Walter said. He was feeling so depressed and generally unwell that he blurted to me one morning, "I should just swallow some poison and get it over with." And then I read that Shadow novel I've already mentioned, the one with arsenic murders in the story. I remembered Frank telling me that his brother-in-law was a pharmacist. So, I said to myself, he'd have access to arsenic. I felt like Sherlock Holmes, I felt like my own creation, the Broadway Prowler, but it wasn't any fun.

I had my suspicions, but to get proof I'd have to catch Frank Sweeney actually poisoning Walter. Surely it was too much to expect that I'd just look inside Frank's portfolio and find the evidence. Not at all! Sometimes—very rarely, I think, but sometimes—the world actually works the way it should. I untied the strings, opened the side boards, felt around in a pencil pocket, and came out with a tiny brown unlabeled bottle. There were a lot of small gray crystals inside.

I took it to a drugstore in Chelsea, and they confirmed what it was, so then I went down to police headquarters on Centre Street and had a chat there with a homicide cop named Gus Pearle. He had a brother in the American Fiction Guild, and most of the pulp guys I knew who wrote crime novels used Gus to get background information. I'd used him a few times myself, mostly for my series of Prowler novels in *Dime Detective.*

After I'd told him about discovering the arsenic and what I figured was going on, Gus said that I had a couple of options. I could have Frank arrested, and Gus offered to do it himself, or I could have the little shit killed. He could steer me to some-

body, he said, and it would cost thirty-five dollars. I was star-tled—even a tough-guy writer like me. "Gus," I said, "why the hell would I want to have him killed?"

"Then your friend wouldn't have the embarrassment and trouble of a noisy trial."

"He's not a friend, he's just a guy that I work for."

"It was merely a suggestion."

The next day, it was a Friday, Walter called Frank down from the studio. When he came into the office, he was surprised to find me there, and looked terrified when I introduced him to Lieutenant Pearle of the New York City Police Department. When Gus produced the tiny bottle, Frank dropped into a chair. He seemed dazed. His breathing got labored.

Walter sat behind his desk and calmly said, "You tried to poison me, you little bastard!"

"I didn't!"

That's when Gus placed Frank Sweeney under arrest.

Frank began to whimper, he didn't want to be arrested—no! He couldn't be under arrest. No, that was impossible! He pleaded with Gus to let him go, he begged Walter to say that it was all a big mistake. He wouldn't look at me; by then he knew this was all happening because I'd gone snooping in his portfolio.

"Walter, please. I'm your friend! I wouldn't do this!"

Walter Geebus just looked at him blankly. "I'll be seeing you," he said.

Clearly it wasn't a promise. It was a dismissal.

MY "SISTER" VISITS

"I hope I did the right thing, Mr. Bready, but I let your sister wait in your room for you. I checked a couple of times, and she's sitting right there, so I didn't let in a thief or anything. Is it okay, sir?" Dick Barthorne, on the lobby desk, had hailed me the moment I came back to the DeSoto after taking my supper alone at a paprika joint on Fourth Avenue. It was around seven o'clock. You could tell that Dick had had second thoughts and was afraid that I'd chew his head off or report him.

"No, that's all right. When did she come?"

"Almost right after you left. About an hour."

"How'd she seem?"

"Seem? Fine. We had a nice chat before I took her up."

"You had a chat—with Jean?"

"Is that her name? She didn't say. But she has a wonderful smile."

My sister had the saddest, dreariest smile I'd ever seen; nobody would ever call it wonderful. So it couldn't be her that Dick Barthorne had let in, it had to be Jewel, and so it was.

She'd cleared off my bridge table and replaced the big Underwood with a bottle of Pinch, two striped glasses, and a green ceramic ashtray in the shape of a cabbage leaf. I didn't own such a thing. She'd brought her own ashtray? She had. There was still a Kresge's price sticker on it.

"I learned that sister trick from a detective novel," said Jewel. "You probably wrote it."

"I probably did."

She was wearing lip rouge, which ordinarily she did not. A heavy dusting of face powder made her dark eyes look shadowy and matte. A bit too mysterious for my liking. I wanted her to smile. But so far she hadn't. Smile, Jewel. Please? She had on a dark blue dress pinned with a glittery clustered-glass brooch. It was a dress that I'd told her once I thought was pretty.

"Shut the door, Al."

I hadn't realized I'd left it open. "I don't think they allow this at the Martha Washington," I said.

"We're not there."

I shut the door.

"Who's Blaine?" Jewel said then, glancing toward the "Butch Burlap" strips that I'd pinned to my wall; gone were Sacco and Vanzetti and the *Dinner at Eight* gang.

"That's Howard Blum's new name."

"He changed it?"

"Apparently. What do you think?"

"Why Blaine?"

"I didn't mean that. I mean, what do you think of the strip?"

"It's fine."

"You didn't read it."

"No." She broke the seal on the scotch and poured us both a couple of fingers. "We're leaving next Tuesday. On Monday Jimmie signs everything at our lawyer's, and we leave Tuesday morning." Jewel unzipped the red cellophane strip from a package of Herbert Tareytons. She'd brought along my brand, not hers. That did not escape my notice. "Sit down, Al, we're going to get drunk together. I hear that you don't get very drunk very often. A little birdy told me. Tonight, though." She gripped her glass by the rim and swung the bottom to gently clink mine, still on the table. "Tonight, though. It's a farewell party. Let's make believe this is the *Normandie.* Bon voyage!"

"You look so unhappy."

"You want me to smile?" Then she did. " 'Lady's got some great smile, don't she?' You know what I think? You're a coward, Al Bready."

I sat down across the table. "The other night when I wasn't, you rang off."

"Same as you rang off on me, last month." She took a swallow of her drink.

"All right."

"All right?" She lifted her penciled eyebrows. "What's that supposed to mean?"

"It means I got feelings for you, Jewel."

" 'But so what'—is that what that shrug just meant? 'I got feelings for you, but so what?' "

I'd shrugged?

"No, that's not what it meant. 'But what can I do about them? I got feelings, but what can I do about them?' I guess *that's* what it meant."

She put her hand on the package of cigarettes, then turned it slightly like it was an oven dial. "I'd stay if you asked me to."

"What?"

"What do you mean, 'what'?" She finally looked at me again; till then she'd been talking at the Herbert Tareytons. "I'd stay. If you asked me to."

"Tonight?"

She mugged a face. "What the hell is it with us? We start talking, and it's like we're on the radio. Burns and Allen. Bready and Rodgers. Yeah, tonight. Sure, tonight. If you want. But that's not what I meant. And you know it."

"We'd be crazy."

"Yeah? So why can't we be crazy? Everybody else is."

"You really . . . would?"

"If you asked me."

"And Jimmie? What about Jimmie?"

She poured more scotch for herself. "Aren't you drinking?"

"I asked you about Jimmie."

"And I didn't answer you. What *about* Jimmie? We'll break his heart. He'll haunt us like a ghost, he'll never leave us alone. He'll take poison. He'll shoot the pair of us. Al, I don't want to talk about Jimmie right now."

"Jewel, do you ever . . . ?" I pushed my hand across the top of my head. "What would you call it exactly, what we are to each other?"

"I don't have a word for it." She laughed.

"Neither do I. But if. Say you didn't go back to Midvale—"

"Megville."

"—and say that you and me. Just suppose. We got together. Then it wouldn't be the same. It would be something different."

"You're not going to ask me, are you?" Jewel put a cigarette between her teeth and reached for the paper of matches. She tore one out and snapped it across the strike board. It didn't flame. She tried again, brusquely. "You're not, are you?"

Then her match flared, and a moment later the whole paper of them went up in a yellow flash.

The day Frank Sweeney was arrested, Walter stayed in a clenched rage. He'd told Sadie to go take a room at the Plaza, which she did, but I kept him company at the house. After the first three or four calls from newspapermen, he left the receiver off the hook. Wouldn't answer the door. And I wasn't allowed to, either. I watched through a studio window as a couple of photographers took flash pictures of Walter's brownstone. It got dark outside.

He'd been drawing, and I'd been reading magazines, and we probably hadn't exchanged more than a hundred words since Frank was bundled into a prowl car. But finally Walter capped the ink bottle and threw away his crow quill—plucked it from the holder and dropped it in the wastebasket. Then he turned to me and said, "This is the worst day of my life."

"Yeah, I'd have to say it's one of my worst."

"But not *the* worst?"

"No, I don't think so. No."

Twenty minutes later we were drinking coffee at the picnic table, and he said, "Well? Are you going to tell me?"

"Tell you what?"

"The absolute worst day of your life."

"No."

"We're colleagues," he said, "practically family. So spill it. The evening is young. And Frank Sweeney is crying in the Tombs. You were saying?"

"But I wasn't."

"About your worst day ever."

"All right. Why not? That would have to be the day my old man and his lady friend got shot. I was fifteen."

"This is true?"

"True story. My dad was seeing this lady in the neighborhood, couple times a week, and one day somebody shot them both in her bedroom. She was dead right there, the old man lived for another month. I found them."

"Jesus Christ, Al. I don't know what to say. Did they know who did it?

"The husband. Of course. Johnny Meatro."

"Burn for it?"

"He wasn't convicted."

"Tried?"

"He had some kind of phony alibi. No, he was never even arrested."

"Yeah, I can see how that might've been your worst day. How'd you happen to find them?"

"When he didn't come home for supper, I knew where to look."

"And this all really happened?"

"It really happened."

"What about your mother? I mean, what happened to her?"

"She had a cancer, but nobody knew. She died two weeks after the old man," I said.

"You and Derby Dugan."

"What about me and Derby Dugan?"

"My two little orphan boys," said Walter. "Jesus Christ. I'm sorry as hell."

"It was a long time ago."

"But some things . . ."

"Sure. But I don't dwell on it."

"I would."

"I know you would."

"And I *will*. This business. I want Frank's blood."

"I know that, too."

"This is the worst day of my life." But immediately after he'd said that, he started laughing.

"What?"

"Imagine that little scumbag saying he was my friend! 'Save me, Walter, save me!' The fucking nerve!"

"You're dwelling."

"I know I am! So what? I got a right, if I want to." He got up and walked over to Frank's table. There was a white business envelope lying on top. Walter picked it up, opened the flap. Frank's paycheck.

"My mother," said Walter, "drowned. An excursion boat. She and my twin sister. I was ten. Just a kid. Same as you. Almost."

"And *that's* not the worst day of your life?"

"The worst day of your life changes, Al. If you live enough, it changes."

"I can't imagine you as a kid."

"I was a great one. For what seemed a very long time."

"Get along with your old man?"

"Why do you ask?"

I shrugged.

Walter said, "Since we're talking? That why?"

"Yeah. Since we're talking. You get along with your old man?"

"Loathed him."

"The doctor."

"The physician!"

"I liked mine. He was a little roughneck, but yeah, I liked him. And I could understand him wanting—I think it was more for some peace and quiet than for anything else. Mrs. Meatro was nobody you'd notice. Believe me."

Walter nodded. Then he took out his lighter and lit a corner of Frank's paycheck. He held it over an ashtray, watching the yellow flame nibble at the paper and curl it. Walter smiled, looked at his wristwatch. "Ten past nine. What do you think Frank's doing just about now? Lights out already? Would you think? He's lying in the dark, Al, with his eyes open wide. Panel one. Panel two . . ."

"You're dwelling again."

"I can't help it. I'm only human."

"Lucky you," I said.

He glanced in my direction. "It was your mother, wasn't it?"

I stared back at him.

Then Walter gave a surprised yelp, swore an oath, dropped the fiery check, and stuck his thumb to his lips.

EPISODE TWENTY-SIX

THE END OF THE EVENING

I made Jewel stand at the sink with her fingers under the cold running water. "Are we going to laugh about this someday?"

"I think we should probably laugh about it right now," I said. "If we're going to laugh."

"I'll pass." She turned off the faucet, then pushed her blistered fingers into a jar of Vaseline that I'd found in the medicine chest. I went and brought in her drink; I thought she could use it. But she poured the rest of it down the sink.

Putting her into a cab a short time later, I didn't even kiss her good night. I stood at the curb for half a minute, then went back to my room, pulled the presentation strips off the wall, and stuck them in the mailing envelope along with my pitch letter. I sealed everything up and addressed it to the NEA Service in Cleveland. Frank Sweeney's old outfit. But to hell with Frank Sweeney.

I went to the late window at the General Post Office and shipped the package. Then I walked back downtown along Eighth Avenue, and just kept going till I got to Fifteenth Street. I hadn't done any business with the Sullavan sisters in nearly two months; I just hadn't been in the mood. Tonight, though . . .

"It's that kidnapping son of a bitch, Al Bready! Nobody talk to him. Girls, he's got a drip."

Besides Clarky and the three sisters, present that evening in the parlor were an elderly man and young Floyd Olsen. The old man would've appeared dapper in his three-piece brown suit except that he'd taken off his shoes and was sitting on the sofa with his legs stretched out and his white-socked feet sticking up. His eyes moved to mine, then moved away. Olsen looked embarrassed to see me. The girls were at the card table, doing a jigsaw puzzle. It was a red barn, silos, farmland, blue skies, white clouds. Grazing cows.

Clarky had been in the midst of fixing himself a drink at the bar cabinet. He had an ice cube held in a wooden pincher; he brandished it like a sword. "I mean it, nobody talk to him! First he kidnaps my favorite little boy—he steals away my Howard Blum—and *then! Then* he impugns my reputation. Bready! How dare you tell people that I'm dishonest! How *dare* you!"

I scowled at Floyd, and he seemed relieved when Ruth Sullavan got up and took him by the hand and led him down the hall.

"How could you say that about me, Al? And to a nice youngster like Floyd. I've been fair to him. How could you tell him that I'm dishonest?"

"For Christ's sake, you still owe me over a hundred bucks."

"You want a hundred bucks?" He reached for his wallet.

"Forget it."

"You want a hundred bucks? Here's your hundred bucks."

He threw the money at me. I caught it and put it away. Of course I did.

I asked him then, "So, are you buying it?"

"What?"

" 'Mr. Z.' Isn't that what it's called? Floyd's strip."

" '*The* Z.' "

"What the hell does that mean?"

"Means. Who cares what it means. It *sounds* better. 'Mr. Z.' That could be Mr. *Zielinski*. It could be Mr. *Zabriski*. But *The* Z."

"Yeah? What?"

"It *sounds* better."

"You're crazy. Call it 'Mysterious Jones.' "

That caught him by surprise. "You serious?"

"Of course I'm serious. What, it's not better? 'The Z!' *That* could stand for The Zipper! Or The Xylophone."

"Xylophone starts with an X, Al. But you got something there. 'Mysterious Jones!' I like it. Everyone in Bigburg could call him Jonesy."

"They could do that," I said, feeling suddenly juiced, almost giddy, the way I'd get whenever somebody, usually Walter, gave me an idea and I shook it up, juggled it, goosed it, petted it, grabbed it for my own. But then I came back to my senses. "I don't care what they call him!"

Clarky laughed, pulling a new-looking pebbled artist's port-folio from behind the sofa. "I think Floyd's got something here, Al. Trouble is, the pictures are terrible and the story's no good. Hint, hint."

He passed me a couple of Floyd's strips; you could tell that they'd made the rounds—the bristol board was wrinkled and grimy and spattered with old bursts of coffee.

The drawings were stiff and crude, totally charmless, and in the balloons a dozen words were misspelled. Nothing hard like "xylophone," either. Words like "innocent" and "penitentiary" and "executed."

"You're not really going to try to publish this, are you?"

"Try?" said Clarky. "I'm *doing* it. We'll cut up the strips and paste 'em down for a comic book. 'Mysterious Jones,' number one! But if you and Howard wanted to, you could take over after that. Till Floyd gets a little more polished."

"Howard's going to be too busy. And I'm not interested."

"You're such a snob, Al. For a cheap hack writer, you're such a little snob." He waved me away, then something seemed to strike him all of sudden, something troubling. I could see it in the set of his mouth. "You think the guy could sue me? The real guy?"

"What real guy?"

"Mysterious Jones. If I use the name, could he go to court and sue me?"

"And I'm saying to you again, *what* real guy? A guy wears a mask, he's not a real guy. Anybody could put on a mask and say it's him. I wouldn't worry about it."

"You're right, what was I thinking? Guy wears a fucking mask, he's not a real guy. I'm using the name!"

"Of course, if he can't sue you, he just might shoot you."

"I think this conversation has gone on long enough. I've said everything I have to say to you. Except that you're passing up a golden opportunity. I was ready to give you this strip, you could write every single story!"

"Gee, Clark, I don't know what to say."

"You smirk! All right, go ahead and smirk, you big stupid dope, but I was going to put your name on the strip. 'Mysterious Jones,' by—by!—Al Bready. No matter who drew it, it's

your name up there on the page. You like it? You do! I can see it! You're tempted! All right, the offer's back on the table."

"I'm not tempted. And what about Floyd's name?"

"You're tempted! And what *about* Floyd's name. I seem to recall he created a strip called 'Mr. Z,' which nobody bought."

"Oh, for crying out loud," said Judy Sullavan, "you two are starting to give me a headache."

"Al? Last chance."

"What do I know about masked men?"

"Last chance."

I said, "Pass."

Clarky gave me a look of disgust, then turned his head at Floyd's reappearance. "Well. That was quick!"

The kid flushed from his hairline to his shirt collar.

"It's a magical experience, isn't it, my son? And it only gets better."

"Aw, cut it out, Mr. Clark. I done this before."

I decided to forego the magic and left a few minutes later.

Back at the DeSoto, I washed out the two glasses, put the top back in the Pinch bottle, and shook the ashes from the ceramic tray that Jewel had brought. I wiped it clean, then put it away in the bottom dresser drawer, along with all my wrapped pennies, some "Derby Dugan" dime-store merchandise, a tin of Bayer aspirin, a stick of Black Jack gum, Clarky's Zippo, and a candy-coated Beechie in a cufflink dish. Then I set my typewriter back on top of the bridge table. It was only ten o'clock, a few minutes past. But it felt much later.

"Howard?"

"Who is this?"

"For Christ's sake, it's me. It's Al. Al Bready."

"Oh," he said. "Yeah? What do you want, Al?"

I sat on the side of my bed, wrapping the telephone cord around my index finger. "I thought I'd try out your new telephone."

"Guess it works. Good night."

"While I got you on the line, Howard. We should talk."

"About? *About?* You still there?"

"Sure. No, I thought maybe we should talk about week three."

"Week three?"

"What happens next. You got a sketch pad? 'Butch Burlap,' week three. Howard, you with me? Panel one. Myrna's house."

"Al . . ."

"Flower garden. White picket fence. Daytime. Butch approaches the front steps. Lugging his duffel bag. You might want to doodle this out. Panel two. He's on the porch, he's ringing the bell. Panel three—"

"Hey! Al! Hey!"

"Butch's face. Startled as hell. Panel four. Butch is twisting around, but his hands are up. He's reaching for the sky."

"Al, I'm going to ring off."

"There's a shotgun barrel pressed to his back. You like that? And not one word of dialogue, Howard. Not one single word. You notice?"

"I'm going to hang up. Because I'm exhausted and because I got some company."

"You got company? Who?"

"None of your business."

"Howard, wait!" I said. "I mailed off our strip."

"Good night, Al."

"Don't hang up!"

But he did, and three seconds later, Sadie called.

Walter Geebus was dead.

She had been cutting his hair earlier in the evening; well, she'd been reading to him at first—that's what she told me on the telephone: she'd been reading him *Drums Along the Mohawk,* then all of a sudden Walter asked her to give him a haircut, which she'd thought was downright peculiar and a little creepy—at nine o'clock at night? a haircut?—but he'd said please, just a trim? and Sadie went along with it. Sat him up and commenced to clip, but then he'd started weeping. That hadn't lasted long—barely a minute—then he'd sent her to the kitchen for a glass of beer.

When she came back with it, he was sitting propped against a pillow with Sadie's barber shears squeezed in his right fist, and he'd passed away. Except for what little bit of light crept in from the hall sconce, the room was dark. Somehow he'd managed to switch off the lamp.

I don't know why I went up to the house after Sadie called. She didn't need me—we both knew that—and there was nothing for me to do there, but still I went. When I arrived, all the lights were on, or seemed to be on, upstairs and down. Walter's body had already been removed, and the big house felt cold and empty; it felt *emptied.* Or maybe that was just Al Bready's vivid imagination.

I found Sadie in the front parlor with Dr. Gleason. He'd filled out the death certificate and was trying now to convince Sadie to take a light sedative. "I don't need anything," she told him. "I'm just going to close up here in a few minutes and go on home. Al!" she said. She lifted her arms, and I moved into

them. For a moment she felt like a statue, then her hands touched my back and she pressed.

I stepped away from Sadie and nodded to Gleason. He was a thick-set man with nicotined fingers. We'd met dozens of times, December and January, at the hospital. He said he was sorry for my loss, and I thanked him, and he took his black bag and left.

"Sadie . . ."

"I'll be fine, Al. Just let me sit for a minute."

I went upstairs.

In Walter's room, there were clumps of gray-and-black hair scattered on the hardwood floor; there were still more on the pillow. The barber shears lay across a novel open on the bedside table. I picked up the scissors, and put them back down. I looked at pill bottles. I read the labels. Sadie finally called up the stairs. "Al? You just about ready?"

"Be right down," I said. Then I took out my set of keys, detached the house key, and flipped it into the table drawer, next to the pistol. I checked. It was loaded.

The pistol and drawer got vague then, and so did the table, and so did the lamp, and so did the bedstead. Everything got all vague and blurred and watery.

It had suddenly hit me that Walter Geebus no longer existed anywhere. And I never felt closer to him.

"Al—?"

I went back down the stairs and met Sadie in the foyer. On our way out to the street, I took another glance, I guessed my last, at that big oil painting of those stupid French cows in that shaft of yellow daylight. And still I couldn't see the point of making pictures without any people in them.

All of that happened a long time ago. Yet every day, some time every single day, I still think about those years I spent partnered up, in my own fashion, with Walter Geebus and Jewel Rodgers. I suppose you could even say that I dwell on them. I just can't figure out why. I really can't. All I know for certain, those few years were the most important in my life. But what actually happened to me then is still confusing, a big strange mystery, and I figure that's how it's going to remain. I'll be sixty-seven next month, or I will be if the emphysema doesn't kill me first. Don't get me wrong, though, I'm not kicking. I'm not complaining. I'm just wheezing. Al Bready has done all right for himself.

We sold "Butch Burlap" to the NEA Service, Howard Blum and yours truly, but for the six-plus years that we did it together, the sucker ran in fewer than one hundred newspapers; at least that's what the syndicate told us. It was a decent strip, a

good crime strip, only it never clicked. Over time, Howard and I became the best of friends, but as partners? We never clicked, either. He drew his heart out, drew beautifully, and I wrote the best stories that I could—it simply wasn't meant to be. I made a funny speech at Howard's wedding (I told the guests how surly he'd been when I first met him, and how skinny), and I played uncle to Howard's four kids, and right up until he moved his family out to California in the late 1950's, I went to dinner every Sunday at his tiny house in Baldwin. But as partners, we couldn't make a real go of it.

We probably shouldn't have tried, and I blame myself. I've always felt that Clarky would have done what he promised when he'd attempted to keep Howard from quitting The Kamen Studios—made the kid half-owner. So if Howard Blum had stuck it out there, in time he would have been all set, filthy rich. We didn't talk about it, never, but it must've galled him when Clarky made a fortune later with the line of dime comics that Howard, for all practical purposes, had launched. During the war years, circulation for Top-Drawer comic books surpassed twenty million copies a month; all by itself the "Mysterious Jones" title accounted for three million of those.

The last I heard about poor Floyd Olsen, by the way, he was clerking at a hardware store that belonged to his father-in-law, in Poughkeepsie or New Paltz or Hastings-on-Hudson. Well, I'd warned him! And the real Jonesy neither sued nor shot Clark Kamen. In fact, he and his flowery gladstone bag disappeared from the streets of New York forever shortly after the first issue of "Mysterious Jones" hit the stands. Nobody ever saw him again, and he was gradually forgotten.

But I was talking about Howard Blum—the point being I imagined that he fumed in private, and fumed often, about his missed opportunity, his golden chance, at Top-Drawer Comics.

Of course, I'd been pretty deeply involved myself in setting up Clarky's empire, but missing out on the big bucks never fazed me. Because I'd never expected them. Never wanted them. I've lived my life strictly work-for-hire. Listen, I haven't missed a meal in fifty years. I've done all right for myself.

Although comic books were never what Howard Blum wanted to draw, after he got out of the army in 1946, he drifted back into the field, just to make a living till he could work up a newspaper strip of his own. As Ward Blaine, he ended up staying in comic books forever, hacking for Timely and Dell, then moving over to D.C. He drew "Green Lantern" for a while. He drew "Superboy." He drew "Aquaman." But Howard never drew another page for Clark Kamen, and I quit writing for him in '41 after Marty Planet was gunned down in Keansburg, New Jersey. With Marty dead, I decided that the promise I'd made to him at the Even Twenty Club was null and void.

During the war, I was drafted, but my service record isn't much worth talking about. They had me write a weekly enlisted-man's strip for *Stars and Stripes* and caption automotive and ordnance manuals done as comic books. I've still never seen Europe, and that's quite all right. To hell with Europe! Joe Wein died an infantryman there, in France. So did Frank Sweeney. Sprung early from Sing Sing and stuck into a uniform, he was killed by an artillery burst at Cherbourg. The son of a bitch. That poor, rotten, impatient son of a bitch.

After the war, everything changed. Except for "Joe Palooka," all the adventure strips that I'd been scripting were eventually canceled, then I lost even that last one in 1955 when Ham Fisher put a pistol to his head on Christmas Eve and blew his brains out.

Come the Eisenhower years, newspaper comics turned dull, they turned into boring little soap operas about doctors and lawyers, Air Force colonels, men in suits and uniforms, or else they were gag-a-day things—"Beetle Bailey," "The Wizard of Id," "Peanuts"—and that just wasn't for me. I couldn't get the hang of it, and when the last of the pulps finally expired, I started writing cowboy novels for Whitman—Roy Rogers, Gene Autry, Red Ryder—and I did a lot of seduction-and-sex fiction for the cheesier men's magazines. Well, I've always had a good imagination! I even wrote a few paperback spy novels for Lancer Books, and a couple of space operas for Ace. Al Bready conquers the universe. In between jobs I lived on my savings.

I heard somewhere that Leonard Duveen became Buddy Lydecker's ghost writer, but I never found out for certain. Not that I was terribly interested one way or the other. After I quit, I never followed "Derby Dugan." As far as I was concerned, the strip came to its abrupt finish on February 14, 1937, with Walter's final Sunday page, published three days after he was buried in a cemetery in Hoboken.

Funny enough, I ended up back in New Jersey myself. By the early 1960s the DeSoto had turned too seedy even for me. After the Sullavan girls closed up shop and went on to other careers (for a while Ruth Sullavan was the weather lady on WPIX-TV, Channel 11), I found it convenient living in a hooker hotel; all I had to do, if I got the urge, was traipse down the hall and tap on a door. But then I got mugged, and robbed twice, and finally I checked the hell out.

I moved in with my sister. I paid a good rent to Donald and took care of Jean. She wasn't so bad, she was sweet, and the only real problem that I had, and it wasn't that big a problem, was sleeping in the same bedroom with her practically every night.

No, listen—don't get any funny ideas. It was nothing like that! She always took my old bed, and I always slept in Donald's. And what the hell. I made up stories with her.

Jeannie died Easter Sunday, 1970. My mother once told me, when an aunt of hers died on Easter, that it was a fine day to go. The best day. Heaven is supposedly open to anyone and everyone on the day Jesus Christ rose from the dead. Not that my sister had anything to worry about. I miss her company, but I get along all right without it.

So. Thirty years have passed—more than that, thirty-four—and I pay less and less attention to the world outside. Vietnam. Nixon. Rod Stewart. For crying out loud, I couldn't care less. I write a little, I smoke a lot, I got this damn emphysema. I'm not kicking, but I already told you that. My neighbors all think I'm a queer old buzzard, but a harmless one. They wave whenever I go out for groceries, and they call me "Alfie" or "Mr. Brady." I'm Alfred O. Brady again. And why not? Why not?

Walter, though. Jewel, though. I still think about them, and about those depression days, and now I've written about them, because I hoped that if I did, then maybe I could figure out some things. One thing in particular: why do I feel that nothing that happened to me after Walter died and Jewel left New York ever meant a damn thing?

You know, I really never did much like Walter Geebus, and if I loved Jewel, I wasn't *in* love with her. How could I have been? You don't let somebody you're in love with just go away! So I've always heard.

What Jewel was to me, though, and Walter, what I felt about Walter Geebus, I'm still not certain. But I know that our time together was important. Yet when our time was up, when it blew away, when it floated off, when it died, it didn't destroy me; it didn't even hurt very long. I continued on doing pretty

much the same things I'd always done. But none of them meant a damn thing.

I lose sleep. I sleep poorly. And sometimes—sometimes when I do sleep for a long stretch, I'll dream that I'm climbing a flight of stairs and floating down a long, curving hall. I turn in at one doorway, the door is painted scarlet, and I find Dad on his back on the bedstead pressing a hand to his belly and fat Mrs. Meatro sprawled impossibly across the floor, and the papered walls are lined with glass-fronted display cases crammed full of "Derby Dugan" paraphernalia. I force myself to wake up, and when I do, I'll lay in the dark for a couple of hours thinking about Jewel and about Walter. About Walter and Jewel. Sometimes I wish I'd been there with them at the moments of their deaths. Sometimes I think I was.

And sometimes—those times when I'm more asleep than awake—I even think that I killed them both. Which is stupid, of course. It's crazy. Walter died of heart failure, and before that he'd had a stroke, so how could I have been responsible? And Jewel. She stayed with her husband and went back upstate and lived the rest of her life in perfect health till she died.

While Jimmie Rodgers operated his little stationery store, Jewel taught at the Megville public high school, and mailed me Christmas cards, and once or twice a year a long, chatty, funny letter. She never talked about the old days in New York, except once.

In a letter dated October 14, 1956, Jewel was writing about having raked her yard the day before and burned all the dead leaves in a great big pile, saying how much she'd loved watching the blaze, and the white foaming smoke, and then suddenly, apropos of nothing and in the very same paragraph, she wrote: "I've always thought it was peculiar, Al, and a little bit sad, that I never met your friend Walter Geebus. When he was

in the hospital that time, I kept expecting you to invite me along with you some evening to visit, but you never did. I suppose I could have asked you to *take* me along, and often I considered doing just that, but as you once told me, I didn't always say what was on my mind. I would have liked meeting him, and strange to say, it nags at me from time to time that I never did and remains a vaguely sweet regret. Oh, don't I sound silly! Enough of that! Now let me tell you something I never told you before. Although I never actually met Walter Geebus, I saw him once. It was a weekday, and it must have been around this same time of year. I remember it was a chilly bright afternoon and there were leaves blowing. School had just let out and I was about to walk home when I got it into my head that I'd go over and take a stroll through the Morgan Library. (Remember I took you there once or twice? It was one of my favorite places, but you always complained that it was too dark inside to see any of the stuff on display! You were right, too!) Anyhow, I was on my way there when all of a sudden I heard two men arguing, and I looked across the street and there you were, Al. You were walking in lockstep with a man who was a head taller than you, and you were shouting at him and he was shouting right back. I realized immediately who the man was—I'd seen his picture once or twice in the Saturday rotogravure, or maybe it was in Nosy Natwin's old column. (By the way, did you see in the paper last month where Nosy retired? Tuberculosis! The poor man.) I guess Walter had taken you to lunch again at the Union League Club, and now here you were on the street shouting at each other. And do you know what the pair of you were shouting about? I'll never forget, Al. You said something like, "The goddamn kid is fourteen!" and he said, "Ten! He's ten, you son of a bitch!" I stood there amazed, just watching, and then Walter said "Ten!" and shoved you. You shoved him back

and said, "Fourteen!" And then the two of you were laughing
and shoving and shouting, and my goodness, Al Bready, you
both seemed twelve. Twelve! Twelve!"

When Jewel died, Jimmie wrote to me, in the most perfect
Palmer penmanship. She drowned, he said, while swimming in
Lake Oneida. She got a cramp and she drowned, he said, on
July 25, 1961. He thought I'd want to know. Sincerely, James
Rodgers.

I sent off a mass card.

Now I'm finished. The first true thing that I've ever written
in my career, in my whole stupid life, and now I'm finished.
But after everything is said and done, what it finally comes
down to is that Sunday page of Walter's, that dream that was
never drawn. That story I never could tell. Derby's in a rowboat.

And so, I guess, is Al Bready.

It's night.